SORREL

Also by David Randall

Clovermead: In the Shadow of the Bear
Chandlefort: In the Shadow of the Bear

Margaret K. McElderry Books

DAVID RANDALL

SORREL

IN THE SHADOW OF THE BEAR

MARGARET K. McELDERRY BOOKS

NEW YORK   LONDON   TORONTO   SYDNEY

Margaret K. McElderry Books
An imprint of Simon & Schuster Children's Publishing Division
1230 Avenue of the Americas, New York, New York 10020
Book design by Steve Kennedy and Greg Stadnyk
The text for this book is set in Cochin.
Manufactured in the United States of America
2 4 6 8 10 9 7 5 3 1
Library of Congress Cataloging-in-Publication Data
Randall, David, 1972-
Sorrel / David Randall. — 1st ed.
p. cm. — (In the shadow of the bear)
Summary: Clovermead, a shape-shifting fifteen-year-old girl, must not
only convince others to join the fight against evil but also rescue the
people of her best friend from enslavement.
ISBN-13: 978-0-689-87872-5 (hardcover)
ISBN-10: 0-689-87872-9
[1. Fantasy.] I. Title.
PZ7.R5638Sor 2007
[Fic] — dc22
2006032220

To my wife,

Laura Helen Congleton,

always my love

ACKNOWLEDGMENTS

As always, my editors, friends, and family have read, commented upon, and improved this novel; I am grateful to Lisa Cheng, Emma Dryden, Simon Lipskar, David Rosen, Sarah Sevier, Ariane Randall, Francis Randall, Laura Randall, and, always and especially, my wife, Laura Congleton. This book is dedicated to her, but she has been essential to all of them.

CONTENTS

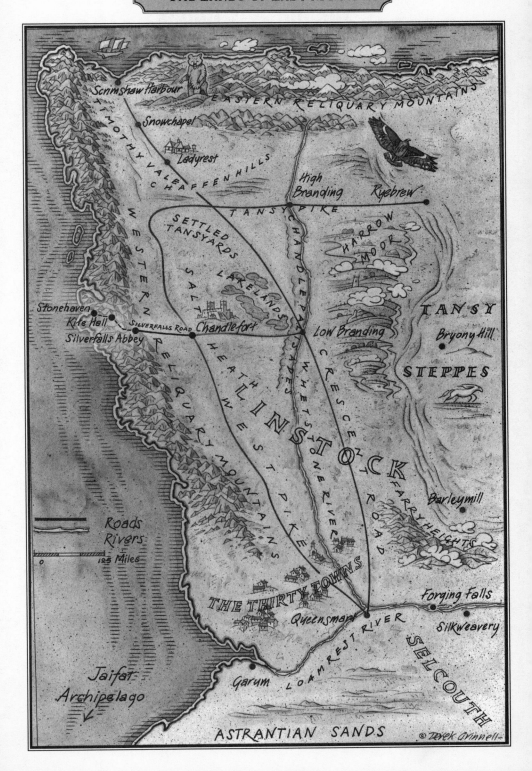

THE LANDS OF LADY MOON

Chapter One

THE EMISSARY FROM THE STEPPES

"I DON'T KNOW WHO HE IS, BUT HE'S COME ABOUT something important," said Clovermead. She squeezed Auroche with her knees, and her horse moved forward a few inches. "He's a Tansyard, so he looks a little like you, Sorrel. I saw him ride up to the Castle yesterday afternoon, and he's six and a half feet if he's an inch, with a face like a marble statue. The guards at the Castle door whisked him up to Mother's study, and I haven't seen either of them since. I tiptoed to her doorway toward midnight, in case she'd left the door open, so I could peek in. She hadn't, but I saw light under the door and heard them talking. He had a low voice like a bull—Auroche, what are you doing? Don't stop now." Auroche neighed nervously and refused to budge.

"He thinks you are not paying attention to your riding or to him," said Sorrel. He trod softly through the mud to Auroche, patted him a moment, then stepped away again. "He thinks your jaw is so busy moving that you will send him galloping into the water before you notice anything is wrong. I agree with his suspicions. Stop thinking about this stranger, Clovermead. You can be scatterbrained when you have a saddle and reins to help you, but not when you ride bareback. Keep your back straight and help Auroche to reach dry land."

"Why? He's thrown me three times today." Clovermead glowered at her horse, but she followed Sorrel's instructions. Auroche whinnied apprehensively as he took another step on the plank laid over the pool of water that filled up half the back courtyard after the latest spring rains. "Shh, Auroche," she whispered. "That puddle's only a few inches deep. Please don't send me into the mud again. It's cold and it squelches." Auroche took another step forward, then stopped. Clovermead pressed his flanks again. "Aren't you curious to see him, Sorrel? I don't think I've seen another Tansyard besides you in all the time I've been in Chandlefort. And he is such a sight! He doesn't just sound like a bull, he's as big as one too."

"I am not a Tansyard any longer," said Sorrel. He plucked at the yellow sleeve he wore. "I am a Yellowjacket and a Chandleforter now. My compatriots are here."

"That doesn't stop you from talking about the Steppes all the time," said Clovermead. Auroche teetered forward another step. "I know every inch of them, just from listening to you talk. I'd think you'd at least want to say hello to a countryman."

"I love the Steppes," said Sorrel. "That does not mean I wish to chatter with every Tansyard who shows up in Chandlefort. And even if I did—Clovermead, to you Chandleforters I am simply a Tansyard, but my nation was the Cyan Cross Horde. The other Hordes were not as strange to me as you farmer-folk are, but they were foreigners too. And not friends. Most of Cyan Cross' wars were with other Hordes. No, I do not need to speak with this man." He clucked his tongue and Auroche straightened up from a dangerous wobble. "Be careful, please! Your mind is wandering. And do not press Auroche so hard. You need only a gentle touch."

"I'm doing my best," said Clovermead. "It's not as easy as you think. Still, I do think I'm getting better at this—" But as she spoke, Auroche's front legs rose into the air, Clovermead tumbled from his back, and there was a loud splash and a fountain of muddy water as she landed. When the fountain settled, Clovermead sat sprawled in the puddle. She looked very bedraggled and very brown.

"Phooey," said Clovermead. Grimy droplets trickled down from her yellow hair and over her eyes. She glared at Auroche. "Unruly beast! Back into the saddle you go!"

"You cannot become a bareback rider in a day," said Sorrel. Fastidiously he flicked a murky globule off his hand. He had managed to dodge most of the mud and to keep his clothes dry. "It is a difficult skill to learn, even when you are not chattering about fascinating strangers." He walked around the puddle to the far end of the plank and clapped his hands. Auroche trotted briskly to him, off the plank, and onto dry earth. Sorrel stroked his ears, and Auroche happily rubbed his nose against Sorrel's face.

"Riding bareback isn't a skill at all," said Clovermead. She let herself sit in the mud puddle. It was satisfyingly melancholy just to let the cold water ripple against her clothes and seep into her skin. "It's something you're born with, like your hair or your eyes. You Tansyards have it, and you can ride without saddle or reins from one end of the Tansy Steppes to the other without wobbling once. We Linstockers don't have it, and we end up in puddles. I give up. I know my limitations."

"It is not three days since you climbed atop a gargoyle on the roof, and then discovered that you could not clamber off so easily as on. I had to haul a ladder up two flights of stairs to get you down, so I remember the incident vividly. Whatever your limitations are, I am sure you are ignorant of them." Sorrel laughed. "I assure you, Clovermead, you are perfectly capable of riding bareback. All it takes is effort and perseverance. Now, I will grant you that I am particularly expert with horses, and that Chandlefort's Demoiselle rides like a sack of potatoes"— he sidestepped a sudden splatter of mud shooting toward him from the puddle—"but that is the fruit of experience, which you will have in time. Please don't muddy my jacket just now, Clovermead. I must go on parade in an hour, and the captain thinks badly of soldiers in dirty uniforms. Are you staying in that puddle?"

"Why not? I'm better at riding puddles than riding horses. If I stay here long enough, I'll grow webbed feet and learn to swim like a duck." She sneezed and jumped up hastily. "Or maybe I'd just get a cold." Clovermead stalked toward Sorrel and glared at him. "I'm through riding today! I've had enough mud for a good long time." Then she stomped over to Auroche while the Tansyard hastily retreated from her muck-stained clothes.

It was already daffodil season in Chandlefort, and summer would be along soon, but a north wind out of the Chaffen Hills had brought a wintry blast to the town this morning. *I'm growing soft down here in the southlands,* thought Clovermead. *Back in Timothy Vale I'd have gone short-sleeved in weather like this. Now I shiver and complain about the cold.* She had put on a quilted scarlet jacket and gray flannel trousers that morning to protect her against the chill, but now their wet cloth clung to her from her shoulders to her ankles. Her equally damp locks of hair lay limply against her neck.

Clovermead's hair stretched past her shoulder blades. She was as freckled as when she had come to Chandlefort three and a half years ago, but she had grown much taller. She was five feet and seven inches high—almost as tall as Sorrel. She hadn't acquired much grace with her height, though. The twelve years she'd spent believing she was Clovermead Wickward, daughter of the innkeeper Waxmelt Wickward, had ingrained country manners into her bones. The last three and a half years as Demoiselle Cerelune Cindertallow, daughter and heir of Lady Melisande Cindertallow, had provided her only a veneer of court manners, which tended to rub off when she wasn't concentrating on etiquette. Which was frequently.

Clovermead had also acquired a figure lately. She would never be as buxom as some of the young ladies of Chandlefort, and exercise kept her sinewy, but by now she curved almost as much as her equally athletic mother. Clovermead didn't much care for these changes. All the lordlings in Chandlefort who'd pointed at the scar on her arm or her missing tooth a few years ago gawked at different parts of her now. They stared so much that she'd taken to wearing clothes that were shapeless and large.

Clovermead heard a noise from the parapet at the far end of the courtyard, and she whipped her head up—but it was only the wind rustling through pebbles.

"It could have been Lord Turnbolt or Lord Pattock," Clovermead whispered to her horse. "They're pimply pests, and they've been following me everywhere and

peeping at me. Why do they stare like that, Auroche?"
Clovermead took a somewhat muddy sugar-cube from a
leather pouch in her pocket and fed it to him. Auroche
gulped the sugar down without demur: He wasn't a
finicky eater. "You're a boy—tell me, would you lose
your manners and act like a complete nincompoop the
moment you saw a mare? No, don't answer that, you
probably would. You're all alike."

"Even on the Steppes," said Sorrel from across the
courtyard, "we do not talk to our horses as much as you
do, Clovermead. That is because we know they do not
speak. Sometimes I think you are astonishingly ignorant
of the basic facts of horseflesh." He chuckled. "Or astonishingly willing to carry on one-sided conversations."

"You are snide," Clovermead informed Sorrel as she
began to brush the mud from Auroche's mane. "You have
been snide ever since I met you. I have never told you
this, but I think you need to know that you will die a
snide-bound old coot." Sorrel looked at her blankly.
"Hidebound old coot, snide-bound old coot. Oh, never
mind. And I'd been saving that one up for days now."

Sorrel rolled his eyes. "I will complain to Milady," he
said. "My snide is not tough enough to endure such terrible puns." His smiling eyes met Clovermead's, and
then his easy chuckle got her to laughing too.

Sorrel's eyes never wavered from Clovermead's face.
Her damp clothes pressed against her body, and any
other young man in Chandlefort would have looked at
them. Clovermead wasn't indecent or anything, but it
would have been embarrassing. But Sorrel was a perfect
gentleman, without any fuss at all, and Clovermead
didn't have to be embarrassed.

Sorrel doesn't stare because he's too busy looking at himself in the mirror, thought Clovermead. Sorrel had always taken care of his appearance, but he had become quite the dandy ever since his promotion last summer to regular trooper in the Yellowjacket Guards. His yellow jacket was always spotless and his boots gleamed in the sun. He put musk on his long brown hair, tied up in a yellow ribbon, and he had taken to daubing yellow paint around the crisscross blue tattoos on his cheeks that declared that he had been raised with the Cyan Cross Horde on the Tansy Steppes. He had even bought a new hat to replace the one he had brought with him from the Steppes so many years ago. The new one was also edged with a fox's face, paws, and tail, but the fur was redder, and it shone splendidly in the sun. There wasn't a twenty-year-old in all Chandlefort, Sorrel had assured her more than once, who looked as magnificently handsome as he did.

You are *nice to look at*, Clovermead thought wistfully, as her eyes darted to his delicate features, his fine brown hair, and his laughing eyes. She didn't let herself look for too long—it would be far more embarrassing to be caught looking at Sorrel than to catch him looking at her. She brushed Auroche's mane even more vigorously. So far as Sorrel knew, Clovermead just thought of him as a friend.

"Excuse me, Demoiselle," Clovermead heard, and she turned to see a redheaded maidservant in a white dress curtsy low to her. "Milady your mother sent me to ask you to her study. You too, Master Tansyard," she said to Sorrel. "I'm glad to find the two of you together. You're to come at once, she said." The maidservant bobbed her head apologetically.

"Do I have time to change?" asked Clovermead. The

maid shook her head. "Is it something to do with that Tansyard giant?" Clovermead asked, rather eagerly.

"He was in the study with Milady, Demoiselle, but I'm sure I don't know what their business is." The maidservant took a step toward Clovermead and Sorrel and whispered to them. "I don't know how Milady has the nerve to be alone with him! He looks like an ogre who's going to pop me into a stewpot and make me his dinner."

"You do not look like you would make more than a snack," said Sorrel. Thoughtfully he licked his fingers. The redhead glared at him, not certain whether to pout or to laugh. "Do not fear," Sorrel continued blithely. "We Tansyards only consume flesh in the evening. You should be safe for some hours to come." The servant looked at him with round and horrified eyes, and Sorrel burped. She squeaked and fled.

"You're terrible," said Clovermead, as she and Sorrel began to walk Auroche to the stables. "I'll have to ask Father to tell her you were only joking. Otherwise she'll tell everyone that she heard it from a Tansyard himself that they really do gobble humans."

"Most will not believe her," said Sorrel. "And those who do will never think well of Tansyards." For a moment anger flickered in his voice. Then it passed. "I should not let it bother me. Some Tansyards will never think well of Chandleforters, either."

"Has anyone been giving you trouble?" asked Clovermead anxiously. "I'm awfully sorry. You'd think people would have gotten used to you by now."

"My comrades in the Yellowjackets respect me, but some townsmen and townswomen always find amusement in baiting a foreigner." Sorrel shrugged, patted his sword, and grinned. "Do not worry. I can take care of myself."

"Well, if ever you do need help, I'm always up for a brawl. Or I think I am—I haven't been in one yet." She lifted up her right hand and turned it into a large clawed and golden-furred bear-paw. "I bet I could make a tavern full of lowlifes turn and run!"

"I am sure you could, Clovermead," said Sorrel. "However, your mother will evict me from the Yellowjackets as soon as she finds out I have led you into a tavern brawl. Regretfully, I must decline your help." Sorrel didn't bat an eye at Clovermead's furry paw. He had turned quite pale three and a half years ago, the first time Clovermead turned into a bear, but he had long since conquered his fears. Now he was the only person besides her parents and her cousin Saraband who never looked at Clovermead with terror in his eyes.

They settled Auroche in the stables, then hurried to Lady Cindertallow's study, up on the top floor of Cindertallow Castle. As they opened the door, her mother looked at Clovermead's mud-spattered clothes and laughed. "You're going to give the laundry maids ulcers. I thought you weren't getting dirty so often lately. What happened?"

"Spring, Mother. I fell into snowbanks during the winter and got wet instead of muddy, that's all." She went to her mother and kissed her on the cheek.

Lady Cindertallow turned her head to keep Clovermead from bumping against her new spectacles. She had worn them for a year now: Her eyes were martyrs to the papers strewn upon her desk. Her hair had faded entirely from golden to straw the last few years, and her crow's-feet had grown deep. She wore a black beaver stole over her emerald gown. A roaring fire kept the room uncomfortably warm, to keep Lady Cindertallow from complaining of freezing fingers and chilled toes. She was still a strong fighter and an expert rider, but she had slowed lately.

Clovermead heard a cough behind her, and she turned to look at the giant from the Steppes. He really was enormous — a foot taller than Clovermead, twice as broad, with muscles bulging in his jacket of white leather trimmed with ermine. He was in his midfifties. His square face had been darkened and his chestnut hair bleached by years of wind and sun. He wore two braids down to his waist, and on each cheek was tattooed a white star. He looked at Clovermead, looked at Sorrel — and his dark eyes suddenly went wide as he saw the blue crisscross on Sorrel's cheeks. He shot out a question to Sorrel in Tansyard.

Sorrel answered in common tongue. "I wear my tattoos by right. The bear-priests and Low Brandingmen did not catch every warrior of the Horde that night in Bryony Hill."

"Did any other Cyan Cross warriors survive?" the giant rumbled. His accent was thicker than Sorrel's, but comprehensible. "You are the first I have seen these seven years."

"I fled that ambush, that night of slaughter, like a cowardly child, and I survived by sheerest chance. I saw the bear-priests take some of our women and children to Barleymill as slaves, and perhaps a few of them still live as well. But all of Cyan Cross' warriors were killed but me." Sorrel scowled. "I hear White Star Horde is foremost on the Steppes, now that Cyan Cross has been destroyed. Perhaps your Horde Chief takes pride in that fact, though White Star never defeated us in war, save that one battle at Sundew Creek. Tell him not to worry: Cyan Cross Horde will not challenge him again."

"Perhaps the Horde Chief does think such things as he roams the Steppes," said the giant slowly. "But I am here in Chandlefort, and I was only surprised."

"Of course, warrior," said Sorrel, with the faintest edge of disbelief in his voice. "It surprises even me that I am still alive." He turned to salute Lady Cindertallow. "I am at your service, Milady. I beg your pardon for neglecting the proper ceremonies."

"Granted." Lady Cindertallow gestured the three of them to seats in the middle of the room, and they all sat down. "Sir, my daughter Clovermead and Trooper Sorrel. Clovermead, Sorrel, our guest is Fetterlock of the White Star Horde."

"I am an emissary from the Horde Chief," said Fetterlock. He smiled a little. "Perhaps I should say that I am an emissary from the Horde Chief's wife. It is more her will than his that I should come. He would not have sent me without her prompting."

"Why are you here?" asked Clovermead. She frowned. "I suppose it's trouble of some sort. Powerful people don't ever seem to send messengers to say they're doing well and to ask after your health."

Fetterlock chuckled. "I am afraid you are correct, Demoiselle. I think you know that the bear-priests built a wooden fort on Bryony Hill after they destroyed Cyan Cross Horde?" Clovermead nodded. "When we came north from the southern Steppes this spring, we found that the bear-priests had brought vast quantities of granite blocks to Bryony Hill over the winter. Slaves are erecting a stone fortress there, and the bear-priests will dominate the Steppes when it is completed. Then, one way or another, the Hordes will have to submit to Lord Ursus' rule." Clovermead's scar ached at the sound of Lord Ursus' name, and her jaw throbbed where her missing tooth had been. They were the ineradicable reminders that Lord Ursus had once seduced Clovermead with dreams of blood and killing, had once possessed her, body and soul. "Yet we cannot evict the bear-priests from Bryony Hill by ourselves," Fetterlock continued. "I have been sent to Chandlefort to ask for your mother's aid."

"I have decided to give it," said Lady Cindertallow. Her voice rang clear but her head was bowed. "As Fetterlock pointed out quite eloquently"—she grimaced—"Ursus' bear-priests will be able to invade Linstock from the east once he has a fortress in Bryony Hill as a base. I've put enough soldiers into the southern forts that Lord Ursus will take serious losses if he sends his main army north from the Thirty Towns, but I don't have nearly enough men to garrison the eastern frontier as well. We need to raze the fort at Bryony Hill this year, before the fortress' stone walls go up. I will be sending an army to the Steppes this summer."

"Am I going to fight with you, Mother?" asked Clovermead. Her stomach was queasy. Once she had thought of fighting as a grand adventure, but that was before she had fought and before she had killed. She was good at fighting, but it disgusted her.

She was afraid it would disgust her less the more she fought. Clovermead had vomited the first time she'd killed. She didn't think she would the second time.

"Perhaps," said Lady Cindertallow. "But I need you

for another mission first. Fetterlock will explain." She nodded to the Tansyard.

"I am definitely an emissary from the Horde Chief's wife," said Fetterlock. "I am in some sense an emissary from the Horde Chief. I am not an emissary from the White Star Horde. The Elders have not yet decided to fight Lord Ursus. Before they do, Chandlefort must formally request an alliance with the Horde — and before they accept such an alliance, the Elders will need to be persuaded that Chandlefort will be their ally not just this year, not just next year, but until Lord Ursus is driven entirely from the Steppes. We are very near to Lord Ursus' citadel of Barleymill, and you are far away. The Elders must be convinced that after we have retaken Bryony Hill you will not leave the Horde to face his retaliation alone. Chandlefort must send an ambassador to them." His eyes fell on Clovermead.

"Me?" asked Clovermead. "Mother, do you want me to head out to the Steppes?"

Lady Cindertallow nodded reluctantly. "The White Star Horde will require that I send a high-ranking ambassador." She glanced at Sorrel. "Isn't that so, Trooper?"

"We Tansyards have a high opinion of ourselves," said Sorrel. "If we are to ally ourselves with foreigners, we wish to talk with their leaders, not with servants. Ideally, Milady, you should go to the Steppes yourself. We are told in our stories that your great-grandmother's great-grandmother rode to every corner of the Steppes herself to gain our alliance. If you cannot come yourself, no one of lower rank than the Demoiselle will do."

"I must stay here to ready the Yellowjackets to ride

13

to the Steppes," said Lady Cindertallow. "I'll also have to twist the Mayor of Low Branding's arm to send some of his mercenaries to join us. Sending an army into the Steppes isn't covered under our defensive alliance, but I think I can convince him to help us. After all, Bryony Hill is nearer to Low Branding than it is to Chandlefort."

"Let Ursus do to the Low Brandingmen what he wills," Sorrel whispered, but only Clovermead heard him. His eyes snapped with uncontrollable hatred. He had never forgiven Low Branding for its role in helping Lord Ursus destroy Cyan Cross Horde, even now that the Mayor had allied himself with Chandlefort.

"I don't like the thought of you gallivanting off into the wilderness, Clovermead," Lady Cindertallow continued, "but it seems necessary."

"I don't quite understand," said Clovermead. "I thought Mr. Fetterlock came here to ask for your help, but now I'm supposed to go ask the White Star Horde to help us?"

"And all the other Hordes as well," said Fetterlock. "White Star has influence with the other Hordes, but it does not speak for them. It would be well for you to make your request to every Horde on the Steppes." He shrugged his shoulders. "It is all very roundabout, Demoiselle, but it is the best way to proceed. The Horde Chief's wife asks you for help, you ask the Horde for help, and everybody feels flattered and needed. And those Elders who waver between fighting Lord Ursus and submitting to him perhaps will fight to aid Chandlefort, from pride, when they would not fight to save themselves."

"You are a very puzzling people," said Clovermead.

Fetterlock smiled and shrugged. "What happens if the Hordes turn me down?"

"Then we march our armies back home," said Lady Cindertallow. "We pray to Our Lady that the bear-priests don't ambush us while we are on the Steppes. We settle down inside our walls and wait for the bear-priests to come after us." She frowned. "Don't let the Hordes turn you down, Clovermead."

"I'll do everything I can," said Clovermead seriously. "I swear by Our Lady."

Lady Cindertallow nodded. "Ask the Hordes where we should meet them, and send me word in Low Branding. I'll be there with my Yellowjackets within three weeks. From there we can get quickly to any spot in the western Steppes."

Clovermead's eyes lit up. "Sorrel's coming with me, isn't he? That's why you told him to come here too?"

Lady Cindertallow nodded again. "Trooper? I want you to accompany Clovermead—you're the only Yellowjacket who knows the Steppes. But I won't order you to go. I recollect that you told me once that you would have trouble returning to your homeland."

"I fled from the bear-priests and I lived," Sorrel said slowly. "The other warriors were brave and they died." He touched the tattoos on his cheeks. "Anyone who sees these tattoos will guess the truth, that I was a coward, and therefore know that I am an outlaw. On the Steppes, any Tansyard warrior will be able to kill me with impunity."

"That is so," said Fetterlock. "But you wear a yellow jacket, and the Hordes will respect the Cindertallow livery. At least while you ride with the Demoiselle."

"Then I will go," said Sorrel. He smiled at

15

Clovermead. "How can I miss this opportunity to show you the Steppes? You will not appreciate them properly without me to educate you as to their beauties." Then he looked thoughtful, and turned back to Lady Cindertallow. "The Hordes do not like to have foreigners wandering on the Steppes, Milady. No more than two handfuls of soldiers should accompany the Demoiselle."

"Fetterlock said the same." Lady Cindertallow glanced with anxious love at Clovermead, then sighed. "I'll send ten Yellowjackets to accompany you, including Sorrel, and I'll write a letter requesting the Mayor and his men to give you a safe-conduct through Low Branding. Can you leave the day after tomorrow, Clovermead? Once I've given you some lessons in diplomacy, you'll need to leave immediately." Clovermead nodded. "And, Clo? I know you mean well, but you have a tendency to be impetuous and hare off on your own. We can't afford any impulsiveness on this mission. Your first priority is to get the Hordes to agree to an alliance. Remember, no one but you can do this."

"You can count on me, Mother," said Clovermead. "I don't flibbertigibbet when it's important." Her eyes were large. "But I've never done diplomacy before."

"I'll start teaching you now," said her mother. "We can start with the basics."

"Always be polite, never promise anything, have an army on hand to get people in the mood to do what you want them to do, and when all else fails, lie," Clovermead rattled off. She smiled. "I'm a fast learner."

Fetterlock laughed, a booming rumble. "I do not think she needs any lessons, Milady," he said. He stood, his head nearly scraped the ceiling, and he bowed low to Lady Cindertallow. "Please excuse me, Milady. You will want to give your instructions in private." Sorrel stood and bowed too, and then he and Fetterlock left the room.

Lady Cindertallow waited until she heard their footsteps recede. "The first thing I want you to keep in mind," she said, "is that I'm sure Fetterlock isn't telling the entire truth. Be wary of him until you find out what he's keeping back from us."

Chapter Two

THE PROMISE

"BOTHER THE WHITE STAR HORDE," CLOVERMEAD said around a mouthful of lamb stew the next evening. With her free hand she patted down a wrinkle on her sky-blue sweater. "Bother the Green Spike Horde and the Red Bar Horde and the Paisley Curlicues Horde and the rest of them. I am bored by Hordes. Oh, Saraband, did you ever have to memorize which Horde is which?"

Lady Saraband Sconce took a dainty bite from her own bowl. "Yes," she said, when she had finished swallowing. "When I was Demoiselle, I could tell you the name of every single Horde, where their grazing grounds were in summer and winter, and how each of them felt about the other Hordes. Tansy politics was one of the first things I forgot when I renounced being Demoiselle, and I am happy to say that I have known nothing at all about the Steppes for a good seven years." She took another delicate nibble of stew, and smiled wickedly. "Don't despair, Clovermead. There aren't more than two dozen Hordes to keep straight." Clovermead groaned.

Saraband, tall, dark, and pale, was dressed in a lilac dress that complemented her complexion perfectly. She looked as lovely as ever. Clovermead had never stopped being envious of her cousin's beauty, but she remained best friends with the nineteen-year-old. Saraband was a dancer and a healer, a quiet lady who loathed fighting, but she and Clovermead got on well despite their differences. Sometimes Clovermead wanted to put away her sword and talk about how to style her hair, or go into town to buy a new dress, or do anything that didn't have to do with fighting and politics, and Saraband was the perfect companion then.

"I know how you feel, Clo," said Waxmelt Wickward. He sat across the table from her and spooned down his own stew with a hearty appetite. The three of them were eating dinner in Clovermead's room. "My first day working in the Castle, I was told to memorize ten patterns of porcelain stored in three different pantries, and then I was told I had a week to learn the shortest route from each pantry to every room in the Castle. All I could think to myself was 'Help!'" He smiled at Clovermead—then clucked his tongue as he saw that his eyes were above hers. "Don't slouch. I know you're taller than me."

Clovermead straightened up, and now she could look down at her father's head, half-bald and half-full of graying hair, his lined face lit by a wry smile, his goatee gone fully white, and his eyes that always looked at her with love. Waxmelt was now a good three inches shorter than Clovermead. He wore a soldier's attire of scuffed brown leather and chain mail this evening, as he did habitually now that Lady Cindertallow had appointed him General of the Regiment of Servants.

"Mother also tells me I should have better posture. It's difficult to remember. Anyway, I'm tired." Clovermead slumped down again, so her elbows supported her on the table. Out of the corner of her eye she could see Saraband sitting marvelously upright, and she sighed. "Cousin, stop setting a good example!"

"Yes, Clovermead," said Saraband dutifully—and for a moment her arms were sprawled and her back bent, and she looked like a particularly ungainly monkey spread out around her bowl of stew. Then she straightened up again, with only a twinkle in her eyes and the ghost of a giggle to hint that she had ever moved. "Do you also want me to stop eating my vegetables and to stop cleaning my room?" Her eyes took in the clothes strewn across Clovermead's floor, and she winced. "I will forgo vegetables, but I cannot make my room look like this. I . . . do not have your talents in this direction."

Clovermead glared at Waxmelt as he tried to stifle a laugh. "Did you have anything to say, Father?"

"Me? It's your mother's Castle, not mine. Do what you will to it. All I want from you is good posture." He turned to Saraband. "I blame that Tansyard. He's always hunched over that horse of his, Brown Barley, and he makes a bad example. Do you think that's it?"

"Doubtless so," said Saraband, and no one but Clovermead would have caught the slight coolness in her voice as she spoke of Sorrel. Only Clovermead knew how close Sorrel and Saraband had been to each other three years ago in the Reliquary Mountains. Their romance had ended badly: She and Sorrel were civil to each other now, but they weren't friends. Saraband smiled stiffly. "The young man can have quite an influence on impressionable minds," she continued. She glanced self-consciously at Clovermead—and then her eyes widened as she saw Clovermead blush.

Clovermead yawned, so that her hand could cover her mouth and obscure her cheeks. "I am dead tired," she said, and suddenly she realized how true it was. "I've been up since dawn, and I'll have to be up at dawn tomorrow. We're riding off to the Steppes early. I know it's awfully rude, but do you mind if I go to bed now?"

"Of course not," said Waxmelt. He pushed his chair back and rose slowly and carefully. He leaned heavily on the table and favored his right foot. "Blast my ankle! It's stiffened up again."

"Poor thing," said Clovermead. Tired though she was, she ran around the table and put Waxmelt's hand on her shoulder. "Here, Saraband, support his other side."

"Gladly," said Saraband. She wiped her mouth with a napkin, then glided around to join them. "You will be well soon, Lord Wickward, I assure you."

"I've become a soldier too late in life," said Waxmelt, as they began to limp to the door. "I bruise, I sprain, and I will break all my bones soon enough. Blast sword-practice! Blast all those hulking stable-boys who are twice as fast and strong as me. And blast my pride that made me try to run and parry at the same time. Ouch! Not so fast, Clo!"

"Sorry, Father," said Clovermead, and she slowed down her pace.

"The stable-boys sprain their ankles too, Lord Wickward," said Saraband. "They come limping to my sickroom, and they don't stop howling while I bandage them up. You're no more foolish than they are, and you're a sight more pleasant to have as a patient. Don't worry—you'll be well in a fortnight."

"Thank you for the encouraging words, Lady." Waxmelt smiled at Saraband. "If my ankle is cured by midsummer, remember I've claimed a dance at the Ball with you. A general is allowed such privileges."

"Then I'll be sure to doctor your sprain away as quickly as I can," said Saraband. "We shan't miss the pleasure of a dance together." She batted her eyelashes at him.

"Your friend is a coquette," Waxmelt informed Clovermead. "But a silver-tongued coquette who is quite a lovely dancer. I will call on you for ointments, Lady Doctor, to be sure my sprain is gone."

Saraband laughed. "Did you know your father has danced with me at each of the last three Balls, Clovermead? He dashes out onto the dance floor ahead of all the young men to ask me to be his partner. La, sir, you will make a spectacle of yourself."

Waxmelt turned a little pink. "I'd be more conspicuous if I didn't try to dance with you, Lady. I'd have to fight against a tide of men rushing toward you." They were at the door now, and Clovermead swung it open. "Back to bed with you now, Clo. You need your sleep, and I'm sure Lady Saraband can act as my crutch without you."

Clovermead stopped to hug her father tightly and kiss him on the cheek. "It'll be a rush tomorrow morning, so let's say good-bye now. I hope I'll be back before summer's over, but I don't know for sure."

Waxmelt hugged her just as tightly, then reluctantly let her go. "I won't be going to the Steppes to join you," said Waxmelt unhappily. "Milady has told me she plans to take the Yellowjackets with her and leave the servants to garrison Chandlefort. I'm honored that she trusts us enough to leave us to guard the town by ourselves, but I wish I could come. I hate the thought of staying here while you're risking your life out on the Steppes." Lines of anxiety wrinkled his face. "You will take care of yourself? You won't do anything foolish?"

"Why does everyone seem to think I might?" asked Clovermead in an injured tone of voice. "Don't answer that. I will be so good and cautious and mouselike, you will think I've had a spell cast on me. I will come back to Chandlefort healthy and whole, and I'll bring you back a recipe for horse soup, Father. Satisfied?"

"Not in the slightest," said Waxmelt, laughing. "But I guess I have to trust you."

"I'll say good-bye to you in a little while, Clovermead," said Saraband. "First I'll escort your poor, decrepit father to his room"—Waxmelt yelped protestingly—"and apologize for calling him decrepit. Lord Wickward, don't you know that impudence is the prerogative of young ladies?"

"So I have learned." He gripped Clovermead's hand in his, then turned away. Clovermead watched him hobble down the hallway, leaning on Saraband. They waved to each other a last time as he turned the corner, and then Clovermead shut the door.

She staggered back to the armchair by her bed, and collapsed into it. "Don't be too long, Saraband," she said. "I'm falling asleep already." She yawned and curled up around a cushion. "In a good world, pillow-grass would grow wild on the Tansy Steppes, right by the bed-trees and the blanket-bushes. But it's not a good world, and I just know that this will be my last comfortable sleep for months." Her eyelids drooped shut. "I'll just nap for a second," she mumbled. Then she was asleep—

Clovermead was a white bear. She was twenty feet long, broad in proportion, with claws like kitchen knives and teeth like pike-heads. She ran through northern woods on a summer night, and her enormous paws trampled bushes to the ground, sent birds and weasels and even wolverines running from her path. Snowcapped mountains loomed in the distance, blurry through her tears. "Ursus," she roared. "Son, where are you?"

She was Boulderbash, Ursus' mother. Save in dreams, Clovermead hadn't seen her for three and a half years, but she recognized her instantly. It was a much younger Boulderbash who called out to her son. This was a dream from a long time ago.

Boulderbash came to a cave in the mountainside, a rotten hole in the rock, and she stopped on the ledge of black rock outside. "Ursus!"

"Hello, Mother," Boulderbash heard from inside the cave. The roar was loud as thunder, and hot and fetid breath came out of the hollow in the rock. "I've been waiting for you."

"Come outside," said Boulderbash. "Oh, Son, what have you done?"

"Not enough," said Ursus, and then he emerged from the cave mouth. He was scarcely recognizable. He had been larger than Boulderbash for years, but now he bulged with a glowing darkness. His claws were rakes dripping poison into the earth, and his fur was matted with filth. His teeth dripped with blood. Boulderbash weeped to see him, and Clovermead was screaming—

"Wake up, Clovermead!" said Saraband. She was shaking Clovermead's arm. "You're having a nightmare." Clovermead blinked and she was in her armchair again. "You were roaring," said Saraband, and she looked down at Clovermead's hands. Long bear claws sprouted out of them, and Clovermead had slashed her cushion to ribbons. Clovermead pulled her claws back into her fingers, and Saraband sat down gingerly on the hassock by the armchair. "What on earth were you dreaming about?"

"Bears," said Clovermead muzzily. She tried to clear her head. "I dreamed I saw Lord Ursus." She shuddered, and Saraband shivered too. "Never mind. It's over now. Thank you for taking Father back to his room."

"I'm always glad to. He's a sweet man." She looked curiously at Clovermead. "Now, speaking of men we like . . . I think I saw a suspicious blush at dinner." Saraband had a hint of mischief in her voice. "I suppose I should be polite, and pretend I didn't see anything, but I can't resist the opportunity to embarrass you thoroughly. Clovermead, have you finally noticed how attractive Sorrel is?"

"We're just friends," said Clovermead. "That's all we've ever been." Saraband raised an elegant eyebrow, and Clovermead's cheeks suddenly flamed quite red again. "Sometimes I do wish we were more than friends," she confessed. The words clattered out of her mouth, and even to say that much out loud made her heart race. "I daydream about him, you know, kissing me—oh, Lady, now I must be scarlet down to my toes! But I do think about that an awful lot, when I should be doing home-work, or when I'm reading in the library, or just when I'm eating dinner. Other times, though, the thought scares me stiff. I mean, I like him an awful lot, but how do I know if it's, it's—"

"Love?"

"Serious. Real." Clovermead hunched into herself in embarrassment. "I—You know, I first thought I might care for him, that way, that much, the summer we were riding in the Reliquaries."

"I never guessed," said Saraband. She suddenly laughed. "Though I shouldn't be surprised. You seemed awfully angry at me then and I couldn't quite understand why. Now I think I do." She looked at Clovermead with sudden compassion. "You've felt this way that long?"

"I don't know," said Clovermead. "I was awfully jeal-ous of you, but then when you and Sorrel stopped seeing each other, it seemed like I didn't care so much about him. Not the same way, anyway. Then I thought maybe I'd just had a stupid little-girl crush on him, and it wasn't really l-love." She stuttered a little as she said the word out loud for the first time. "I mean, I wasn't even thirteen yet. And then I thought, I keep on thinking, I'm only fifteen now, and maybe it's still just a little-girl crush. How can I tell?" She shook her head shamefacedly. "I spend hours asking myself, 'Is it a crush or isn't it?' I am such a noodle-head."

"I see," said Saraband. "You've spent hours a day for the last three years thinking about Sorrel, and wondering whether it's just a crush."

Clovermead rolled her eyes. "I'm not that bad! Sometimes there are days, or weeks, when I don't much think about him at all. But then it all comes back to me. He's so kind and funny, he's such a brave soldier, and he never forgets that I'm really Clovermead Wickward, and not Cerelune Cindertallow, the Demoiselle of Chandlefort. Mother and Father aren't bad about that, and neither are you, but I'd lose my balance without Sorrel." Clovermead blushed. "And he is so handsome! I'd be horribly frightened if he even looked at me funny, but I would very much like it if he kissed me. That would be lovely." She looked helplessly at Saraband. "If you want to be kissed, is that being in love or just a crush?"

"Oh, now I'm being called in as the voice of experience? I feel like an old crone." Saraband smiled, and took Clovermead's hands in hers. "I don't know much more than you about the subject. All that my immense age suggests is that you don't need to worry so much about names. Call it a crush, call it love, it doesn't matter."

"That's entirely too sensible a piece of advice. I couldn't

possibly follow it." They both laughed. "Do you mind, Saraband? That I like him like that?"

"Me? I don't care." Saraband laughed again, but now her laughter sounded a little sad. "Not much, anyway. It's been three years. And Lady knows we were no match for each other, while you two ruffians clearly are. No, no regrets on my part, Clovermead, no jealousy."

"You don't have cause to be jealous anyway," said Clovermead. "He's never looked at me the way he looked at you. I like to think that it's because I'm the Demoiselle of Chandlefort, and I'm so exalted that he's afraid to say anything, even if he does like me." She grimaced. "But maybe, when you get right down to it, he only thinks of me as a friend."

"He is discreet—he always was." Saraband smiled. "But you needn't despair. I think I have seen him give you several admiring looks lately."

Clovermead's eyes went wide, and she was blushing worse than ever. "Really?"

Saraband hesitated. "I *think* so. I haven't spent much time with him of late, you understand." She giggled. "You'll have plenty of opportunity to find out this summer."

"Don't say that," said Clovermead. "Now I'll be embarrassed all the time, and I'll make a fool of myself, and I'm going to blame you." Then she took Saraband in her arms and hugged her. "I hope you're right," she whispered.

"I do too," said Saraband, as she hugged Clovermead back. "But don't fret yourself. A watched Tansyard never boils." She released Clovermead and kissed her on the cheek. "Take care of yourself out on the Steppes."

"And you take care of yourself here," said Clovermead.

They made their last good-byes, and then Saraband slipped from the room.

"That wasn't nearly as embarrassing as I'd feared," said Clovermead. She fell into her bed, kicked off her shoes, and scrunched up the blankets about her. "Maybe saying something to Sorrel won't be so bad either. 'So, Sorrel, did you know I think you're awfully handsome? And I love the way you smile. So, would you like to kiss me?'" She groaned, and pulled the blankets over her head. "No," she said through the cloth, rather muffled, "that would be just awful. I suppose I should have read more of those sappy love poems that Saraband likes—they must have some tips on what to say to someone you like. But they're dreadfully boring. It was all so easy in *The Astrantiad*—Sir Tourmaline rescued Queen Aurette single-handedly from being devoured by a sand dragon, and she just *knew* that he was in love with her, and of course she was rather fond of him after being rescued from the dragon, so they didn't actually have to talk about the matter. I wonder if there are any grass dragons on the Steppes?" She started thinking about how precisely to rescue Sorrel from a grass dragon, and then she fell asleep—

Clovermead was in the northern woods again, trapped in the same dream. Ursus stood in front of her again, in front of Boulderbash. He was dark, he was huge, and he was terrible. Blood and filth besmeared his black fur. His eyes were dark holes.

"It is true," said Boulderbash, in horror. "I heard, but I couldn't believe. Until now." She looked at her son, and more tears trickled down her fur. "What have you done to your eyes? They shone so beautifully in the moonlight—"

"No more," growled Ursus. Blood dripped from his mouth and he caught it in midair with his tongue. He gulped down the red

liquid. "There is no moon. There is no light. There never was. Only darkness, Mother." He chuckled. "Darkness for everyone."

"There was light in your eyes," Boulderbash repeated stubbornly. "I saw it when you were born. Oh, Ursus, you were lovely."

"I am magnificent now," said Ursus. He rose onto his hind legs and reared up against the sky. His claws scrabbled against the stars. When he came back on four legs, he had grown. He was twice the size of Boulderbash, and still growing. "I am power, I am pain, and I am destruction. I am killing and I am the end of light. I am the end of everything. Oh, Mother, you have given birth to a god." He smiled. "Lord Ursus." Blood streamed out of his teeth. It spread along the rock ledge, pouring toward Boulderbash.

"I have given birth to a monster," said Boulderbash, and her heart was breaking. "Lady, what did I do wrong?"

"There is no Lady!" Ursus howled, and the roar made the mountains tremble. And the blood rose from the rock. The red liquid spun in the air, formed tendrils—and one strand lashed out to grab Boulderbash. Red threads were spinning into a net, and Boulderbash reared up in sudden fear and anger and slashed at the red tendril with her claws. Her claws bounced off the blood-net and another tendril attached itself to her. And her son laughed, cruel and mocking. "Beg for help, Mother. Ask your Lady to help you."

Another tendril came questing for Boulderbash, and she snapped at it with her fangs. Her teeth slid away from the red line. "Help me, Lady!" Boulderbash roared in terror. "Keep me free." But there was no light in the darkness, no aid for her, only more tendrils attaching themselves to her limbs, her torso, her head. And somehow the tendrils were going into her, and her muscles were no longer moving at her command. Ursus moved her instead. All that was left was her brain—to see, to hear, to know what he was doing with her body. "How can you do this to your own mother?" she roared.

"I will bring the gift of darkness to everyone," crooned Ursus. "You are my first servant, but I will have many more. In time all bears will serve me and all humans worship me." He laughed. "There is no hope, Mother. You will never be free." The blood-net was tight around her now.

"Our Lady will not leave me in darkness forever," said Boulderbash. "I will be free."

Then darkness swirled down, endless darkness, and when it lifted, Boulderbash had grown old, and she was looking at Clovermead, Clovermead as she had been three and a half years ago. Clovermead stood by a prison cart in the Army of Low Branding and she held a bear-tooth in her hand, glowing red with blood. "Come help me," she said to Boulderbash. "I need your strength to free Father." There was another blur of darkness, and then Clovermead wavered back into view. "You can go free when you're done here."

Clovermead was suffused with blood, Lord Ursus' darkness covered her, but the clouds overhead parted and her eyes glowed with moonlight. It was Our Lady's light, the light Boulderbash had seen so long ago in her infant Ursus' eyes, and the words repeated inside of Boulderbash, a promise fulfilled at last. You can go free. You can go free.

Clovermead faded from view. Now there was only darkness and pain. "More than three years have passed and I am still waiting," said Boulderbash, and she was very tired. "Redeem your promise. Free me."

"That wasn't what I meant," cried Clovermead. "I just meant I'd free you then, from my own compulsion. I didn't mean I'd free you from Ursus, too. You aren't remembering this properly." She gulped. "I've sworn to free all the bears, Boulderbash. I'll free you when I can, with the others —"

"You promised to free me, Clovermead," said Boulderbash. "I heard you. Don't tell me I dreamed it. Don't tell me you never gave me hope." She was crying in the darkness. "I saw the light in your eyes. Our Lady will not abandon me forever. You promised."

"I didn't," cried Clovermead. "This isn't fair of you. You can't expect —"

"You promised!" Boulderbash repeated, and she roared in sorrow and in loneliness. "I heard you, changeling. Our Lady was in you."

"It's not fair," Clovermead repeated, but it was only a whisper now. Boulderbash ached so, and Clovermead tried to refuse her again, but she couldn't. "I will free you," she said wearily. "It won't be just a dream. It will be real. I promise you that, in Our Lady's name." She sighed. "Stop weeping, Boulderbash."

Now Boulderbash roared with sudden joy. "I will, changeling. Thank you. I am waiting for you. Come quickly."

"Where are you?" asked Clovermead. "How can I free you if I don't know where you are?"

"Come quickly," Boulderbash repeated. Her voice was softer now, dwindling in the darkness. "I am waiting."

Chapter Three

ACROSS THE WHETSTONE RIVER

CLOVERMEAD CAME TO THE TOWN GATES AT DAWN the next day. She had put on her traveling outfit of black leather boots, gray woolen shirt and trousers, and an outer jacket of boiled brown leather laced with steel wire. In the square in front of the gates Fetterlock, Sorrel, and nine other Yellowjackets waited for Clovermead. The Tansyards were talking to each other quietly while the rest of the Yellowjackets said farewell to their children and their wives. High above, Yellowjackets and armed servants lined the formidably thick walls of Chandlefort. The gates themselves were the walls' only weak point. Mallow Kite had shattered them three years ago, and so far the town blacksmiths had only welded back together the first ten feet of iron. Above the ironwork, nothing more than a palisade of wood protected Chandlefort from its enemies. The city was fortunate that Lord Ursus had been busy subduing the Thirty Towns since Mallow's assault: Save for the odd raiding party of bear-priests, Lord Ursus had left Chandlefort in peace.

Clovermead swung up onto Auroche and checked to make sure her true father Ambrosius' sword was still tightly cinched to her belt—she was now tall enough to wield it comfortably. It had been broken once, but now it was whole again, and as strong and supple as a new-forged blade. Three years ago it had blazed with Our Lady's light, and Clovermead had freed two hundred bears from Lord Ursus' slavery—but there'd been no chance for it to shine lately. Ursus had kept his bears prudently far from Chandlefort since then. Clovermead still called it Firefly, in memory of when it had shone in the night. She patted the sword, and waved to the distant Castle, where her mother was watching from the window of her study. Then she and the Yellowjackets rode out onto the Low Branding road.

They galloped along a highway of gray flagstones straight east toward the distant line of the Chandle Palisades. A slight rise of twisting hills hid the riders from the green fields of Chandlefort almost at once, and then they were riding across the flat Salt Heath. Knee-high thorny bushes pockmarked the brick-hard ochre earth, and a thick blanket of fine red dust whipped back and forth in the breeze. The land was empty of human beings, of animals, of everything but the occasional thornbush.

Clovermead looked two or three times at Sorrel as they rode, to see if she could catch him being discreetly admiring of her, but he was always quite busy watching the road, or soothing Brown Barley, or drinking water from his flask. *Saraband doesn't know what she's talking about,* Clovermead decided. *He spends more time looking at Brown Barley than he does at me!* Clovermead's heart twinged, but only a little. *At least I know how to be just friends with Sorrel. It'll be easier to talk with him that way.*

The morning was briskly cool and the sky a pale,

clear blue. As the sun rose in the sky, it warmed the land, but not much. They stopped for a lunch of water, hard cheese, and oat bread by a cluster of teardrop-shaped pillars inscribed with the burning bee. Five Yellowjackets kept watch while the rest of them ate their lunch; halfway through lunch the watchers and the eaters changed places. The sergeant in charge of the Yellowjackets paced restlessly by the pillars when he'd finished eating; he was a lanky, fair-skinned man with graying chestnut hair. *What's his name?* thought Clovermead. *Oh, yes, Algere. He's from the Lakelands.* Near the horses a laughing, freckled redhead barely older than Clovermead fenced with a scowling, bald-headed corporal with a jet-black goatee who was twice his age. Sorrel sat near Clovermead, and glanced eastward as he ate.

"Are you happy to be going back to the Steppes?" asked Clovermead, between swallows. "I would be. Chandlefort's home for me now, but I still miss Timothy Vale awfully, and I wish I could go back there for a visit. But nobody will be taking potshots at me in Timothy Vale because they think I should have died bravely and stupidly, and I can see how that would make me less eager to pop on by."

"I am not afraid," said Sorrel. He looked at the desert around him and shook his head. "Except, perhaps, of disappointment. I always talk about how much I love the green grass of the Steppes, and how much I dislike this dry land, but I have grown used to it over the years. I wonder if I will love the Steppes so much when I see them again. I wonder if I have forgotten what they are really like."

"I'm sure they're wonderful. And I want you to show me what you like best about them! Anyway, you won't be half as disappointed as I will be if it turns out that the Steppes aren't as ravishingly beautiful as you've always said."

"You need not worry," said Sorrel, smiling. "I am sure the Steppes are more beautiful than anything you have ever seen. It is just that they may not compare with my fond memories." Then he sighed, and his eyes strayed eastward once more.

Fetterlock sat, listened, and said nothing as they ate. His eyes met Clovermead's, and he smiled and nodded. Clovermead tried to smile back at him as casually as possible.

I don't know what he's hiding, Lady Cindertallow had said. *I don't believe he's lying about the fortress going up on Bryony Hill—that fits with other reports I've had from my spies. I even believe he's an emissary from the Horde Chief's wife—that will be too easily checked for him to lie about that. But he's keeping something important hidden. Watch for it, Clovermead. Don't let him realize you're suspicious, but find out what's the truth he's keeping hidden. I suspect it will matter a great deal.*

Do you think he's an agent of Lord Ursus? Clovermead had asked. *Is he leading us into a trap?*

I don't think so, her mother had said. *Too much of what he says has the ring of truth. Still, don't let him lead you too close to Bryony Hill.*

Fetterlock finished his food, wiped his mouth, and stood up. Clovermead wondered what would happen if she wrestled him in bear shape. There weren't many humans who could tussle with a bear, but Fetterlock looked like he might be one of them.

They rode through a thickening scrub all through the afternoon. The Heath grew more pleasant the farther they were from Chandlefort, and by day's end they had come near to the forests before the Chandle Palisades. Birds flew in the air and small animals scurried through the trees. The freckled redhead, Habick, blew his horn and galloped after a jackrabbit, until Sergeant Algere grew annoyed and summoned him back with a ferocious whistle. He dressed Habick down with a lashing tongue, but the sparkle in the eyes of the young Yellowjacket showed he was unrepentant. The scrub turned into a hardy grass, sprouting new and green in the spring rains. They camped for the night a mile from the edge of the Heath.

"I do like the land better here than in Chandlefort," said Clovermead as they ate dinner around a fire. "It's nice to see greenery that doesn't come out of an irrigation ditch. And I can smell sheep! It's not what I'd call perfume, but when I smell them, I think I'm back in Timothy Vale, and I feel warm and cozy. I'm glad we rode this way."

"It's a fair stretch of earth, Demoiselle," said Sergeant Algere. Tonight he sat near Clovermead, between Fetterlock and Sorrel. He tore a hunk of bread from the loaf in his left hand, and gulped it down. "And good sheep country, as you say. My da used to graze his flock here, when I was a lad. I remember when the grass was taller than I was."

"Back in Timothy Vale I used to scuttle through the tall grass and sneak up on the sheep," Clovermead confided to the Sergeant. "I was heartbroken when I got too big to hide. Of course, by then I was large enough to leap ewe-back and pretend I was a knight on horseback." She winked at Algere, and he laughed.

"I think I have heard the end of that story, Sergeant," said Sorrel. "She tried to rescue a maiden lamb from a dragon of a ram, but he sent the gallant knight flying and cracked her forehead. This explains many things." The Tansyard looked at the grassland around him and smiled. "It is like the Steppes in a dry season. It reminds me of a time one very hot summer when a sudden flood had swollen the stream in our way and blocked the Horde's wandering. My father saw that some animal had slept the night before on the grass where we pitched our tent, and he took my brother Emlets and me away from the Horde for a day, to follow its tracks. The three of us left the camp and followed the animal's tracks all day, rustling our way through sere, yellow grass until we came to a broad hill. We climbed to its summit, and there, on a meadow very much like this one, we saw a red fox crouched down, coolly watching us, with a look on his face as if to say *What took you so long?*

"Emlets wanted to kill it. He drew his knife, danced up and down, and began to warble a death-challenge to the fox. I had no knife yet, but I capered up and down too, imitating Emlets as best I could. For a moment I wanted nothing more than to scramble and fight with the fox, to prove my valor against its claws and teeth—and then Father cuffed us, just hard enough to return us to our senses.

"'What do you want to do that for?' he asked us. Emlets muttered something about being a brave warrior, but Father walloped his backside. 'Measure your courage against a wolf or a bobcat,' he said roughly. 'A fox is no challenge to your strength.'

"'What do we do instead?' Emlets asked.

"Father shrugged. 'We sit and wait,' he said. 'Our Lady will tell us what to do.'

"So we sat and waited. The shadows lengthened and

37

night descended and we fell asleep. It was a hot night and comfortable enough. The next morning—" Sorrel grinned mischievously at Clovermead. "I will tell you some other time what happened the next morning."

"You're joking," said Clovermead disbelievingly. Sorrel shook his head. "Is this something else they do in the Cyan Cross Horde? Stop telling stories halfway through?"

"No, this delightful stratagem has just occurred to me. You will never dare dismiss me from the Yellowjackets while the end of the story is untold, and perhaps I can invite myself to meals with you, and eat well while you dance in tantalized agony from one foot to the other, hoping that this time at last you will hear the tale's conclusion. Then, when I do at last finish this story, I will also begin a new one, and leave that one unfinished as well. I will continue the practice until I have reached a ripe old age."

Clovermead hit Sorrel on the arm, hard enough to sting but not hard enough to hurt. Sergeant Algere snorted, and Fetterlock laughed. "The fellow is canny, Demoiselle," said the giant Tansyard. "Hit him again! It is the only way to keep these clever boys in line."

"Do not hit me," Sorrel protested. He rubbed his arm. "I am a delicate creature. He speaks from inveterate malice—White Star and Cyan Cross have always been rivals, so he seeks to have you drub my weak flesh. Do not let him put the cotton in your ears."

"Pull the wool over my eyes, you mean," said Clovermead. "Don't worry. I'll only hit you when you need hitting." Sorrel groaned, and Fetterlock chuckled again.

"Don't bruise my trooper too badly, Demoiselle," said

Algere. "I need young tongue-wagger to stay in fighting trim." He brushed bread crumbs from his fingers and got to his feet. "Beg pardon, Demoiselle. I should go see which of our sentinels is napping. Sorrel, don't stay up too late telling stories—you'll be sentinel with Habick on the third shift." Sorrel ducked his head obediently, the Sergeant saluted Clovermead, and he ambled off toward the slumping silhouette of a Yellowjacket.

"I once had a baby fox for a pet," Clovermead continued, when the Sergeant was out of sight. "Card Merrin killed its mother and he would have killed her, too, but I made him give her to me. I kept her in my room and fed her scraps from the table. I called her Satin, because that's what she looked like in the evenings when she was licking her fur. I wanted to tame her, but I never could— she got to be friendly enough with me, but she never stopped being a wild fox. She stayed all winter, but in the spring I left the bedroom window open one day, and she jumped out and ran away. I saw her once or twice in the next few weeks, but then she disappeared. I hope she's had a good life since." She elbowed Sorrel in the ribs. "And that's the end of the story. Unlike some Tansyards I could mention, I don't leave people on tenterhooks."

"I am a wretch," said Sorrel unabashedly, and he wandered off to make his bed.

"I see you do not sit on your dignity, Demoiselle," said Fetterlock. "You are friendly with your troopers."

"I try not to be stuck-up," said Clovermead. "I don't know how to be properly haughty anyway—when I stick my nose in the air, I can't see anything, and I bump into people. I wasn't brought up to be Demoiselle, you know, and mother says I'm hopelessly common. Anyway, how could I be snooty to Sergeant Algere? He's three times my age, and besides, he was my drill instructor that awful day I managed to disarm myself and trip over my feet at the same time. I'd be too embarrassed if I tried to play the snob with him. And Sorrel's my friend. That won't change if he's a trooper or a general."

Fetterlock raised an eyebrow. "A Tansyard general of Chandlefort! There is an idea! Do you think it likely he will rise so high?"

Lady Cindertallow's consort commands the Yellowjackets, thought Clovermead. She blushed in the darkness, and made herself speak in an even tone. "I guess there's no telling. We'll just have to wait and see."

"An undeniable truth," said the Tansyard. Then he lapsed back into silence.

The next day was damper, and gray cloudbanks filled the air. The band rode into the forest and soon they came to the Chandle Palisades, gray granite cliffs that stretched to the north and south horizons and plunged down four hundred feet from the forest to the Whetstone Valley. The road switchbacked steeply down the cliff-face, and they had to go slowly as they descended. Oaks and cedars rose high above them, and they lost sight of anything but the trees around them. The day grew warmer as they left the plateau of the Heath behind. Halfway down the slope Clovermead saw snowdrops beginning to bloom, and toward the bottom she saw crocuses. By the road a stream fat with spring rains surged exuberantly over rock overhangs to make small waterfalls. At the bottom of the cliff, the party stopped at a fort garrisoned by Yellowjackets that marked the boundary of Lady Cindertallow's realm.

Fetterlock looked at every corner of the fort as they ate their evening meal, so casually that only Clovermead noticed what he was doing. "Taking notes?" she whispered to him. "I'll tell Mother to change the locks."

Fetterlock chuckled softly. "The Horde Chief's wife wanted me to keep my eyes open, Demoiselle. She wants to know if Chandlefort is prepared to fight against Ursus."

"Quite well, thank you. I trust the gleam on the garrison's pikes satisfies you?"

"Eminently," said Fetterlock. He bowed respectfully to Clovermead, then sauntered over to the barracks where he had bunked down for the night. His saunter took him close by the stables, and the Tansyard couldn't suppress a gleam in his eye as he passed the soldiers' steeds. The Hordes were notoriously addicted to purloining horses.

"And we keep our horses well guarded, too," said Clovermead softly to herself. "So don't even think of trying to abscond with any of them, you horse thief!"

The third day a steady drizzle poured down on the riders as they rode through the close-packed fields between the Palisades and the Whetstone. Soon they came to the small riverport town of Widder Brand, just opposite Low Branding. A troop of Low Branding soldiers waiting at the harbor brought up their spears as the Yellowjackets approached, but Clovermead had the letter from Lady Cindertallow in her pocket that she showed to the wizened patrician at the head of the soldiers. He squinted at it, gave it back to Clovermead, and then escorted the Yellowjackets to a large barge. "Take us to South Harbor," he told three sailors in oilskin jackets. He got onto the barge with the travelers, and the sailors began to pole them across the river.

The Whetstone was a quarter of a mile across here,

broad and gentle. As they crossed the fog-shrouded river, Clovermead saw other boats poling through the water, and then the dim shine of a lighthouse lantern. Soon the lighthouse itself emerged from the mist, followed by the long stone breakwater that stretched from the lighthouse to the shore. Then they were among dozens of boats, ranging from small fishing boats to great traders a hundred feet long. Ahead were wooden piers, the great Customs House of Low Branding, and the low sprawl of warehouses and taverns that formed the shorefront of the city. The sailors steered them to the south end of the harbor, and then they had landed among a hubbub of longshoremen and merchants.

"I'm going to the Mayor, to let him know you're passing through our lands," said the patrician. "Take the road to the right—that will take you around the walls, so you don't have to go into the city itself. The main road east to the Moors is easy to find. Don't dawdle: We'll all be happier the sooner you're out of our territory." He gave Clovermead a sketchy salute, then turned and strode into the town.

"You'd think he could be nicer to his Mayor's allies," said Clovermead.

"Allies are astonishingly ungrateful to one another," said Fetterlock. "The need for the alliance galls." He scowled. "Me, I do not like to ask Yellowjackets, farmerfolk, to help us defend our Steppes."

"You came to us," said Clovermead.

"The Horde Chief's wife sent me," said Fetterlock. "I did not want to go." He scowled again, and kicked his horse so that it sprang ahead of the rest of them on the road.

"I would not care what Low Brandingmen think of

you," said Sorrel. "They are a nation of murderers." He spat at the ground. "I will never forgive them for their destruction of Cyan Cross Horde."

"They're not all responsible," said Clovermead. "It was the Mayor who ordered the Low Branding soldiers against your Horde. I'm not fond of him, either. He's been a sight too fond of assassinating and kidnapping Cindertallows in his time, and I still remember how he locked me up in a cage. But the rest—"

"They doff their hats to their butchering Mayor. They pay the salaries of their soldiers whose swords are stained with my nation's blood. They are all murderers." And he looked so angry that Clovermead didn't dare to say another word to him.

They rode around the southern walls of the city, and Clovermead could see great merchants' halls rising to her left, their tops covered in mist. Soon the travelers came to the east road and began to ride away from Low Branding, leaving the river and the rain behind them. Here there were hundreds of small farms, each with a narrow strip of earth extending several hundred feet from the road. Occasionally the group passed a troop of soldiers marching across the countryside. The soldiers warily eyed the Yellowjackets and peered at Lady Cindertallow's letter, but they were content to see the Yellowjackets ride away from Low Branding. But there were few soldiers: It was a peaceful realm. The farmers walked around without weapons.

The travelers stopped for the night in a fallow field. Fetterlock had dinner with the Yellowjackets, while Clovermead and Sorrel ate together at their own campfire. Sorrel had scared up a chicken—Clovermead tried not to think too hard about where it had come from—

and had spitted it over the fire. Clovermead gathered the firewood, and they sat companionably side by side as they waited for the chicken to roast. Every now and then Clovermead could hear Sergeant Algere quiz Fetterlock about the lay of the land ahead, as his words floated over from the Yellowjackets' campfire. Most of the time Algere was drowned out by the bald corporal, Naquaire, who was singing the old ballad "Leathwake's Ride," and of how the healing draught came too late and Lady Vermeil died in Leathwake's arms. Towheaded, burly Bergander accompanied Naquaire on the lute, his thick fingers strumming with astonishing delicacy. Young Habick listened to the song with wide eyes and an open mouth.

"They make so much noise over there!" said Sorrel. "And they sing a song to make a man cry, though I am in no mood for tears. But we are alone at our campfire, so I will valiantly ignore our companions and pretend we are traveling alone through Linstock once more—you just an innkeeper's daughter and I just a messenger boy for Milady. Do you remember how we cooked as we traveled through the snowstorms?"

"I remember you were awfully afraid of me turning into a bear," said Clovermead. She wiggled her hand at Sorrel, and let it turn furry. "You thought—"

"I thought you would be possessed forever, which almost turned out to be the case, so do not recriminate at me," said Sorrel. He batted Clovermead's paw aside. "You are a much more pleasant bear now—roly-poly and ruggish. I did not expect I would ever be so complaisant to see a golden bear growling at me, but the world is full of surprises. And our tracking games have made me a better hunter than I ever expected to be. On the Steppes we had no intelligent bears to stalk, or to stalk us. I have learned tricks training with you that would surprise the Hordes."

"Like climbing trees," said Clovermead. Her eyes danced. "Do you remember when I leaped out at you from the darkness, over by the hayfields? You went up twenty feet in about two seconds. I'd have caught you if I hadn't been busy laughing."

"I told myself that I would look back on that moment and laugh," said Sorrel. "Clearly, I do not need to bother, since you are laughing for me. But while we speak of fond memories, I am particularly proud of the bear-trap laden with honey that I set for you. It is not merely the look of surprise on your face as the net closed over you, or even the smear of honey on your mouth, but the poetry of the moment. A bear ought to be snared in a honey-trap. The traditional aspects of that incident delight me still." He smiled. "And the fact that it was only a jar of your breakfast honey."

"You don't know how wonderful it smelled," said Clovermead. "Wait until you have a bear-nose—then you'll understand."

"I trust I shall wait a long time," said Sorrel. "I have grown used to you being a bear; still, I would rather not become one myself. It is an unreasonable prejudice, perhaps, but I prefer my skin and my shape."

"Will you tell me the rest of that story about the fox?" asked Clovermead. "I've been waiting very patiently, but I'm dying of curiosity."

Sorrel chuckled. "Patience will never be your strong suit, Clovermead. If I told you that you would have to wait a year, you would die of apoplexy."

"I certainly would," said Clovermead. "So how does

the story end? Did the red fox end up as the trimmings for your hat?"

"No!" Sorrel touched his hat-brim self-consciously. Then he glanced at Clovermead with curious intensity, and fell silent for a moment. His eyes dropped. "I wish," he began—and then he fell silent once more. He looked up at Clovermead again, and for a moment she thought she saw something stronger than friendship in his eyes. They were sitting alone in the dark, and Clovermead was suddenly aware just how near they were to each other, and how far away everyone else was. At the other campfire all the Yellowjackets were singing the chorus of "Leathwake's Ride," singing of how Leathwake fell in love with Lady Vermeil the moment he set eyes on her. Clovermead wanted to smile, she wanted to reach out and take Sorrel's hand in hers, but she just sat still. She was blushing, but Sorrel couldn't see that in the dark.

Sorrel's eyes dropped a second time, and now he was the same Sorrel as ever. "You will just have to wait a little longer," he said in his familiar teasing tone. "You are not nearly frustrated enough yet. You will hear the entire tale one day, but for now you will just have to wait."

"After all this buildup, the story had better be worth it," said Clovermead. Her heart was still beating double-time. *Did I imagine that?* she asked herself. *Oh, Clovermead, you must have. He'd never look at me* that *way outside of dreams.*

"It is a wonderful story," said Sorrel. He smiled at her, friendly and safe. "You have my word, Clovermead. You will be quite happy when you hear the end of it."

Chapter Four

THE HARROW MOORS

THE NEXT DAY GRAY CLOUDS FILLED THE SKY. THE wind had shifted and a biting breeze blew from the north. Through the chill they rode east on land that sloped gently upward. Here the farms were farther apart, and the farmers carried spears with them as they went to patrol large paddocks where sheep, cows, and horses nibbled at the new grass. It was largely horse country: Clovermead saw no end of them in the rolling greensward.

A farmer bringing hay out to a dozen horses looked suspiciously at Sorrel and Fetterlock as the Yellowjackets passed by. Sorrel said quietly to Clovermead, "These are our raiding grounds. Whenever we Tansyards feel short of horses, we head through the Harrow Moors to seize a horse or five from these farmer-folk. Then they come back through the Moors to reclaim their horses—and if they cannot find the proper thieves, they take them from whichever Horde they find."

"That hardly seems right," said Clovermead. "That means they're just stealing horses from somebody else, not taking back what really belongs to them."

Fetterlock laughed and said something to Sorrel in

47

Tansyard. Sorrel laughed too, then switched to common tongue: "Fetterlock reminded me of the time that Curvet of the White Star Horde stole a mare from the Horde Chief of Cyan Cross, and left false evidence to convince him that the thief was actually a Red Bar warrior. Five warriors died in battle between Cyan Cross and Red Bar before the truth came out, and by then the White Star Horde was halfway across the Steppes. The Elders deposed the Horde Chief for folly, and since then White Star has had an excellent story to tell about Cyan Cross."

"And this is something to laugh about?" Clovermead rolled her eyes. "Never mind. It still doesn't excuse the Low Brandingmen."

Sorrel shrugged. "You think horse-stealing is a crime; we regard it as a warrior's virtue. We kill any Low Brandingmen we catch when they come for our horses, but we give them a proper burial. It is a jolly game, and we have killed a great number of each other over the years, like good neighbors. Ah, how little that farmer suspects that I have become an honest soldier of Chandlefort! And what a fine herd he has!" Sorrel tipped his hat to the glowering farmer, and rode on in a good humor.

"These Tansyards are very peculiar," Clovermead declared loudly. "I don't think I'll ever understand them properly."

"You farmer-folk confuse us just as much," said Fetterlock.

In the afternoon the clouds parted and a wan sun came out. The riders passed a low stone fort of Low Branding mercenaries, who cantered out quickly to see who the strangers were—looked at Lady Cindertallow's letter, grunted, and returned to their stronghold. East of the fort the stone road turned into a dirt track. Here the farms were few indeed, and each had a wooden palisade around it. The farmers all were mounted, and they watched the Yellowjackets with surly suspicion. Clovermead saw that some of them had white tattoos in the shape of pikes on their foreheads.

"Are those Tansyards?" she asked Fetterlock.

Fetterlock snorted. "The pike is the emblem of Low Branding. These farmers ape our ways, but they are not Tansyards. The tattoo says that the farmer has killed a Tansyard. It is a new custom: The farmers did not practice it when I was young. I do not care for it. Farmers are farmers, not Tansyards, and they should not try to look like us."

"Sorrel wears a Yellowjacket's uniform," said Clovermead. "Why can't they have tattoos?" Fetterlock did not reply. "Fetterlock?"

"He will have to insult me if he speaks, Clovermead," said Sorrel. "Let him be silent. He thinks it is a disgrace to see a Tansyard in this livery. I do not agree, but it took me years to convince myself that I was not shamed by a yellow jacket. And you know that I would not have put on Cindertallow livery if my Horde still lived."

"*I* don't think it's a disgrace," said Clovermead. "I think it's an honor to fight for Chandlefort, and if any Tansyard tells you otherwise, they'll have to fight me."

"Well said," said Sergeant Algere, and the other Yellowjackets rumbled approval of her words.

"I will tell the warriors of the White Star Horde to be discreet," said Fetterlock, after an appraising glance at Clovermead and the Yellowjackets. "At least your yellow coat brings you a loyal leader, Sorrel. That much of your choice I respect."

"I have no worries there, Fetterlock," said Sorrel. He smiled at Clovermead, and she blushed with pleasure to hear his good opinion of her.

That evening they ate barley porridge from their stores. Clovermead wrapped a blanket around her, but she was still cold. She let herself grow furrier, grow bigger, and the cold lessened. Fetterlock looked at her and he hissed in wonder. "Then the tales are true," he said. "You are a changeling?" Clovermead nodded. "I do not know that the Elders will be pleased to know they must ally with a bear one way or the other."

"I'll stay human in front of them, but I won't lie about what I am." Clovermead couldn't help growling her anger for a moment, and the Yellowjackets sitting by her side, Sergeant Algere and Corporal Naquaire, hastily retreated from her. Fetterlock held his ground. "Our Lady gave the ability to turn into a bear to my true father, Ambrosius Beechsplitter, and to all his descendants. I'm a bear at Our Lady's pleasure, I'm grateful to her for the gift, and I've sworn to use it to fight for Our Lady. I figure that if Our Lady gave me that gift, there's nothing to be ashamed of about it, and I haven't hid it since I learned where it came from. If your Elders can't accept that, they can deal with Lord Ursus by themselves."

"You just have to learn how to stay out of arm's reach when the Demoiselle gets hot-tempered and bearish, Tansyard," said Algere. He looked at the grass he and the Corporal had crushed in their hasty retreat from Clovermead's side, and he smiled ruefully. "Not so difficult to do, is it, Naquaire?"

"Just a short scuttle on my arse, Sergeant," the Corporal growled. "Begging your pardon for the language, Demoiselle. Are you in temper again?" Clovermead nodded, and the Corporal and Sergeant sidled back to their places beside her at the campfire.

"I will inform the Horde Chief's wife that Chandlefort's Demoiselle is indeed a shapechanger," said Fetterlock. "If the fact is brought up in our counsels, perhaps she will know how to mollify the Elders."

The next day they rode into the Harrow Moors. The Moorland was a half-submerged plain interwoven with ridges of chalky gray stone. In the valleys, shallow ponds filled with dun reeds alternated with sheets of mud covered by leafless bushes and studded with stubby thorn trees. On the ridges, sturdy brown grass just turning to green covered the land, save where swellings of stone pierced the grass coverlet. Herons and wild ducks swam among the reeds, and a brown mink appeared on the crest of a nearby hill, twitched his whiskers, and fled from the sight of the soldiers.

"What a desolate place," said Clovermead out loud. "Does anyone live here?" She had meant to ask Sorrel the question, but Sorrel wasn't by her side. He had fallen back to the rear guard, and rode fifty yards behind her.

"The Harrowmen," said Fetterlock. He spurred his horse and came to ride by Clovermead's side. "They live in villages set up on islands in the ponds. They hunt, they fish, they rob anyone who ventures through the Moors without a strong escort. Sometimes we hire them as guides through the Moors on our way to raid Low Branding. Sometimes the Mayor likewise prizes money from his cash-box for their aid." He looked around the Moors. "I believe the Harrowmen find their land quite beautiful."

Clovermead wrinkled her nose. "No arguing with

taste, I guess, but I'm glad I didn't turn out to be the long-lost daughter of the Queen of the Harrowmen. That would have been a lot more depressing than turning out to be Demoiselle of Chandlefort."

"Yes, and then you would have been a were-beaver or a trout-changeling," said Fetterlock. His eyes danced. "You would not frighten the Elders then."

Clovermead groaned. "I thought it was just Sorrel who mocked me, but now I find out that it's Tansyard humor. It's going to be a long summer on the Steppes." *And a long summer away from Mother and Father,* she thought wistfully. *I like being out seeing new places, even if they are damp and muddy, but I miss them already. The worst part about traveling is all the people you leave behind.*

They rode on a curving track that was barely more than a rut in the ground, and soon they were surrounded by pools and mud, reeds and grass. A thin white haze curled over the pools and obscured the travelers' vision. As the denizens of the Moors grew used to their presence, mournful quacking filled the ponds and the rustling of small animals grew louder in the grasses. Fetterlock kept them to the thin track, sometimes orienting them by blazes scratched on rocks. As they rode deeper into the Moors, the pools grew larger and the dry land smaller. Soon they had to line up single file. Sorrel rode in the vanguard.

They came to a large meadow of brown grass that lay amidst three large ponds—and Sorrel suddenly reined in Brown Barley. He peered at something in the grass, then swung to the ground to examine it more closely. After a minute he gestured the others to come closer. Clovermead trotted up on Auroche, Fetterlock close behind her—and she gasped in horror. Two men and a woman had been struck down, and their bodies lay sprawled on the grass. Clovermead saw great gashes all along their bodies. Their mouths were opened to scream.

Fetterlock hopped down from his horse and looked closely at the corpses. "Harrowmen," he said grimly. "The beadwork on their jackets says that they are from one of the southern villages. They were struck from behind. I think they were running away when they were killed."

"Who killed them?" asked Clovermead. Her guts were squirming and she turned away from the dead bodies. "Bear-priests?"

"I do not think so," said Sorrel. "I have never known them to burn their victims. Look, the grass is charred black all around the bodies, and the flesh around these cuts has been burned. There is some sort of silver ash on their wounds. I think they were struck by torches as they died. What else could make injuries like this?"

Clovermead looked back at the bodies, and now she saw the silvery sheen all along the gashes on the dead Harrowmen. It glistened like liquid fire, even in the overcast light. Clovermead swung down from Auroche and knelt by the corpses. Hesitantly, fascinated, Clovermead reached out a finger to touch the silvered flesh—"Ouch!" She drew back her finger. It stung. She looked at her fingertip: It had been charred as black as the grass around the bodies. "That silver still burns."

Sorrel shivered. "I would like very much to know who killed these poor people."

"I would like to know if the killers are still around," said Fetterlock. He looked around at the meadow, whose emptiness suddenly seemed ominous.

"Can we bury them?" asked Clovermead. "If we have time, we ought to."

Fetterlock looked at the sky. The light was dwindling and it would be dusk soon. "We might as well camp here. Let us put earth on them and ready ourselves for night."

The Yellowjackets buried the bodies by sunset, Algere said a few words over their graves, and then they set up camp at the opposite end of the meadow. There were no songs this night, though Bergander strummed his lute for a few minutes in a vain attempt to counter the gloom of the thickening night mists. Clovermead looked nervously back at the fresh graves and at the darkness around them. She ate in silence and quickly fell asleep. In the cloudy night, Clovermead dreamed—

She ran in darkness and pounded through thick mud that sucked at her paws. She could not see and she raced terrifyingly blind. A bit in her mouth pulled her viciously left and right. She ached from a dozen cuts on her sides, and now a nailed whip sliced through her fur and pierced her flesh so that she howled in agony. Clovermead heard laughter. It was a familiar voice. It came from a man riding on her back.

"I want to be free," said Boulderbash. "You promised me. When will I be free?"—

"Where are you?" gasped Clovermead as she woke. "Are you near? Answer me!" She listened, but there was only silence. "I will try to save you, Boulderbash," Clovermead repeated. "Just as soon as I can find you."

It was gray already, nearly dawn. Clovermead rose unsteadily and put on her jacket. The old Yellowjacket Golion, unshaven and potbellied, was standing sentry; he yawned as he saluted her. Clovermead saw Sorrel fifty feet from the camp, looking into the thick fog roiling on the Moors.

"I had bad dreams," said Clovermead as she came up to him. "How about you?"

"I, too," said Sorrel. "I do not remember them, but I woke weeping." He shivered. "In the Cyan Cross Horde, we knew that dreams hold meaning, but we also knew they are difficult to understand properly. We went to the Shaman-Mother to tell us what they meant. Even she could not tell all dreams, but she relieved us of much perplexity."

Sorrel smiled in sudden reminiscence. "She was kind to small children. When our parents were busy, she would take us on walks, tell us the names of plants, and say what medicines they could be used for. She told us stories, too—not the great histories of the Horde, not tales of Our Lady's time wandering on the Steppes, but small, silly things that had happened to our fathers and our grandfathers. I learned from her that my mother once chased a hedgehog into a river, and that my great-grandfather had been terrified by a chipmunk when he was very small. Shaman-Mother had always loved such stories, even before she began to study the shaman arts, and she was glad for a chance to tell them."

"What about young Sorrel? Was he terrorized by a starling?" Sorrel chuckled, but said nothing. "I'll bet there's a story to be wormed out of you." Clovermead looked eastward into the mists. "How far are we from the Steppes?"

"Some twenty miles," said Sorrel. "The Moors are sometimes narrower than that, sometimes wider. I never went through the Moors until after the Horde was destroyed. Then I fled, half-mad, only knowing that I would be in danger until I came to the far, dry place where horsemen wore yellow coats and the town walls were ruby-red. I was many days coming to Chandlefort, and I do not remember them distinctly." The breeze turned, so it came from the east, and a scent of green grass came with it. Sorrel inhaled it longingly. "This is the first time since then that I have come this close to the Steppes."

A soft and distant sound carried through the Moors. Sorrel cocked his ears. "What is that?"

Clovermead let her ears grow big and furry, and she heard water splashing. "Something's swimming. Maybe an otter."

"It would have to be an animal. The Moors suck people into their depths." A cold breeze blew through the meadow, and Sorrel shivered. "We have a tale of how Our Lady walked upon the surface of one of these ponds, to rescue a pure white foal of the Red Spike Horde trapped in the mud. The whole Horde bowed down to worship her, and a Harrowman slave was the first to kneel. When Our Lady returned the foal to dry land, she asked the Horde for a gift to recompense her. The Horde Chief said she could have anything she wanted, and she chose the Harrowman slave. She touched his shackles and they sprang open. He cried with delight and ran into the Moors, skimming lightly over the water. His former mistress could not bear to see him go free, ran after him to catch him, and sank into the mud. Our Lady did not want to rescue her. Only when the entire Horde had fallen to its knees and begged her for mercy did she return to the pond to rescue the woman. Afterward she said she would rescue no more Tansyards if they went slave-catching among the Harrowmen. Since then, we have not touched them."

"Our Lady only walked through Timothy Vale once,

on her way to Snowchapel," said Clovermead. "There were just a few flocks of sheep on the meadows then. She stopped for a night at a shepherd's croft. He learned she had come from the Thirty Towns, and he asked her what they were like. She told him of the crowded cities, the wealthy princes, and the rich fields. The shepherd listened to her thoughtfully, then said, 'That's all well and good, but what of their sheep?' She told him that they had shepherds, too, although none with flocks as fine as his. The shepherd smiled. 'Thank you,' he said. 'You know, I would love to see this valley white with their fleece from one side to the other, like a garden filled with flowers.' 'You will,' said Our Lady, and by the time the shepherd was an old man, the Vale was solid white with lambs every spring. And it's been that way ever since."

"Long may it continue that way," said Sorrel. The distant sound had become louder, and Sorrel frowned. "That is not an otter." Clovermead poked up her furry ears again, and now there were two sounds. Nearby, something was splashing in the pond, trying to come quickly, but slowed by the muck. Farther off there was a low pounding. It came along the grass, still very quiet, but louder and louder. Sorrel whistled loudly, three long bursts, and the Yellowjackets stirred from their sleep and staggered to their feet. "Clovermead, I think you should withdraw behind these soldiers."

Clovermead took a step backward—but Sorrel hadn't moved. "What about you?"

"I should not go," said Sorrel. He shook his head. "Someone calls me to stay."

"I don't hear any voices," said Clovermead. Sergeant Algere and Corporal Naquaire led the Yellowjackets as they rode toward Clovermead and Sorrel, Fetterlock was leaping onto his horse, his braids untied and his hair swinging loose, and Clovermead put her hand on her sword hilt. "You don't really think I'll let you fight without me?"

Sorrel smiled vexedly. "I have no such fear." His smile faded and he looked anxiously again at the Moors. "I know that voice," he told himself distractedly.

"What voice?" asked Clovermead, but now she heard the splashing loud and clear. Through the haze, she saw a figure struggle through the pond. The heavier, pounding sound was approaching swiftly.

"What's happening?" asked Fetterlock. He had overtaken the Yellowjackets and he reached Clovermead before them. He reined in his horse and drew his broadsword, a monstrously long blade at least five feet long that looked delicate against his bulk.

"I don't know," said Clovermead, and then the figures came into sight.

A woman fled toward them through the pond. She held a large bundle in her arms, and made sure never to let it drop. Behind her four bear-priests came out of the mists. They wore wolf-skins, their scimitars were upraised, and each rode a bear. The bears were saddled with reins, bits, and eye-patches to blinker them in a world of night. All around them Clovermead saw with her mind's eye the tight, enslaving crimson bonds of Ursus' blood-net sunk into their skulls and entwined in every muscle. A cinnamon bear came first, then a pair of black bears, and finally a huge white bear.

Boulderbash, thought Clovermead numbly. The last rider pulled on the bit in the white bear's mouth, and men and bears came closer to the fleeing woman. *Is it really you?*

58

It is, Clovermead heard in her head. The old bear had never sounded so weary. *Have you come to free me at last?*

Yes! cried Clovermead. *I'm sorry you've been in darkness so long.*

Rescue me now, little cub. That's all that matters.

"Don't wait for them," Sergeant Algere cried to the Yellowjackets. "Keep them away from the Demoiselle. Tansyard, will you cover my flank?" Fetterlock nodded, and the Yellowjackets started to ride around the edge of the pond to intercept the bear-priests. The woman saw them and cried out something. The words meant nothing to Clovermead, but Sorrel gaped. "She is a Tansyard," he said. "She asks us to help her." Now she was only fifty yards away, hip-deep in water. She had silver hair and a worn face, and held a small girl in her arms. Sorrel looked at her again and his eyes went wide.

"Mother," he said disbelievingly. "Can it be you?" The Tansyard woman looked at Sorrel, and she gasped in shocked recognition. Sorrel looked at the child. "Mullein?" Then he hurtled into the pond, his sword drawn, and he was yelling in Tansyard to his mother and the girl. *His mother's name was Roan,* Clovermead remembered. *Mullein was his baby sister.* She wanted to free Boulderbash, she wanted to go with Sorrel, and she hesitated at the edge of the pond, uncertain what to do. Boulderbash's rider pulled at the bit again, Boulderbash moaned with pain, and then the rider came into clear view.

It was Lucifer Snuff—bear-priest, one-time aide to the Mayor of Low Branding, the savage, silk-tongued man who had convinced Waxmelt Wickward fifteen years ago to steal the baby Clovermead away from Chandlefort. Clovermead hadn't seen him since he fled

59

from Chandlefort three and a half years ago with the remnants of Ursus' army of bears and bear-priests, but his bald head, brown goatee, and filed bronzed teeth were instantly recognizable. He crouched low on Boulderbash, and his face was alive with the pleasure of the hunt. He wore polished leather with his wolf-skins, his black cape flared behind him in the breeze, and his scimitar's hilt glittered with rubies. He knifed Boulderbash in the side with his spurs and sent her leaping ahead of the other bears after Roan.

Why do you let him ride you? Clovermead thought frantically at Boulderbash. *Rise up! Throw him to the ground and tear him apart!*

I can hear you, girlie, thought Lucifer Snuff, and his bubbling laughter splashed through her mind. *She would if she could, but she can't. Lord Ursus has given me the whip hand over her.* He lashed Boulderbash's shoulder, for the sheer pleasure of the blow. *How delightful to see you again, Demoiselle. Now you can watch your friend die.* Boulderbash leaped toward Sorrel.

Sorrel had reached his mother. Their hands touched for an instant, and then Sorrel leaped between Roan and Snuff. Snuff brought down his sword with vicious fury, and Sorrel parried desperately. He half-slipped in the mud, and Snuff lashed out again. Sorrel fell backward into the pool. Fetterlock and the Yellowjackets were halfway around the mud banks of the pool, but now the other bear-priests on their bears had turned from the chase and were blocking their way. Habick and Bergander tried to charge them, shouting "Chandlefort! Chandlefort!" but their steeds' hooves sank into the mud and they could not advance. Only the bears' broad paws were able to keep a footing in the muck. Clovermead drew Firefly, swung it toward the blood-net, and a dagger of light flew from Clovermead, out through Firefly's tip, to shatter against the crimson bonds. The blood-net shivered but stood still.

My master has made preparations, brat, Snuff cried. *You won't undo his knots that easily this time.*

We'll see about that, thought Clovermead. She looked at the blood-net again. It wasn't really a single set of tendrils, the way it had been the last time, but a hundred smaller tendrils intertwined within each shackle. The bonds were flexible and resilient, but if Clovermead concentrated, she could make out the weak points in each bond. She swung Firefly again, focusing fiercely, light jabbed out of her—and the bond around Boulderbash's jaws snapped loose. She roared with delirious joy at her newfound freedom and bit at Snuff's hand. He jerked it hastily away.

The rest now, Boulderbash begged. *Hurry!*

Clovermead wanted to, but then Snuff kicked Boulderbash hard in the side and sent her running into the pond toward Sorrel, jaws still snapping at her rider. Sorrel was standing in front of his mother with his sword drawn, but he looked helplessly small against Boulderbash's huge bulk. Sergeant Algere, Corporal Naquaire, and Golion sparred with two bear-priests, cursing as their horses shied from the snarling bears. Fetterlock tried to turn from the mud bank to help Sorrel, but a black bear snapped at his arm, and he whirled back to slash at its snapping jaws with his sword. "Sorrel," Clovermead moaned, as she staggered into the pond to save him from Snuff. She couldn't focus on more than one thing at once, and she abandoned the white bear.

I'm sorry, Boulderbash, Clovermead whispered. As she ran to the Tansyard, the blood-net's tendrils greedily reattached themselves to Boulderbash's jaw. *There's no one else who can help him in time.* Snuff hammered down against Sorrel's blade, the Tansyard's sword spun into the water, and Sorrel went sprawling. Then Snuff was closing in on Sorrel's mother, she screamed with desperation, and she tossed the child Mullein through the air toward Clovermead. Clovermead dropped her sword into the pond's muddy water as the girl hurtled toward her, and she caught her in her arms as Snuff scooped up Roan.

"No one escapes from Barleymill," Snuff cried out in triumph. "Back to the mines with you, slavey. You'll suffer for this escapade, and then you'll die slowly, where the other slaves can see what happens to runaways." He looked at Clovermead and he grinned. "Someday we'll bring back the little girl, too. Soon all the world will belong to Lord Ursus. You have no hope." He roared, and Ursus' growl echoed thunderously in his voice. The other bear-priests turned from Fetterlock and the scrambling Yellowjackets, and set their bears hurtling through the mud. Snuff cuffed Roan unconscious, laid her body on Boulderbash's back, and raced off after the other bear-priests. In seconds he was gone.

I am still a prisoner, Boulderbash thought as she disappeared from view. *You said you would free me, but you abandoned me.* Terrible disappointment tinged her voice.

I'm sorry, said Clovermead. *He looked like he was about to kill Sorrel. I couldn't just stand there.*

You chose the human over me, snarled Boulderbash.

Next time I'll free you, said Clovermead. *I promise!*

You promised before, said Boulderbash, and then her thoughts faded away.

"We must make sure they do not double back to attack us again," said Fetterlock. "Shall we follow them a little while?" Sergeant Algere nodded agreement, and the Tansyard and the Yellowjackets cantered after the bear-priests into the Moors. Sorrel scooped up his sword from the pond, struggled toward Clovermead, and rapped out quick, fierce questions to his sister in Tansyard. Mullein still clung tightly to Clovermead. She was a girl of eight, dressed in rags, and terribly thin. She answered in frightened monosyllables, and then Sorrel spoke a quick last sentence to her and turned to Clovermead. "I must go," he said. He whistled loudly.

"Go where?" asked Clovermead. Sorrel was splashing toward the dry grass.

"To rescue my mother," said Sorrel. "You heard him. Snuff will take her back to Barleymill and he will kill her." He whistled again, and now pounding hoofs came closer. Brown Barley came running from the meadow. Sorrel looked at Clovermead with suddenly pleading eyes. "Come with me, Clovermead. I will need your help."

Yes! was on the tip of Clovermead's tongue. *Of course. All you have to do is ask.* She opened her mouth.

We can't afford any impulsiveness on this mission, her mother had said.

You can count on me, Mother, Clovermead had said. *I don't flibbertigibbet when it's important.*

"I can't," Clovermead faltered. "I have to go to the Steppes. Mother said—"

"Are you actually saying no?" Sorrel looked at her in

shock. "Clovermead, do you remember how I abandoned my duty to your mother to help you save your father? He would have died if I had not come with you when you asked."

Your first priority is to get the Hordes to agree to an alliance. Remember, no one but you can do this.

Soon all the world will belong to Lord Ursus. You have no hope.

"I can't, Sorrel," said Clovermead. "I would if it were just me, but I'm the Demoiselle, too. Everyone's depending on me."

"Mother depends on me, and I also depend on you, to come to Barleymill. Please. I beg you. Do not refuse me."

"You can go to Barleymill if you want," said Clovermead. "I'm not asking you to stay with me any longer. But I have to keep going to the White Star Horde."

"I understand," Sorrel began—and then he scowled. "No. I do not. I have asked you to help me save my mother's life, and that should be reason enough for a true friend. I thought I could count on you." Sorrel looked at her with disappointment, bitter resentment, and then all affection slid from his face. "I was mistaken. You are no friend at all." He leaped onto Brown Barley. He urged his horse a step toward Mullein, reached down to take her from Clovermead—then hesitated. "It is too dangerous to bring her with me," he muttered. He glanced at Clovermead, and he scowled again. "I do not wish to ask you for help, but I must. Since you will not come with me, at least take care of Mullein. You owe me that much."

"I will," said Clovermead. Tears ran down her cheeks. "You have my word, Sorrel." Sorrel nodded acknowledgment of her words, spoke again to Mullein, then turned to the south. The last Clovermead saw of him, his face was fixed with cold distaste for her. Sorrel tightened his legs, and Brown Barley was off at a gallop.

You always promise, Boulderbash whispered in the distance. *And you always are forsworn. Faithless girl, you abandoned me.*

Mullein tightened her arms around Clovermead's chest.

Chapter Five

MULLEIN

HE'S GONE, THOUGHT CLOVERMEAD NUMBLY. SHE fished her sword from the muddy bottom with one hand, then carried Mullein to the side of the pond. Fetterlock, Sergeant Algere, and the Yellowjackets rode back to rejoin her, swords still drawn in case the bear-priests should return. Mullein shrank from them and pressed herself against Clovermead. "Don't be scared," said Clovermead, but the girl only babbled in Tansyard. Clovermead turned to Fetterlock. "Tell her not to be afraid," she said. *I'll never see Sorrel again.*

Fetterlock sheathed his sword and knelt, his knee squelching in the mud. He spoke softly, and after a while Mullein said a few words to him, loosened her hold on Clovermead, and reached out to him. He lifted her to the bank.

"I could use a hand up too," said Clovermead. *He's gone.* She couldn't stop thinking that. *He's gone, he's gone,* the words hammered at her.

"At your service, Demoiselle," said Fetterlock. He reached down, grasped Clovermead's outstretched hand, and pulled her out of the pond in one smooth motion. She was light as a feather in his grasp. He gazed, distracted, at the spot in the Moors where the bear-priests had disappeared. "Lucifer Snuff," he whispered.

"Yes," said Clovermead—and the name drove Sorrel from her thoughts for a moment. "You know him?"

"He has been on the Steppes before," said Fetterlock. "You are acquainted with him too?" Clovermead nodded. "He is not a friend of mine, Demoiselle, so remove that suspicious look from your face. Where did Sorrel go?"

Away from me forever. "This is Sorrel's sister, Mullein," said Clovermead. "The woman the bear-priests caught is his mother, Roan. They must have survived all these years in the Barleymill mines, after the Cyan Cross Horde was destroyed." Fetterlock gazed at Mullein in wonder. "Sorrel went to rescue his mother from the bear-priests. They're going to kill her when they bring her back to Barleymill."

Fetterlock glanced at Clovermead. "Did you give him permission to go, Demoiselle?"

"Yes," said Clovermead. "She's his mother." *I'll never hear his voice again. I'll never hear what happened to that red fox. Oh, Lady, I've lost Sorrel, who teases me, who tells me stories, who can't ever stop loving the Steppes. My friend.* Her eyes were hot, and she spoke tonelessly. "We can't leave Mullein here in the Moors or take her back to Chandlefort, so we'll bring her with us to the White Star Horde."

"That is good," said Fetterlock. "She can stay with the Horde until her brother returns. There are many women who would be glad to take her into their tents."

"I didn't say I'd leave her there," said Clovermead. "Sorrel asked *me* to take care of her. He didn't say to dump her with the first people I met."

"We are her own kind. She should stay with us, Demoiselle."

"She's your kind, is she?" Clovermead could see Sorrel in her mind's eye as clear as ever, his brown eyes still looking at her with icy revulsion. She wanted so much to moan out loud, and now her guts were churning. "Then why'd you leave her for seven years in Barleymill? Seems to me you'd have tried to help her if you cared that much."

Fetterlock's cheeks flamed red. "That is not a just accusation, Demoiselle."

"I don't care." Clovermead took a deep breath. "Sorrel is a subject of Lady Cindertallow, and Mullein is his sister. That means she's a Chandleforter. If anyone in the White Star Horde lays a hand on her, I'll take it as kidnapping and fight."

Fetterlock looked down at Mullein. She stood between the two of them and stared up uncomprehendingly. "Let us continue this discussion later," he said. "I will inform the Horde Chief's wife. Perhaps she can persuade you otherwise."

"I doubt it," said Clovermead fiercely. She put a protective hand on Mullein's shoulder. The little girl flinched, then let herself relax into Clovermead's grip. "I won't fail Sorrel again."

"The Horde Chief's wife is quite persuasive," Fetterlock said, with an ironic smile. "And do consider whether your friend would have preferred to have his sister stay with you or with other Tansyards. But we can argue that matter again later. Let us get to our horses and ride. Now that the bear-priests know we are here, we are vulnerable to an ambush. I would like to get to the Steppes as quickly as possible."

Mullein spoke a sentence in Tansyard. Fetterlock looked puzzled for a moment, then he burst into sudden laughter. "She wants to know why you have straw for hair. She says it must be very itchy."

"It does not look like straw!" said Clovermead. She touched her hair, and was reassured to find it hadn't suddenly become rough and dry. "Tell her my hair is just hair, but yellow."

"*Iore-le ne imali ta peluwa, siu Mullein,*" said Fetterlock. "*Iore amon ea, neo la.*"

"*Peluwa ea,*" said Mullein. "*Peluwa, peluwa, peluwa!*" A faint smile drifted onto her face for a moment.

"Let me guess," said Clovermead. "*Peluwa* means 'straw.'" Fetterlock nodded, and Clovermead couldn't help smiling herself. For the first time she let herself look the little girl full in the face. She was thin and short, with terribly large eyes, and when she gazed up at Clovermead it was just like Clovermead was looking at a young Sorrel. Her face was wonderfully familiar and Clovermead never wanted to part from her. She held out her hand, and Mullein put her tiny fingers in Clovermead's. "I'll just have to convince you otherwise, Mullein. Come with me. We're going to go riding."

Oh, Lady, I've lost Sorrel. She was hard-pressed not to weep.

Clovermead told Sergeant Algere and the other Yellowjackets quickly about Sorrel's departure, and then they all rode eastward through the Moors in a steady, drenching rain. The mist was thicker than ever, and Fetterlock led them slowly and single file through the highest, roughest land, where there was least chance of slipping into the mud and the ponds. Mullein rode in front of Clovermead, huddled up next to her to stay dry.

She looked around with wondering eyes, and gaped at the dank Moorland. Sometimes she spoke half to Clovermead and half to herself in incomprehensible Tansyard. Other times she would stare at nothing at all and shiver, frozen by something more than the chill of the rain.

They stopped at midday beneath a copse of sodden beeches that provided a feather of protection from the downpour, for a cold lunch of biscuits and beef jerky. "I'll have to tell Mother that Sorrel ran off," Clovermead said quietly to Mullein as they ate. "I allowed him to go after your mother, but he's a Yellowjacket in her service, and, really, Mother will say that he's deserted. If he comes back to Chandlefort, she'll have to punish him."

"I'll ask her to be merciful," said Sergeant Algere. Clovermead started, and Algere ducked his head. "Begging your pardon, Demoiselle, I didn't mean to surprise you, or to eavesdrop. I'd come to tell you the rain got into one of the saddlebags and dampened our food, so we may need to ration our meals out in the Steppes, and I overheard you talking to the girl. Sorrel does need to be punished, for all he's your friend. We can't let troopers ride off whenever they feel like it. But he's a good lad. He's a swaggerer, even for a Yellowjacket. When I sprained my ankle once, he was the one who thought to come to my wife to help do the chores I couldn't. I'll tell Milady that, when he comes back."

"Thank you, Algere," said Clovermead. "That's kind of you." The Sergeant nodded uncomfortably, saluted, and hurried away from her. Clovermead stared southward, where the Tansyard had disappeared. "But he won't be back. He'll never return." She wanted to run after Sorrel, more than ever, and her hands had already turned to paws before she caught herself. She forced them back into hands. She looked down at Mullein, still eating industriously, and she sighed. "I don't even care that we're never going to kiss, or anything. It's losing my friend that hurts." Mullein ignored the meaningless words, concentrating on wolfing down her food, and Clovermead couldn't help but laugh a little. "All right, I'll eat too. No point in being lonely *and* hungry." She stuffed another piece of jerky into her mouth, and made herself chew and swallow.

The rain lightened as they rode that afternoon, and the mist lifted. Here the ponds widened to enormous lakes separated by thin causeways of land. Far away, in the middle of one lake, Clovermead saw a Harrowman village of ramshackle huts huddled on poles and roofed with a shiny mixture of pitch and straw. A few expressionless Harrowmen in canoes watched them pass. The Yellowjackets kept their hands close to their swords.

Midafternoon two Harrowmen suddenly appeared before them as the group rode along the neck between two ponds. The two men were short, scrawny figures wrapped in slick furs, with drawn knives in their hands. Clovermead heard splashing, and she saw canoes with more figures in them appear in the ponds to either side of her. The rowers' hands were on their oars, but they also had knives. She heard footsteps scampering behind her.

Clovermead brought Auroche to a halt. *I guess I'm our leader,* she thought to herself. *I'd better speak.* "What do you want?" she called out. Her voice wavered through the gusting wind. She held tight to Mullein with her left hand.

"Tolls, rider," said one man in front of her. His face was pale and his hair stringy and nearly white. His eyes

71

were pink. "Harrowman land here. You must pay us to pass." He spoke the common tongue with a scratchily sibilant accent, like a saw sliding on silk.

Clovermead fumbled in her purse, drew out two silver shillings, and tossed them to the pale man. He caught them expertly in his hand and pocketed them. "There's your toll," she said. "Let us pass."

The pale man smiled. "Tolls are higher than that this year, rider."

"Not too high, I trust," said Fetterlock. He rode up to Clovermead's side, and his hand was also resting on his sword. Sergeant Algere and Corporal Naquaire followed close behind him. "Make the tolls too extortionate, and travelers will not return. Is it not better to have many silver pieces over the years than a few now?"

The pale man shrugged. "Perhaps I will not be here to collect the silver pieces when you return, Tansyard. Fortune spins her wheel and who knows what the future will bring? I would rather take advantage of the present." He grinned. "The toll is your horse, lady rider. Your pack and your purse, too. Get down, lady, give them to us, and your party can pass. We don't want to hurt you."

"It would be a pity to have to burn your village," said Fetterlock calmly. He pointed back toward the tumbledown huts they had passed earlier. "Surely you want a soft bed to come home to at night?"

The pale man's short and bandy-legged companion guffawed. "Not our village," he giggled. "We don't care."

Clovermead lifted her right arm high, so every Harrowman could see it, and let it grow. Soon it was a bear's paw—thick and long, with long claws. She smiled at the pale man. "I believe you are mistaken, sir. I have paid the proper toll."

Mullein moaned in fear, and pulled away from
Clovermead so fast that Clovermead had to grab her to
keep her from falling off the horse. Fetterlock rapped out
quick words to her in Tansyard, so that Mullein stayed
on Auroche, but she turned to stare at Clovermead with
eyes made enormous by sudden terror. Sergeant Algere
trembled a little, and Corporal Naquaire made the sign of
the crescent, but Fetterlock shivered and was hard-
pressed to keep himself by Clovermead's side. The pale
man murmured something to his fellows, and their
canoes began to back away from Clovermead. He
bowed, sheathed his knife, and stepped off the path. His
companion scuttled by his side.

"I beg your pardon, mistress. We mean no harm to
emissaries of the Bear." The Harrowman fumbled in his
shirt and took out a piece of obsidian carved in the shape
of a bear's tooth. "We honor your lord, mistress. Pass on,
pass on."

Clovermead opened her mouth to say she wasn't one
of Lord Ursus' followers, but Fetterlock hissed at her in
warning. Clovermead nodded, and rode past the bowing
Harrowmen. The Yellowjackets rode slowly after her,
their swords bared. She went on for another minute,
then looked back. The Harrowmen had disappeared
from sight.

"Are they allied with Lord Ursus too?" she asked.

"They fear him," said Fetterlock. "They won't get in
his way if he sends an army through the Moors. But I do
not think they will impede our armies either." He looked
at Clovermead's arm, grown human again, and he could
not help but shudder. "I find it hard to believe . . ." He
trailed off.

"That I'm not a servant of Lord Ursus?" Clovermead

felt very much like growling at Fetterlock, but Mullein was still staring at her with terrified eyes, still sitting as far away from Clovermead as she could get on Auroche's back. Clovermead swallowed her anger so as not to frighten the girl any more. "Believe what you like. I don't care." Coldly she set Auroche riding onward into the Moors.

Mullein's terror faded, and she nestled back against Clovermead. But Clovermead could feel her heart still racing, *pit-pat, pit-pat, pit-pat,* and it beat even faster when Clovermead tried to speak comforting words to her. After a while Clovermead gave up, and they rode on in silence.

That night Clovermead and the Tansyards set up one campfire, while the Yellowjackets sat around another. Sergeant Algere came to consult with Clovermead and Fetterlock for a few minutes about their route the next day, then went back to rejoin his troopers. Tonight old Golion and young Habick were sword-dancing for their comrades: The blades whirled around their legs as Golion jumped precisely and Habick enthusiastically capered. Quinch and Sark whistled their approval, Lewth and Dunnock clapped for an encore, and even scowling Corporal Naquaire allowed himself to smile.

Mullein began to speak, and Clovermead turned away from the dancing Yellowjackets. The little girl asked Fetterlock a series of questions in Tansyard. He answered her in a low voice touched with sadness and sometimes with laughter. Then Mullein looked again at Clovermead. She was still suspicious, but she slowly reached out her hand toward Clovermead's and pulled it toward her. *"Gora le ea,"* she said to Fetterlock. *"Mi'ita le seboyara coa vi goru."*

"She would like you to turn into a bear again," said Fetterlock. "But please do it gently, Demoiselle. She is very frightened of bears."

Clovermead let the fur sprout from the back of her hand. Mullein gasped as the hairs poked against her palm, then she hesitantly ran her fingers along Clovermead's long golden fur. Clovermead let her hand grow into a paw once more, and made her claws lengthen. She kept still while Mullein touched every inch of her paw from wrist to claw-tips. Mullein looked up at Clovermead and Clovermead let a wave of fur flow up her arm, across her body, and down her other arm. Then the fur faded back into flesh.

"Tell her I'm a friend of her brother," Clovermead said to Fetterlock, never moving her eyes from Mullein. "Tell her that I would never hurt her, and that I will fight to keep her safe from her enemies." Fetterlock nodded and spoke in Tansyard. Mullein stared at Clovermead a while more, then smiled tremulously and spoke to Fetterlock.

"She says she will trust you," said Fetterlock. He smiled. "She says she knows now that your hair isn't straw, but fur."

Clovermead laughed. "So it is," she said. She ruffled Mullein's hair fondly, and Mullein smiled, her fear gone.

Mullein ate ravenously, and while she bolted down her food, Clovermead tried to learn some Tansyard words from Fetterlock. She had picked up a number of Tansyard phrases from Sorrel over the years, but not enough to do more than make Mullein giggle at her confused attempts to talk in the Steppe tongue. The lesson wasn't terribly successful, and after dinner Mullein set herself to learning common tongue instead.

"*Tebeyu,*" she said, pointing at the fire.

"Fire," said Clovermead. Then, following Mullein's finger, she said, "Tinder. Kindling. Cheese. Beef stew. Buttons. Those are buttons too!"

"Tinda, kindeleen, chis, bif estu, bottenes, thowis ara bottenestu!" said Mullein, laughing. Now she pointed at Clovermead's hand.

"Hand," said Clovermead. She wiggled her fingers. "Fingers." Then, cautiously, she turned her hand back into a paw. "Paw. Claws."

"Gora," said Mullein. *"Kamu po ta seboyara vi goru? Gorai perenjiu heva Ursus."* She stared intently at Clovermead.

"What was that?" Clovermead asked Fetterlock. "Something about Ursus?"

"Gora is 'bear,'" said Fetterlock. "She said, 'How can you turn into a bear? Bears are the servants of Ursus.'"

"Tell her I'm not a servant of Lord Ursus," said Clovermead. She looked Mullein full in the face as she spoke. "Tell her that Our Lady gave my father the ability to turn into a bear as a gift, and gave the same power to all his descendants. Tell her we were given that gift so we could free every bear from Ursus' slavery."

Fetterlock spoke, and then Mullein spoke back to him. "She says, 'We are slaves too, in the mines. Will you come and free us as well?'"

The spiked whip lashed into Boulderbash. Clovermead felt tears glitter in her eyes. "Tell her I've made too many promises already." She hastily wiped her eyes. "No, don't say that. Tell her we're fighting Ursus, and that if Our Lady blesses us, sooner or later everyone will be free from him." Fetterlock spoke, and Mullein sighed. She looked exactly the way Sorrel did whenever he was feeling cast down, and Clovermead's heart wrenched in her again.

"Tell her she looks very much like her brother."

Mullein became more animated. "She says her mother had told her of Sorrel, in the mines. She said he was very sweet, and that he was dead, like all the other men of the Cyan Cross Horde. Is her father alive too? Are her other brothers?"

Clovermead shook her head. "Just Sorrel." Mullein nodded, awfully solemn, with an expression too old for her years. Clovermead hesitated. "Does she know how she and her mother escaped from Barleymill?" Fetterlock relayed the question.

Mullein looked around at the darkness, and Clovermead followed her gaze. Old Golion had grown tired, and now brawny Bergander had taken his place in the sword dance. He was as oddly dainty in his dancing as he was delicate in his lute-playing. Beyond their two campfires was an immense night. Mullein hunched close to the fire and spoke in a low voice. "She was in the tunnels digging ore with the rest of the women and children when the Shaman-Mother started to sing," said Fetterlock. "A dark cloud covered the torches, and she couldn't see. Then she heard the Shaman-Mother singing inside her head, and she could see in a strange light. Mullein's shackles came loose, and so did her mother's. They started to walk, and the Shaman-Mother sang directions to them until they came out of the mines. The guards couldn't see them. The cloud hid them until they were past the walls of Barleymill, and then it thinned and went away, and so did the Shaman-Mother's voice. Then Mullein saw things she had never seen before, and her mother said they were grass and streams and trees and birds—" Fetterlock could not help but sob deep in his chest. "But her mother made her start to walk at once. They fled through the night and they slept when the sun came out. Sometimes they walked side by side, and sometimes her mother carried her in her arms. They dug for roots, and her mother caught fish in the streams with her bare hands. After a while her mother started to look behind her, and said she was sure there were bear-priests coming to catch them and bring them back to the mines. They left the grasslands and went into the Moors. Then the bear-priests caught up with them, but her mother tossed her away, and said to trust her brother Sorrel and never to come back to the mines, to kill herself before she let the bear-priests capture her. And then Sorrel left her to go after their mother, and he said to trust the straw-haired girl, she would keep her safe." Mullein fell quiet, and tears were rolling down Fetterlock's cheeks. "Oh, Lady, she had never seen grass."

"I won't let the bear-priests catch you," said Clovermead. And she knew she'd given her word too often before, but she said, "I promise you that." Somewhere Boulderbash was laughing bitterly at Clovermead, but Clovermead couldn't help it. "In Our Lady's name. Tell her that, Fetterlock." Fetterlock spoke in Tansyard, and Mullein smiled. Then she yawned and lay down by the fire. In moments she was asleep.

The next day Clovermead and Mullein rode together again in a morning far warmer than the day before. Blustery gusts still blew against Clovermead, but she was no longer chilled to the bone. The grass beneath Auroche's feet was still damp, but he was able to make far better time. Mullein looked around her with interest and enjoyment, gasped at every bird that rose from the reeds, and laughed when she saw a muskrat waddle into a pond. She pointed at everything she saw, and Clovermead told her the words in common tongue. In a few hours Mullein had memorized the words for bird, tree, pond, ride, swim, fly, and everything else Clovermead could show her in the Moors.

Mullein saw a sparrow hop from a thorn tree branch to the ground and she cried out in delight. "Sparoa!" she cried. "Sparoa fly. Sparrow fly," she said more carefully. She laughed. "Mullein ride horoos."

"Mullein rides horse," Clovermead agreed. "Clovermead rides horse. Horse gets tired, wants grass. Fortunately, we'll be in the Steppes soon, where there's all the grass Auroche could ever dream of." Mullein stared at her in puzzlement. "Let's go back to language lessons. I wonder how long it will take you to learn adjectives and adverbs."

That afternoon they rode uphill through land that grew lusher and dryer by the mile. The ponds grew smaller, the earth grew deeper and darker, and the grass turned from dun to bright, pale green. All along the track lavender and yellow crocuses joined snowdrops in bloom, and green leaves exuberantly burst forth from poplar trees. A herd of red deer bolted away from the Yellowjackets. The wind blew steadily from the south in a cloudless day. The scent of grass was strong around them.

"It is lovely," said Clovermead to herself. "Sorrel wasn't exaggerating. Mullein, do you suppose it's like this all over the Steppes?"

"Steppes?" said Mullein, pointing at the green grass. Clovermead nodded. "Steppes piretty!"

"Steppes very pretty," said Clovermead. "Father would love how green they are. Mother would say Chandlefort is prettier, but she'd still be impressed at how far the grass stretches. I wish Sorrel were here to show them to us." Her heart ached again.

Toward evening they emerged onto the true Steppes. They had come high enough that the air was thinner and chillier than it had been in the Moors or the Whetstone Valley. Now they ran on fertile soil. Clovermead judged it with a shepherd's eye: It would make good grazing land for sheep. The Steppes ran on and on, rolling slightly, but flat as far as she could see. The eye got swallowed up in their immensity.

"You could plunk down a dozen Chandleforts here, Demoiselle, and lose track of them all," said Habick, awed. He was riding to Clovermead's left. "I thought the Salt Heath was big, but it's just a patch of sand next to this. Do you know how far this grass goes on?"

"Four thousand miles, Sorrel once said. You travel for two years, and it gets drier and colder as you head east, and after a while it turns into a desert with just a few scraggly villages around the odd oasis. Beyond that there are mountains, and beyond that is the Sublime Royaume, where the farmers train insects to make their clothes and magicians bring clay soldiers to life to guard their cities." Clovermead's eyes gleamed. "I'd love to see what it looks like."

Habick went very pale underneath his freckles. "You aren't going to take us that way, Demoiselle? I'm already too far from Chandlefort."

"Don't you worry!" said Clovermead. "This isn't a pleasure jaunt. I'm afraid I'm not getting to the Royaume anytime soon." She laughed, a little sadly, and then lapsed into silence.

Mullein ate another huge dinner that night, then promptly fell asleep. Fetterlock looked at her sadly, and he muttered in Tansyard.

"What's worrying you?" asked Clovermead.

"Regret," said Fetterlock. "I suddenly worry that I made a wrong decision once."

"I know I have," said Clovermead. "After I make a mistake, I tell myself I'll make better decisions the next time, but somehow I keep on blundering. Sometimes I just make a fool of myself. Sometimes I hurt other people, and when I say 'Sorry' afterward, it doesn't make up for what I've done. If you have only one decision to regret, you're doing well."

"It was a very important one," said Fetterlock. "People died."

Once Lord Ursus had possessed Clovermead. With one voice they had ordered bears and bear-priests to attack the soldiers of Low Branding and the Yellowjackets. Clovermead had urged them on to more slaughter, and there had been blood everywhere, spattering the snow. The scar on Clovermead's arm and her missing tooth both ached. They were mementos of the time she had let Lord Ursus possess her; mementos of the evil she had done with him.

"I've made mistakes like that too," said Clovermead in a low voice. She glanced up at huge Fetterlock. "Do you want to tell me what you did? I won't be nosy if you'd rather be quiet, but if you want to talk, I'd be glad to listen."

"Perhaps I would," said Fetterlock. He looked again at Mullein, and a tear rolled down his cheek. "Oh, Lady, she has never seen the grass. And I am to blame."

"You?" asked Clovermead, startled.

"In part," said Fetterlock. "Enough." He began to speak.

Chapter Six

THE SILENT WARRIOR

WE HAD FOUGHT THE CYAN CROSS HORDE THE summer before. They challenged us for the use of the meadows along the Sundew Creek, which has the best pasturage for horses in the northern Steppes. White Star Horde had won the use of the Sundew lands from the Tawn Cross Horde when I was a boy, and it had been the pride of our Horde ever since. We fought with desperate love, for our fathers had paid for that grassland with their blood. We also fought with anger, for Cyan Cross already had fine pasturage for their herds by Charlock Lake: They waged war in the arrogance of their power, to take what they did not need. We delivered a repulse to their presumption. At the end of the day the Cyan Cross retreated and left the meadow dappled with the bodies of their fallen. It was a glorious victory, and we shall sing of it for generations.

It was a costly victory too. As many of our warriors as theirs lay on the ground, and White Star was a far smaller Horde than Cyan Cross. One of them was my daughter's husband, Stringhalt. I had not wanted her to marry him, for he was small and clubfooted, but my wife had said, "He can ride a horse as well as you, clubfoot or no, and all warriors in the Horde are short to you. It does not matter: He is a brave warrior and he will make Arman a good husband." He had indeed been a good husband, for he made Arman smile day and night the three months they were married, and he had been a good warrior, for three men of the Cyan Cross lay around his body. I carried his small body back to the Horde in my arms. Arman's face went cold when she saw him dead, and she never smiled again. I think she would have ceased to eat if she had not had Stringhalt's baby growing inside her. Even when my little granddaughter Calkin was born, Arman was barely alive.

So you will understand that I had little reason to love the Cyan Cross Horde as we came north on the Steppes the next summer. They had not behaved dishonorably. I had killed a warrior or two of theirs myself in that latest battle, and I knew that because of me a wife in Cyan Cross wept for her husband as much as Arman wept for hers. Yet I could not help but be bitter. Indeed, I had spent all winter down in the southern Steppes planning a raid on the Cyan Cross when next we saw them. I would bring a string of Cyan Cross horses back to Arman and say to her, "I have brought these back from Stringhalt's enemies for Stringhalt's wife and Stringhalt's daughter. Please, Daughter, let these assuage your grief. Let Calkin know that her mother can smile." I feared they would be no comfort to her, but I could think of nothing else.

I rode ahead of my Horde as midsummer approached, for we were near Bryony Hill, and I knew that Cyan Cross would be there at the sacred hill to celebrate the solstice. I did not intend the sacrilege of attacking them while they worshiped Our Lady—but I thought perhaps that I would surprise them a day or two after the solstice had passed.

Usually there were no raids then, either, but the Shaman-Mothers did not explicitly forbid fighting save on the solstice itself. I knew in my heart that Our Lady would not be pleased by such an action, but I did not care. My daughter's empty face pressed against my soul, and I wanted my revenge against Cyan Cross Horde. I would use any gambit against them that I could.

I came over a hill and there was Cyan Cross spread out before me. I halted my horse in a patch of tall grass and I looked down at the Horde. They walked northward in a straggling line that spread a mile in length. At the center were the packhorses, who carried the tents and what few possessions Cyan Cross carried from place to place. Before them and behind them the old nags bore the Elders of the Horde and the women with babes in arms. The women and children walked by the sides of the Elders and the packhorses, bringing them water and food. The horse-herds grazed a little farther off, and the warriors rode in a great circle around them all, to keep any horse from wandering away and to keep any enemy from wandering in. The younger warriors sometimes strayed into the heart of the Horde, performing handstands on horseback, jumping streams, and showing off as young men will. I almost smiled to see them so innocently happy—but then I remembered how Stringhalt had done the same in front of Arman, and my smile faded from my face. Stringhalt was dead, and the young men of Cyan Cross did not deserve their joy.

I watched, and as I watched, I became aware that there were other watchers near me. A hundred yards down along the ridge I saw rustling in the grass. Then I saw a bear-priest on a white Phoenixian horse dart away from the ridge and ride to the west, toward the Harrow Moors.

My mind was in a whirl: There should not have been any bear-priests in the central Steppes, and certainly none this close to Our Lady's temple on Bryony Hill. I almost shouted at once, to raise an alarm—but then I remembered how far I had wandered ahead of the White Star Horde, and how unlikely the Cyan Cross Horde was to ask questions before they shot a bevy of arrows at me. And it occurred to me that perhaps the bear-priests meant some mischief to the Cyan Cross Horde, and that prospect strangely warmed my heart. I stayed silent.

There was another rustling in the grass and a second bear-priest came trotting toward me. He rode on the other side of the crest from the Cyan Cross Horde, where they could not see him, but through clear, short grass where I could see him perfectly. He kept his empty hands up so I would know that he intended no attack. I stayed where I was. I did not much want to talk to a bear-priest, but I was curious to know what he had to say.

He was a short, balding man with a goatee. He had bronzed and filed his teeth, as bear-priests do, but he wore wool and leather in addition to the normal bear-priest wolf-skins. He smiled as he rode up, but his eyes were cold. "Greetings, Warrior of the White Star Horde," he said as he drew up to me. He spoke in passable Tansyard, though it was thickly accented. "My name is Lucifer Snuff."

"I am Fetterlock," I said. "What do you want with me?"

He laughed. It was unpleasant to listen to him: Small boys who tear the wings off of butterflies laugh the same way. "I am curious to know what you are doing here, Warrior. I hadn't thought White Star Horde was a friend of Cyan Cross. Have you come for a social visit?"

"No," I said stiffly. "And you? What is a bear-priest doing on the Steppes? This is Tansyard land."

"Only passing through, Warrior," said Snuff. He grinned so the sun blazed on his teeth. "I mean no disrespect to the Hordes." He paused a moment. "Save, perhaps, the Cyan Cross Horde. They are an arrogant nation. They don't respect Lord Ursus as they should."

"That little is to their favor," I said. "I do not care for your butchering master either, bear-priest." Snuff shrugged and smiled. "But I allow that they are arrogant. You speak the truth there." I turned from Snuff to glance at the Cyan Cross Horde passing down below. Now the four flags of the legions of Queensmart came fluttering in the hands of Cyan Cross' standard-bearers in the valley below. All the Tansyards had combined to defeat the legions, a century ago and longer, but Cyan Cross had claimed the flags as their own spoil. What should have been the pride of all Tansyards they had kept as their particular boast, and that stuck in the craw of every Horde upon the Steppes. "They should be taken down a notch," I muttered.

"They can be, Warrior," said Snuff. I turned back to him, startled: I had not realized he could hear me. "They will be."

I looked to the west. The first bear-priest was still barely visible as he raced away. I jerked my thumb after him. "Will he be bringing back more bear-priests?"

"Indeed," said Snuff. "Soldiers of Low Branding, too, and bears. They will come secretly, they will surprise the Cyan Cross Horde, and then"—he grinned—"Cyan Cross will not be so cock-a-hoop." He glanced at me slyly. "White Star Horde shouldn't object to that. With Cyan Cross weakened, you'll be the most powerful

Horde upon the Steppes. I should think that would be a feather in your cap."

"I am not fond of Cyan Cross Horde," I said slowly, "but they are our kindred. We worship Our Lady together, and their lives are precious to her. I do not want to see them butchered by you bear-worshipers. Perhaps you should gallop after that other bear-priest and tell him to call off your attack. Tell him that both Cyan Cross and White Star will be waiting for you, ready for a fight."

Snuff stared at me for a long moment. "You wear loops of black cloth around your braids, Warrior," he said at last, most amiably. "Would you be so kind as to tell me for whom you mourn?"

"For Stringhalt," I said. "He was my daughter's husband." I heard a joyful whoop from below, as four young warriors of Cyan Cross began to race one another. "He was slain in battle with the Cyan Cross Horde," I said, and I could not help letting go a few tears. Stringhalt should have been as alive as those young racers below.

"I do not believe your fine words, Warrior," Snuff said. "I think you do not care that Cyan Cross is kindred, or that they worship the sky-crone, or that their lives are precious to her. I think you want revenge for your own dead, that you would be glad to see Cyan Cross' warriors dead in great numbers, and that you do not care who butchers them." He spoke sweetly and his words wormed their way into my heart. I struggled to deny them, but I could not. I was silent, and my silence was the most eloquent assent.

Snuff smiled. "Well, Warrior, I believe we bear-worshipers can be of service to you. We will fulfill for you all your dreams of revenge. You need do nothing— just ride away and say nothing. Wait a week and you will hear word of what has happened to Cyan Cross. Your daughter's husband will be revenged." Laughter bubbled from his bronzed teeth. "I promise you that where Cyan Cross spreads its tents there will be blood high as a horse's head."

I was twice Snuff's size, and I could have broken him in two—yet there was something in him that terrified me. All at once I wanted to be riding away from him, to somewhere leagues away from his terrible eyes and his laughter that sounded of dying men.

I controlled myself. I thought of praying to Our Lady for guidance, but I did not want to. I knew what she would tell me and I did not want to listen to her. I wanted revenge for the grief Cyan Cross had given my daughter, and nothing else mattered.

"Do what you like, Bear-Priest," I said. "I shall not warn Cyan Cross."

"I'm glad to hear it," said Snuff. "Lord Ursus has planned this attack for a long while. It would be a shame to have it spoiled." He turned to go—then checked his horse with a vicious pull of the reins. "If Cyan Cross is warned, Lord Ursus' wrath will fall on the White Star Horde," he said. "If I were you, Warrior, I would not provoke him." Then he was riding away to the west, without so much as a farewell.

His last threat was a grave insult to me and to the Horde. Proper courage demanded that I defy him and go at once to warn Cyan Cross Horde. But he had also terrified me: I did not want to expose the White Star Horde to the anger of Lord Ursus. And, too, there was my daughter's constant grief. That decided me. I looked once more at the Cyan Cross Horde below me, so undeservedly happy, and I turned from them. "They can take their chances," I said to myself as I galloped away.

A week passed. The solstice was three days gone when a scout came galloping into our camp with unimaginable news. The bear-priests had razed Our Lady's temple from the crown of Bryony Hill and had begun to build a temple and a fort of their own there. Cyan Cross Horde was gone. The warriors had been wiped out to a man. Only a few of the women and children had survived, and they were being taken as slaves to Barleymill.

"All dead?" I asked him. "Surely you are exaggerating?"

"Go and look for yourself," he said. "The grass is littered with corpses."

I went at once. I rode my horse at a gallop night and day, and I was at Bryony Hill within twenty-four hours. All around—oh, Lady, I do not want to remember what I saw. There had been near two thousand in Cyan Cross Horde when I saw them a week before; now their bodies lay before me, rotting in the summer sun. The whole nation had been wiped out. I thought to myself, *Stringhalt has been revenged*, but I got no pleasure from the thought. Then I thought, *They are dead because of me.* I wanted to ask Our Lady for forgiveness, but I could not imagine how to begin.

I got down from my horse and wandered among the remains of Cyan Cross. I tried to memorize their faces, for I did not think anyone else would ever remember them. Their clothes had been looted from them, bears had eaten from their flesh, and I wandered among the naked dead. They stared at me with terrified, accusing eyes.

After a while Lucifer Snuff rode up to me. He came from the bear-priest encampment on Bryony Hill. "Is this sufficient revenge for you, Warrior?" he asked me amiably.

"It is too much," I whispered. I knelt by an old man and closed his eyes. "How could you kill them all? Warriors should only fight warriors." I looked around the valley, and tears sprang to my eyes. "I did not mean for this to happen."

"I promised you revenge," said Snuff. "I promised you blood high as a horse's head. I am true to my word. And you, Warrior—you said 'Do what you like.' This is what I like." He looked at the nightmare around him, and he smiled. "I follow Lord Ursus so that one day I will make all the world like this."

"I will—" *resist you, fight you, keep this from ever happening again,* I thought, but I could not speak the words. In that greensward of dead men I was terribly afraid. Perhaps Our Lady would have given me strength, but I had no right to call on her assistance. I dropped my eyes to the ground.

"You have been wise so far, Warrior," said Snuff. "If you had spoken, this would have happened to the White Star Horde as well. Continue to be wise, and Lord Ursus will not consider you his enemy." He paused for a moment, but I could not speak, could not look at him, could not do anything at all for fear and shame. "Take a string of horses with you," said Snuff at last. "Cyan Cross doesn't need them anymore." He laughed derisively then, and walked away from me.

I did not accept his offer. I had enough honor in me not to be a jackal. But I went home to my wife and my daughter, and my infant granddaughter, and I was glad that they were alive. I remembered the dead of Cyan Cross Horde, and I had no trouble imagining my family slaughtered in the same way. I have felt shame ever since then for my silence, but my relief that my family is alive has been even greater.

"I wish I were a nun," said Clovermead slowly. "They know what to say when pilgrims come to them with a story like this—what to say in solace, what penance to impose. I—I won't say there's nothing wrong with what you did, because there is, but you know that already. I still wish I could comfort you." She put her hand on Fetterlock's forearm, and patted it clumsily for a moment. For a moment the Tansyard smiled, and his thick fingers fumbled against Clovermead's. Then her forehead wrinkled. "Why did you come to Chandlefort to ask us to ally with you against Ursus? Weren't you afraid to do that, when you've seen how powerful Ursus is?"

"The Horde Chief's wife sent me," said Fetterlock. "I could not refuse the commission. But, yes, I am afraid for my family still. I am afraid for my Horde, and for all the Hordes on the Steppes. I do not want to go to war with Lord Ursus." He shrugged wearily. "I wish I were a braver person, Demoiselle. But I am not."

"I killed with Lord Ursus," said Clovermead. *So many soldiers had lain dead upon the snow.* It was difficult saying the words out loud, but she wanted to share them with Fetterlock. "I didn't just stand aside. I ordered our bears, my bears, to kill Chandlefort's Yellowjackets and Low Branding's mercenaries, and, oh, Lady, I was filled with joy every time the bears butchered a man. Butchered at my command. I thought I was lost in darkness, Fetterlock, but I wasn't. Our Lady was there waiting for me, and she offered me a way out. There always is one."

Fetterlock smiled, and looked down at the sleeping

figure of Mullein. "I almost believe that now, Demoiselle. A son of Cyan Cross survived the slaughter, here is a daughter of the Horde, and it seems that others still survive in the mines of Barleymill. They live!—a ragged scrap of Cyan Cross, to be sure, but they live. Ah, Demoiselle, I have been in night for years, and to see them is a scrap of light. It almost makes me hope that Our Lady will offer me a way to redeem myself."

"She will," said Clovermead. "She gives that chance to everyone."

"I pray you are right," said Fetterlock. And then his smile faded. "I am still afraid, Demoiselle. That terror has been graven in my soul. I do not think that I can ever drive it from me."

Chapter Seven

HIDDEN BEASTS

THEY RODE DEEP INTO THE TANSY STEPPES THE NEXT three days, curving northeast in a wide circle around Bryony Hill, and the Moors gradually disappeared from sight behind Clovermead. It was early spring still, but the young meadow on the Steppes was already six inches deep. Clovermead was totally lost the moment the Moors slipped beyond the western horizon. The sun traversing the sky told her the directions, small trees provided local signposts, but there were no other landmarks by which to orient herself. Pale green shimmered in her eyes, and every now and then she had to look up at the sky to keep from getting dizzy.

Mullein stared anxiously southward when they first ventured onto the open Steppes, but her fearfulness slowly diminished. She learned enough of common tongue that she could string together a few words at a time into short sentences. In the evening Mullein ran her hands along wildflower petals, and sometimes she cried from joy as she stretched out on the soft grass. But she never wandered too far from the campfires, never ceased to look out into the empty plains around them with a shadow of wariness in her young eyes.

On the third day, Clovermead saw riders in the far distance. They rode parallel to the Yellowjackets for a ways, then galloped away to the south.

"Friends of yours?" Sergeant Algere asked Fetterlock.

Fetterlock squinted after them. "Gray Bar warriors," he said. "They are the first Horde to head north in the spring, and the last to head south in the fall. They spend their summers in the far north of the Steppes, in the foothills of the Reliquary Mountains."

"Should we go talk with them?" asked Clovermead.

Fetterlock shrugged. "It will not hurt, but it will not help. They will follow the lead of the White Star Horde. We are best off hurrying to the White Star's encampment."

They stopped for the evening by a stream bubbling through the Steppes. Clovermead stalked out to the middle of the stream, her legs protected from the chill by luxuriant fur, caught half a dozen fish with quick flicks of her paws, and brought them back for the party. Fetterlock gathered twigs and made a pair of fires for the party, and then Bergander and Habick roasted the fish. Mullein ate as much as Fetterlock, though she was a quarter his size, and she licked the bones clean.

Clovermead looked down at Mullein in the torch-light, and she saw that the little girl's hands were callused from labor, and the creases on her palms inlaid with grime. Flecks of silver streaked her hands. Clovermead reached down, gently took hold of Mullein's hands, and held up her palms. Now she could see that the grime was also silver, filling every line in Mullein's palms. Clovermead ran her fingers over the ingrained silver, and her own skin began to itch.

Clovermead tried to rub the silver away—and gasped, as it burned into her flesh. Mullein stared at her curiously, but didn't flinch.

"They mine quicksilver, mercury, in Barleymill," said Fetterlock. "Down in the Thirty Towns it is used to extract shining silver from dull silver ore. It poisons, it kills, and no one mines it unless they are shackled in chains and driven forward with whips. In Tansyard we call quicksilver Poison Silver, *hwanka-velika.*"

Mullein cried out softly as he spoke the last word. "No!" she said. "Never again. Mother said." She trembled.

"Don't worry," said Clovermead. "Never *hwanka-velika* again, I promise."

"I promise too," said Fetterlock grimly. He made the sign of the crescent, slipped into Tansyard, and Mullein looked reassured. She asked a question and he said "mines."

"Mines bad," said Mullein. "All time dig. Bear-priests—" She broke into Tansyard again.

"Whip," said Fetterlock. Mullein asked him more words. "Blood. Starve. Kill. Die." He shuddered. "She wants to tell us what life is like for them in the mines. I think you can guess from the words she wants to know."

"Velika-gora," said Mullein.

Fetterlock frowned. "I do not know what that is. A silver-bear?" He asked Mullein a question in Tansyard.

"In mines," said Mullein. "Silvah-bera." She thought a moment, then tried another word on Fetterlock.

"Monster," said Fetterlock.

"Monsters in mines," said Mullein. "I no go back. Die first."

"How did you live?" Clovermead whispered. "How is it possible?"

95

Fetterlock asked Mullein a question, and then they spoke back and forth for a minute.

"Shaman-Mother," said Mullein. "Keep Cyan Cross live. Take our poison, into her. Other slaves die. Our Horde live." She paused a moment, then looked up at them with sudden, awful sorrow. "She hurt, all time." A tear rolled down her cheek.

That night Clovermead dreamed of darkness—

She felt spurs on her back and a bit in her mouth. She was thirsty and tired, but she could not stop to rest, could not drink. Her paws fell clumsily on the unseen earth, and she was jarred by every small rise and fall of the ground. Sharp twigs scored the fleshy pads of her paws. The saddle on her back had rubbed sores into her flesh.

"Where are you?" Boulderbash asked wearily. "I have not seen the sun in a week. Little cub, Clovermead, you said you would free me. That was more than three years ago. When will you come?"

"I'll come as soon as I can," said Clovermead. There was no point in trying to contradict her.

"Why didn't you free me?" Boulderbash howled with rage and frustration. "You were there. You sprang one knot of the trap, and then you let me go. You chose the human over me."

"Yes," Clovermead said miserably. "I did. But I didn't have time to save both of you, and I couldn't just let him die—"

"I'm tired of your excuses," Boulderbash roared, howled with the agony of years enslaved. "Save me now."

"I will help you," said Clovermead. "Just as soon as I can. But—"

"But you have other things you need to do first," said Boulderbash, with weary bitterness. "Isn't it always that way, little cub?"

"Mother sent me to the Steppes on a mission," said

Clovermead. "I can't give it up to help you." Sorrow thickened her voice. "I couldn't give it up for Sorrel, either, and he's my best friend."

"No one is my friend," said Boulderbash. "So I am left in darkness."

"You're being unreasonable," said Clovermead. She wanted to be sorry for Boulderbash, but the constant complaints were aggravating her.

"Reason is a pretty word for abandonment," said Boulderbash. She switched her tail angrily. "I am growing tired of coming last, little one."

"I'll come for you," said Clovermead wearily. "I promise, I will."

"I am waiting," said Boulderbash.

And as Clovermead woke, she heard a great and familiar growl. "I have always been true to you, Mother," Lord Ursus roared—

A spattering of hail pelted them at dawn, then turned into an intermittent drizzle that chilled them to the bone. The Yellowjackets wrapped their sleeping blankets around their bodies. Sergeant Algere began to sneeze helplessly as the wet day wore on. Clovermead grew thick fur all over her body, and Mullein jumped as Clovermead's fur poked into her back, but then made herself relax into the warm and golden pelt. Fetterlock cast uneasy looks at her furry body all morning long.

Toward noon a pale sun emerged between thick gray clouds. As it did, a scream shivered over the Steppes. It sounded of pain twined with bloodlust. It wasn't human, but Clovermead had never heard an animal moan like that. The cry sent gooseflesh running up and down her arms.

"Lady preserve us," Naquaire whispered. The bald

corporal had gone dead white. He made the crescent sign with a trembling hand, and Bergander and Golion shakily followed suit.

"*Velika-gora,*" Mullein whispered, and now she shook with fear. "Monster." She tugged at Auroche's reins, and looked up pleadingly at Clovermead. "Please, ride fast."

"I think that is good advice, Demoiselle," said Fetterlock. He looked around at the unnerved Yellowjackets. "That came from the south. Let us ride straight north." Clovermead nodded, and the party galloped northward.

They did not stop for lunch. The sun disappeared again, the clouds thickened, and the drizzle returned. In the dim light, the Steppes had become gray and colorless. Monotonous, interchangeable grassland fell behind their horses' hooves, but, nightmarelike, they never seemed to make any progress. The terrible scream came at regular intervals. It never fell any farther behind them, although their horses were running so hard that the poor beasts' flanks were heaving. Soon it began to edge closer to them.

They rode deep into the twilight. *Let it stop, Lady,* Clovermead prayed. *Let it sleep.* But the screams followed them steadily. Only when the light was almost gone did Clovermead rein in her horse. "The grass is wet and slippery," she said. "If we keep going like this in the dark, we're going to trip and fall. Mullein, can these things see at night?" Fetterlock quickly translated her query and Mullein nodded her head.

"I do not know what we should do, Demoiselle," said Fetterlock. "All courses are dangerous." He sighed. "A Gray Bar warrior could smell his way through the darkness, but I have no such talents."

Clovermead suddenly smiled. "I do," she said. She fumbled in her saddlebag, and brought out a length of rope. She rode in the thickening dusk to Algere. "Do you have more rope, Sergeant?"

Algere brought out another loop of cord and tossed it to her. "Indeed I do, Demoiselle. What do you need it for?"

"To tie the horses together. I'm going to lead them tonight." She jumped down from Auroche, tied one loop loosely around her chest, and tossed the other end to Fetterlock.

"I do not see the point of this," said the Tansyard. He began to loop the strands around his horse. "We would be better off riding."

"You want a good nose?" asked Clovermead. "I've got one." She turned into a bear.

Her bear-form had grown too, these last few years. Now she was nearly ten feet long, and her claws, her jaws, and her fur were thicker and longer than ever. Fetterlock was small next to her, and Mullein tiny. Mullein tried not to flinch, but she couldn't help backing away toward Fetterlock. Clovermead sighed as the Tansyard picked up the little girl, held her in his arms, and whispered comforting words to her. The band quickly lashed themselves together, and then Clovermead took the lead. She began to walk northward through the dark Steppes.

The horses came in a herky-jerky chain behind her. Clovermead tramped slowly through the wet grass, sniffing and listening more than looking. The horses were nervous at first as they followed her, but after a while they got used to her presence. They were distracted anyway by the screaming that continued at irregular intervals behind them. The thing hadn't stopped for the night, but it had slowed down. Clovermead kept it a steady distance behind her.

Mullein fell asleep first: The screams were terrible, but they weren't new to her. After her the Yellowjackets nodded off one by one in their saddles. Fetterlock was the last to drift off, and then it was just Clovermead by herself in the night, with only the tired horses to keep her company.

Just what is a "silver-bear"? Clovermead wondered to herself. *The name sounds sort of pretty, but the creature can't be, the way Mullein looked when she talked about it. I suppose Ursus has done something to the bears he controls—but maybe I'm not being imaginative enough. Maybe it's some sort of great mole that lurks in the depths of the earth, which Ursus has lured up to the surface, so he can use it in the mines. Though what a mole would be doing scampering on the Steppes at high speed and screaming, I don't know. Maybe it's a carnivorous mole that lives in great, lightless caverns! Maybe there are people in the caverns with great big eyes to see in the darkness, who fight the moles in savage duels!* Clovermead shook her head and rumbled with laughter. *Maybe Mother's right, and I do read too many adventure stories. I'm sure it's just a bear.* There was another scream behind her, and Clovermead shivered. *I'd be just as glad not to find out. I hope it doesn't catch up with us.*

She came to a stream in her path, but she could tell by the sound of the water rippling on pebbles that it was narrow and fordable. She descended into the water, felt her paws freeze beneath her fur for a few seconds, and then she was rising onto the other side. *That wasn't so bad,* thought Clovermead. *I wish Sorrel were here, so he could see how good I am at this!* But then she remembered that even if he were there, Sorrel wouldn't have any admiration for her. He had looked at her with such anger.

He shouldn't have gotten so mad at me, she told herself. *But I bet I'd be just as angry if I'd asked him for help like that and been turned down. Oh, Lady, I know I had good reason to say no to him, but I still feel low-down and treacherous. Sorrel's got cause enough to be disappointed in me.* Growling unhappily, she went on into the night.

She grew more and more tired and walked more and more slowly. Mud caked her paws, her eyes started to ache, and she wanted to just lie down and collapse. Even the screams behind her ceased to frighten her, and she moved only from a sense of duty. The clouds cleared, the rain ceased, and for a moment she paused and looked behind her at the dark Steppe. *I know the Demoiselle is supposed to lead the way,* thought Clovermead, *but I wouldn't mind some help.*

"Are you tired, Demoiselle?" Fetterlock was by her side. He had gotten off his horse and walked up to her. "Now that the clouds have cleared, there is enough moonlight that I can see. Give me that rope, and I will take over pulling the horses. You may rest." He was nervous as he stood by her, but he controlled himself.

Clovermead shifted back to human, yawning as she did, and Fetterlock chuckled to see her floppy bear tongue shrink to a delicate human one. "I wouldn't mind," said Clovermead. She took the rope off her shoulders and looked at him curiously. "I was mostly leading the horses, but sometimes I had to pull them a bit. I know you're strong, but can you really do that?"

"My wife has always called me an ox. Now I can prove her right." Fetterlock took the rope and wrapped it around his chest while Clovermead got back onto Auroche. "Sleep while you can, Demoiselle."

"I will," said Clovermead. "Thank you."

"I have ridden horses all my life," said Fetterlock. "It is amusing to pull a horse for once." Then he began to drag the line of horses through the night. Clovermead settled Mullein in front of her on Auroche's back, and quickly fell asleep.

She woke at dawn to the sound of an even louder scream. The Yellowjackets woke with her, Mullein was crying silently, and Fetterlock was undoing the rope, and then the Tansyard giant was running back to his horse. "Time to ride again!" he cried out—and as he yelled, not one but two screams echoed out of the Steppes. Both were to the south of them, but they came from two distinct directions. "Do you by any chance possess any bear-powers you have neglected to inform me of, which might turn those things aside?" the Tansyard asked Clovermead. "If so, now would be the time to use them."

"All I do is turn shape," said Clovermead. *And free bears,* she thought. She sent her mind winging toward the south, to see if some blood-net of Ursus' kept those creatures captive, but she saw nothing in her mind's eye.

They serve me by choice, Ursus whispered in her mind. *They serve me for pleasure.*

"Let's go quickly," Clovermead said out loud.

They fled through the Steppes with the pair of screamers coming after them. Sergeant Algere kept the rear guard, yelling at any trooper who began to fall behind, and whipping each horse as it began to flag. *Like a good sheepdog,* thought Clovermead. Habick took out a crossbow, and began to wind it up as he galloped. Corporal Naquaire stayed in the vanguard. He flinched every time a scream floated over the Steppes.

The unseen monsters loped just south of a low ridge near them, came nearer by the minute, and sang a terrible, raw sound to each other. It sounded like a horrible parody of the song-speech Our Lady's nuns used with one another. The beasts rose over the ridge crest, and now Clovermead saw them fuzzily in the distance. They were silver and black, and they flew like liquid lightning along the heights. They were like bears, but not quite bears. There was something horribly distorted about them. And their shape *changed*, flowed as they ran, from thick and bulky to long and thin. They glowed in the sunlight.

The beasts howled, and came after them with redoubled speed.

I should have hugged Mother once more before I left Chandlefort, thought Clovermead. *Father, too. And Saraband. Oh, Lady, it's too late now.*

"I am afraid that we are about to find out precisely what a *velika-gora* is," Fetterlock said grimly—but as he spoke he smiled, because there were riders ahead, coming toward them at top speed. They carried pennants on flags with them, each one decorated with a White Star.

"I don't think I was ever so glad to see a Tansyard," Naquaire muttered through chattering teeth. The Corporal's whole body was shaking.

I'd rather see Sorrel. Clovermead sighed, but she couldn't help feeling a surge of relief, too. *The nightmare's over,* she thought gratefully. *Thank you, Lady. They came just in the nick of time.*

The things behind them stopped in their tracks and screamed their disappointment as the White Star horsemen came rushing up. Then the creatures turned and ran behind the hills again. Mullein was shivering violently, and she still stared southward where the monsters had disappeared.

"Those banners do shine marvelously in the sun!" said Clovermead. And then the lead horseman, reinless and saddleless, brought his horse to a halt and looked suspiciously at the party from Linstock.

Chapter Eight

THE ENCAMPMENT OF THE WHITE STAR HORDE

TWENTY TANSYARD WARRIORS WHEELED AROUND them. They rode bareback on wild horses, and controlled their steeds with gentle motions of the arms and legs. Each warrior had a white star tattooed on each cheek — but aside from that they wore a hodgepodge of clothing. Most wore leather from the Steppes, some wore wool from Linstock, a few wore broadloom cloth woven in the Thirty Towns. All, however, wore embroidered bright rainbow designs upon their clothes: One had a blue wolf running across his chest, another a soaring eagle on his shoulder, a third an entire herd of buffalo charging across his back. They wore no armor, but all had stout wooden spears with sharp, bright steel tips. Most wore silver crescent pendants on their chests, but some wore obsidian bear-teeth instead. Clovermead looked at the mouths of the latter and was relieved to see that none of them had filed their teeth.

"Enemies?" asked Mullein. She pointed surreptitiously to the warriors with the bear teeth. "Friends?" She pointed to the ones with the crescent.

"I don't know," said Clovermead. "I'm not sure they know yet either."

Mullein frowned. "Tansyards friends Ursus? Ursus slave Tansyards."

"Tansyards aren't all nice to each other," said Clovermead. Mullein stared at her blankly. "It's difficult to explain," said Clovermead.

Fetterlock rode in front of Clovermead and called out to the warriors. They nodded to him respectfully, and a squat middle-aged warrior with an old scar lining his right cheek began to speak with him. They talked with each other for several minutes, while the Yellowjackets nervously eyed the circle of Tansyards around them. Fetterlock gestured to the south, in the direction where the unseen beasts had fled, while the squat warrior pointed a little south of east. Then Fetterlock rode back to Clovermead.

"We are only an hour's ride from the White Star camp. They will escort us back and make sure that we are not molested by the beasts." He frowned. "Breamback tells me that the Horde has been hearing these things scream the last two weeks. One warrior went to find out what they were, but he has not returned. They suspected that they were hounds of Ursus, and now they are sure, for they have fallen silent since Ursus' emissary arrived in the camp. The Horde supposes that Ursus would not want his servants to attack White Star warriors while he was seeking them for allies."

"Ursus sent an ambassador? How long has he been there?"

"Breamback says he arrived at dawn. But you need not worry. He cannot speak to the Elders until the Horde Chief returns, and he is not expected back until later today."

"What will Ursus' man say to the Horde?" asked

Clovermead. "Oh, Lady, he'll have some smooth-talking lie on his tongue, and I don't know what to say to keep the Elders from believing him. Is he going to try bribes? Threats?"

Fetterlock laughed. "Demoiselle, I am not a mind reader."

"Well, what sort of people are the Elders? I want to put my best foot forward, but I just know I'll make some stupid blunder and muff up everything. What is the Horde Chief like? You never talk about him much, and I get the sense that he's under his wife's thumb, because you keep on saying she sent you, not him."

"He listens to her counsel. Some warriors mock him for that, but if they are wise, they do so behind his back. He thinks she is wise, although he does not think she is infallible. He has often rejected her advice." Fetterlock grimaced. "I would not even hint to him that he is, ah, 'henpecked.' He does not take kindly to the imputation."

"Don't you worry. I'll just make clucking noises to you when his back is turned, that's all." Fetterlock looked rather pained, and Clovermead laughed.

They rode off with the Yellowjackets in a tight circle around Clovermead, Mullein, and Fetterlock, and the Tansyards in a loose circle around the Yellowjackets, and by midmorning they came to the camp of the White Star Horde. It sat on a meadow near a ford over a stream high with spring rain. Four hundred hide tents had sprouted on the grass like spring flowers; smoke rose from holes in the centers of the tents. Clovermead saw young girls bringing pots of water from the river to their tents, and older women cooking the animals their husbands had brought back from the hunt. Farther off, guarded by fifty warriors, was the horse-herd of the Horde—hundreds of grown stallions and mares, and hundreds more young foals. They already had chewed down most of the grass in their meadow. There were fresh meadows nearby, but soon the Horde would have to move on.

Clovermead and the Yellowjackets came to a space in the middle of the encampment, in front of a tent filigreed with threads of silver and gold. Breamback spoke to Fetterlock, and Fetterlock smiled. "The Horde Chief has returned to the camp," he said to Clovermead. "Wait here a moment, and I will tell him and his wife that you have come." He called out a loud sentence or two to the Tansyards around him, dismounted from his horse, and went into the gleaming tent.

Clovermead looked around her uneasily. On all sides, warriors and women had begun to gather at the sound of Fetterlock's words. They came drifting toward them in twos and threes, whispering to one another. They pointed at Clovermead, at Mullein, at the tent, and muttered even louder.

"I wish they weren't carrying so many weapons," Clovermead muttered to Algere. "It makes me uneasy."

"Me too, Demoiselle," the Sergeant whispered back. His fingers strayed to his sword hilt. "They don't look unfriendly, exactly, but I wish I knew why they were so interested in us. I'm sure they've seen Linstockers before."

"They must want to see how the Horde Chief will treat us," said Clovermead—and then the tent flap stirred and the Horde Chief and his wife emerged.

The Horde Chief's wife came out first. She was a tall woman with a kindly face, who smiled at Clovermead and Mullein when she saw them. She wore her silvering hair in a single tight braid down to the middle of her back, and held it together with a silver crescent hairpin. She wore a buckskin shirt and trousers, decorated with white and pink beads that formed a field of daisies, and on her finger she wore a gold ring adorned with a huge and splendid white diamond cut in the shape of a star. She had a look of rangy endurance to her, won by years on horseback.

Next came the Horde Chief. The tattoo on his chest caught Clovermead's attention first. Between the two halves of his open leather shirt an artist had etched a galloping white stallion, whose hooves bounded over the open Steppe. The stallion was wild, strong, free, and magnificent; its every muscle bulged on the Horde Chief's own quite muscular chest. He, too, wore a star-cut diamond on a golden ring, but he did not wear a silver crescent. Instead he wore as a pendant a star of white gold, the emblem of the Horde, on a necklace of silver wire. He walked with an air of great majesty toward Clovermead.

He was very tall. He was very broad. He was Fetterlock.

"You're the Horde Chief?" asked Clovermead in amazement. "I'm such a fool."

Somebody who knew common tongue translated what she said into Tansyard, and now a whisper of hilarity swept through the waiting women and warriors. They clapped their hands together rhythmically, applauding the joke, and the nearest warriors bowed to the Horde Chief. Then, grinning, they dispersed into the camp.

Very gravely, Fetterlock clucked at Clovermead.

She was certain that was Bergander's rumbling laugh behind her, and Habick's high-pitched giggle was unmistakable. Even Sergeant Algere was smiling.

Clovermead turned bright red. "I'm sorry, Fetter— Horde Chief. I didn't know who you were. Please don't be offended."

"I am not," said Fetterlock. He gave his wife his hand and presented her to Clovermead. "Demoiselle, my wife, Bardelle. Bardelle, this is Cerelune Cindertallow, called Clovermead Wickward, the Demoiselle of Chandlefort. She has come to the Steppes to ask the Hordes to ally with Chandlefort against Lord Ursus."

"And what do you think of her, now that you have spied on her so well?" asked Bardelle in common tongue. Her voice was low and brisk, with a hint of music in it. She smiled again at Clovermead, and Clovermead's embarrassment faded a little. "You must forgive my husband, Demoiselle," she said to Clovermead. "He was wary of this proposed alliance, and he wished to look at Chandlefort and the Cindertallows himself. I did not think he would see anything to distress him, so I agreed." Her laughing eyes turned to Fetterlock. "Are they not worthy to be our friends and our allies, Husband?"

"Perhaps," said Fetterlock. He looked at Clovermead long and consideringly. "I do not yet know." He bowed to Clovermead, slightly, as one king to another. "Please pardon me, Demoiselle. I have been away from the Horde for many weeks, and I must see how it fares." He turned and strode away from her into the heart of the encampment.

He's seen me just as I am, thought Clovermead. She was still numb with shock. *It's not just that I was snippy about the Horde Chief, Fetterlock, whoever he is. He saw Sorrel leave, and he must think I'm foolish or weak to let that happen. He didn't like that I said I'd keep Mullein with me, and, dear Lady, he told me about letting the Cyan Cross Horde be destroyed! How could he trust me with that story?* She groaned. *I don't understand and I won't understand, so I won't try. At least I didn't call him anything worse than henpecked!*

Clovermead swung down to the ground and brought Mullein down after her. While Mullein stared at the camp with fear, wonder, and delight, Bardelle approached Clovermead with quick yet gracious steps. "Welcome to the White Star Horde," she said softly. "I hope your trip will not prove to have been in vain."

"I don't think I've impressed your husband," said Clovermead.

"You have not alienated him," said Bardelle. She turned to Mullein and looked at her gravely. "This is the little girl who escaped from Barleymill?" She switched to Tansyard and asked Mullein a question. Mullein clutched at Clovermead's hand, but answered her. Bardelle spoke again, and they conversed for another minute.

"She is very sweet and very shy," Bardelle said to Clovermead. "I would like to take her back to my tent for the night. I think she would like to meet my granddaughter, Calkin—they are nearly the same age, and I think they would get along well. And I would be glad to cook Mullein a good dinner." Clovermead looked at Bardelle suspiciously, and the Horde Chief's wife touched her silver pendant. "I swear by Our Lady that I will not steal her away from you. I only wish to make her comfortable while she is here."

Clovermead knelt down by Mullein. "Do you want to go with her?" she asked.

Hesitantly, Mullein nodded. "She nice, like you." She smiled radiantly. "I back soon." She gave Clovermead a quick hug, than dashed over to Bardelle.

"I will send a warrior to guide you and your soldiers to your own tents," said Bardelle. "I will ask you to stay in them this evening. Lord Ursus' ambassador speaks to the Elders tonight, and he must be allowed the courtesy to speak without your presence. He will not be permitted among the Elders when you speak tomorrow night."

Clovermead scowled. "I still don't like Ursus having an ambassador here." Then she couldn't help but ask anxiously, "Fetterlock—your husband was telling the truth when he said you wanted an alliance with Chandlefort? I've come an awfully long way, and Mother's preparing an army, and I don't want my trip to have been a waste of time."

"I do want the alliance," said Bardelle. "And so do many of the Horde. But not yet a majority." She sighed. "Speak well tomorrow night, Demoiselle. Your words will carry great weight." Then she held out her hand to Mullein. "Mullein will see you tomorrow, Demoiselle. Farewell until then."

She walked away with Mullein trotting by her side, and Clovermead looked around. The Yellowjackets had gotten off their horses and were stretching their legs. Some Tansyard children were still watching her, and Clovermead stuck her tongue out at them. They giggled and ran away. A man in wolf-skins was walking toward her—

Lucifer Snuff came ambling toward Clovermead, and he pulled Boulderbash behind him, jauntily tugging at her with long reins. The eye-patched bear stumbled blindly through the camp. She wanted to loll her tongue, but the bit in her mouth wouldn't let her. Her throat was dry, but she couldn't drink. Her white fur was spattered with mud she had been unable to clean, and welts of blood lined the skin underneath her fur. She was drooping misery, and Clovermead was standing up, turning huge and bearish and clawed, and getting ready to lunge at Snuff—

Algere caught her by the shoulder and shoved her back down to the ground. She had already become far larger than he was, and it took a great deal of strength for him to move her mass of muscle. "Don't, Demoiselle," he said urgently. "You can't attack an ambassador. We've come all this way for Milady, and you can't muck it up now. Please, Demoiselle, calm down." He was sweating with fear as Clovermead turned to glare at him with maddened eyes, but he kept a tight grip on her.

"Do hurt me," said Snuff. He tugged Boulderbash, walked up to them, and grinned at Clovermead. His mocking eyes danced to her clenched claws, her tufts of golden fur sprouting from her, her mouth half-everted into a snout and snarling jaws, and he dared her to use her bear-weapons. His every expression was a provocation. "Of course, I am a guest of the White Star Horde, and Tansyards do set great store by treating guests well. You shan't charm our hosts if you hurt me."

We can't afford any impulsiveness on this mission. With an effort, Clovermead made her claws and jaw retract. "I'm all right now, Sergeant," she said roughly. "Thank you." She shrugged out of Algere's grip and made herself step back from Snuff. "Where's Sorrel's mother?" she asked tightly. "Have you killed her already?"

"Oh, she's not yet dead. Once Ursus sent word to me that he needed an ambassador, I dispatched her with the other bear-priests back to Barleymill." Snuff's eyes scanned the party. "Where's your Tansyard friend, girlie? I have so many stories to tell him about his mother's times in the mines! He'll be delighted to hear them."

Clovermead wanted to leap at him again, and only barely controlled herself. "I sent Sorrel back to Chandlefort," she lied quickly. *I won't let him know Sorrel's chasing after his mother. He'd have bear-priests after Sorrel in nothing flat, and then he'd be dead.* "I had to tell Mother there were bear-priests in the Harrow Moors already, and he was the quickest rider with us. He'll come back and join me soon enough."

"I eagerly await his presence." Snuff dismissed him from his mind. "Well, don't let me detain you. I must stable my steed. The Tansyards say she has to go on the other side of the stream, downwind from the horses and out of sight. She alarms the Horde's horses. Come along, steed." He pulled and Boulderbash came. "I've tamed her," said Snuff conversationally to Clovermead. He held up his whip, tipped with an iron thorn, and a cruel laugh bubbled out of him. "Spur and bit, bridle and reins, I've broken her."

Oh, Boulderbash, thought Clovermead, *I'm so sorry.*

I don't care how sorry you are, said Boulderbash. There was sharp resentment in her voice. *When will you free me, Ambrosius' daughter? Will it be soon?*

She can't help you, Snuff jeered in their minds. *She's raised your hopes, but she can't fulfill them. Don't bother yourself with her.* He jerked at the reins, and brought Boulderbash toward the ford over the stream. She growled in pain and shambled forward. Snuff's bit cut into her mouth. With each step a drop of blood fell from her. Boulderbash looked back toward Clovermead, blind, then was pulled from sight.

I begin to believe him, little cub, was the last thought Clovermead heard from her.

A warrior led Clovermead and the Yellowjackets to a line of tents at the far left of the camp. Clovermead looked around, eager to see Tansyards who weren't Sorrel just walking and chatting and living. Tansyard children, still untattooed, followed the Linstockers, and gaped and giggled and pointed at their strange clothes. The children up to age six or so went naked through the camp, the children a little older wore loincloths and moccasins, and from ten on up the children wore leggings and shirts. Grown warriors and women also glanced sideways at the Linstockers—but decorum restrained their curiosity.

When Clovermead reached her tent, she yawned. *I have been up most of the night,* she thought. *A little nap wouldn't hurt.* She crept under some soft furs and promptly fell asleep. When she woke up, it was already evening. She found a pot of hot stew waiting for her in the tent, kept warm by a cup of hot coals underneath, and she happily quenched her stomach's rumbling hunger. She could hear the Yellowjackets talking in the neighboring tent, and she thought of going to join them, but she was still sleepy and didn't feel like talking. She ate and listened to the noises of the camp.

A whisper filled the dusk. Clovermead listened carefully, but she couldn't make out any words. "I suppose that's Snuff telling the Horde Chief and the Elders how lovely it is to drink blood," she said to herself. "'Be Lord Ursus' wolfhounds!' he says. 'Join us and we can loot Low Branding! Join us and we can ravage Chandlefort!'" She shivered. "I wonder if they'll listen to him." Clovermead let her bear-ears poke up. Now she could identify Snuff's voice, but she still couldn't hear what he was saying. She let her ears dwindle again.

The murmur of Tansyard voices came from the center of the camp. Clovermead mimicked a Tansyard accent: "'Oh, yes, Mr. Snuff, we'd love to join you in an attack on Linstock! We can trust you bear-priests!'" Clovermead took another spoonful of stew, but somehow she had lost her appetite. "I wish I'd gone with you, Sorrel. I'm sure I've made Fetterlock think he'd rather be eaten by ants than ally with Chandlefort. What's the good of talking to this bunch? I'd have been of more use if I'd gone to help save your mother."

Rescue me, she heard in her head. Boulderbash's voice was suddenly very loud in her skull. *Please, Clovermead.*

And Clovermead smiled. *Maybe I can do some good here after all,* she thought. *I'm coming,* she called out, and she put down her stewpot and left the tent.

There were no Tansyards near her: Most had gone to listen to Snuff speak to the Elders, and the remainder were in their tents, making dinner. Cooking smoke wafted to the stars from a hundred tents. In the darkening evening Clovermead stole toward the stream where Snuff had left Boulderbash. She flitted inconspicuously from tent to tent.

She found Boulderbash tied to the trunk of a prairie willow. A chain wrapped around the tree extended to a tight metal collar that half-choked the great white bear. The leather patches were still firmly around her eyes, and Snuff had left the stirrups and bit on her. Clovermead ran to Boulderbash and hugged her in her arms. Boulderbash's huge jaws rubbed against her shirt and left bloody smears on it.

Release me, said Boulderbash. *You promised. Let me go free.*

I will, said Clovermead. She drew Firefly and it shone in the night. She saw Ursus' blood-net glow: Its tendrils clung to Boulderbash, insinuated themselves within her brain and into every muscle. Clovermead reached out with her mind, examined the knots, and she knew that she could sweep them clear with one slice of her sword, hack open the metal shackles, and let the bear go free. She raised her blade.

Tansyards do set great store by treating guests well.

Clovermead hesitated. She looked back at the Tansyard camp. Then, slowly, she lowered Firefly. Its light guttered out, and she sheathed the blade. *I can't now, Boulderbash,* she said. *I'm the guest of the White Star Horde. I have an awful feeling that if I freed you, they'd call it stealing from another guest. Any other time, I wouldn't care what they think, but now I'm here to bring the Tansyards into alliance with Chandlefort against Ursus. If I free you and offend them, then maybe they won't ally with us. Maybe they'd even ally with Ursus, and then he'd conquer everyone and there'd be no hope left. Don't you understand? I can't risk offending them by stealing you.*

I do not belong to that man, said Boulderbash, with rising anger. *You are not stealing me if you let me go free. Loose me from my bonds!*

Clovermead's hand clenched hard on Firefly. The power still hummed in her sword, waiting to be used. *You gave me that power so I could free bears, Lady,* thought Clovermead. *I know that.* She wanted so much to take the sword from its sheath.

It would be a disaster if I did, Clovermead thought miserably. *I can't free you,* she said to Boulderbash. Her hand fell away from her sword hilt. *Not here, not now. I don't have a choice.*

I am in shackles, said Boulderbash. *A whip guides every step I take — and you say you have no choice? Don't insult me, little cub. My freedom comes last. My slavery buys the hope for everyone else. That is your choice.* She jerked her head from Clovermead's hands and howled deep rage at Clovermead, to the world, to the moon in the sky. Her teeth snapped at Clovermead, and Clovermead sprang back from her, her heart thumping with sudden fear. *My son hurts me less,* Boulderbash growled. *He tells me openly that I will be his slave. You give me hope, and then abandon me. How can you be so cruel?*

It's for the good of everyone, said Clovermead.

I begin to lose faith in your greater good, Boulderbash snarled. Her teeth snapped again and Clovermead jumped back another step.

I'm fighting for Our Lady, said Clovermead.

I cannot believe that she wants me to remain in bondage, said Boulderbash. Tears leaked from her eyes. *And if she did —* She did not finish her sentence, but growled again, with such bitter despair that Clovermead's skin rose in goose-flesh. *Why should I bother to stay in bondage?* she whispered softly.

You will be freed, said Clovermead. She wanted to comfort Boulderbash, but she knew that would be no kindness now. And she was afraid of her. *I promise you —*

I've heard enough of your promises already, said Boulderbash. *No more words, changeling.* She howled in the darkness, and her claws dug deep into the earth. *Oh, Lady, I have been kept in darkness so long that I am forgetting what the light looks like.*

Good-bye, said Clovermead unhappily. She wanted to say more — but *no more words.* She walked away from Boulderbash.

At the ford two figures stood in darkness. Clovermead stopped a moment when she saw them, irresolute, and then one of them stepped forward. It was Fetterlock.

"She has shown the Horde no disrespect, Bear-Priest," said Fetterlock, and now Lucifer Snuff came forward. "Your suspicion of her was unjust."

"She came close enough, Horde Chief," said Snuff, as jauntily as he could, but he was discomposed. He glowered at Clovermead. "You saw her raise her sword. I think my suspicions had some cause."

"I know the obligations of a guest, Horde Chief," said Clovermead. She glared at Snuff. "I will free her as soon as I can. It's disgusting the way you keep her."

"She is my steed to do with as I will. Isn't that so, Horde Chief?" asked Snuff.

"Yes," said Fetterlock. "But we would not do such a thing." A hint of distaste entered into his voice. "I do not want you as our guest any longer, Bear-Priest. You may stay the night, but I want you gone at dawn. If my warriors find you after noon, you will be killed. You have been warned."

"So you'll ally with Chandlefort? That's a mistake, Horde Chief."

"You assume too much. The Horde has rejected Lord Ursus' offer of alliance, but that does not mean that we have decided to ally with Chandlefort." Fetterlock chuckled. "Perhaps Chandlefort's ambassador will be as unpersuasive as you were, and we will stay neutral in your wars."

"There are hunters and there are prey," said Snuff. "Choose soon, Horde Chief."

"So you told the Elders. Your warning is noted."

Fetterlock nodded slightly to Snuff and Clovermead. "Good night, Bear-Priest. Good night, Demoiselle." He walked through the shallow ford back to the White Star camp.

"I almost hate you more than Ursus," said Clovermead to Snuff. "He's bloodier, but you're crueler. You like toying with people."

"Guilty as accused." Snuff made her a sweeping, ironic bow.

"You'd be nothing without Ursus. You'd be a little torturer in a dungeon."

"I think you are mistaken," said Snuff. "I think I would have risen to conquer one of the Thirty Towns. My abilities are sufficient for that task. But it would have been an unsatisfying success. I prefer to serve something greater than myself." He grinned. "Now I am a great torturer whose dungeon is all the earth. I am grateful to my master for the opportunity to work on so large a scale."

Clovermead shook her head. "I don't understand you. I know how tempting Ursus is, but—he didn't tempt you, did he? You were like this already."

Snuff grinned again. "As you say, girlie, you don't understand me. But I understand you well enough. You moon-rabble are all the same, with a folly that is uniform from the Astrantian Sands to Snowchapel. And so you are easily dealt with."

"We defeated you twice already," said Clovermead. "We'll do it again."

"Now that he's conquered Queensmart, my master can draw on all the Thirty Towns to replenish his armies. You're short of people here in the northlands. Lord Ursus already has twice as many soldiers as he did when you repulsed us at Chandlefort—but Chandlefort hasn't yet made up their losses. You can't afford many more such victories."

"We'll win in the end," said Clovermead. "Our Lady won't let us lose."

"The sky-crone isn't what she was," said Snuff. "Best not rely on her." He bowed again to Clovermead. "Good night, Demoiselle." Then suddenly he screamed at the top of his lungs, shrieked like the unseen monsters. Far away, something screamed in reply.

"Master had to come up with something new, now you and that sword of yours keep him from using bears. Wonderful creatures, they are. You'll be amazed when you see them. And you will see them, girlie. Very soon." Snuff laughed, and he kept on laughing as he walked into the darkness.

Chapter Nine

THE MEETING OF THE ELDERS

CLOVERMEAD WAITED IN HER TENT UNTIL MIDMORNING, to be sure that Snuff and Boulderbash had left. She couldn't bear to look at either one of them. When they were gone, she went out of her tent into the White Star encampment. The scent of horses and verdant grass pervaded the air. Here a warrior was examining the hooves of his horse for pebbles, here a mother and daughter were sewing torn tent cloth with bone needles, here two little boys ran around a tent until Clovermead grew dizzy watching them. Just beyond the boys she found old Golion listening bemusedly as a pair of old warriors sang a rousing tune. The words were Tansyard, but the tune was Chandlefortish.

"That's an old Yellowjacket marching song, Demoiselle," Golion said. "I wish I could remember the words in common tongue—I only heard it a few times when I was a cadet. We sing something else now. These fellows must have fought with Chandlefort in one of our wars."

"Against Cyan Cross," said one of the old men, in heavily accented common tongue. His hair was snow-white, his face was a mass of wrinkles, and he grinned broadly and toothlessly. "They raid against High Branding, Lady of Chandlefort come to punish them. We join for promise of booty, for promise we can fight in vanguard. Our Lady bless us, we earn great renown, great herd of horses, in that war. And learn to sing with Yellowjackets!"

"We fight with your great-grandmother, Dem'zelle," said the other. "Fight with Cyan Cross next year, against her. Send Yellowjackets running from Steppes!" Golion bristled, and the warrior guffawed and pounded him on the back. "Year after that, we run from you. No dishonor in running after defeat in battle."

"I was taught differently," Golion muttered. "Funny people, these Tansyards." Then he shrugged his shoulders, winked at Clovermead, and put a smile on his weathered face. "Do you know any other Yellowjacket songs?" he asked the old warriors.

"Many, many," said the first warrior, and he started up another tune. Golion recognized this one, and he joined them in the song.

Clovermead saw other Yellowjackets, like her, wandering through the camp. Sergeant Algere and Habick admired horses, whose owners were glad to show them off, Bergander chatted with some of the young ladies of the camp, and Corporal Naquaire and the rest simply walked around and gawked at the sights. Each had a trail of children following him—Clovermead looked around, and she saw that she had followers of her own. She tried to shoo them away, but they happily ignored her.

"Good morning, Demoiselle," said Fetterlock, as he strode up to Clovermead. He wore clean, new clothes this morning. His white-gold star jounced against the head of the stallion tattooed on his chest. "Did you sleep well?"

"I lay down, and the next thing I knew it was morning. It's very restful to hear whinnying in the night." She glanced sidelong at him. "I stayed in my tent."

"I would know if you hadn't, Demoiselle," said Fetterlock. He smiled. "Mullein and Calkin were throwing oatmeal at each other during breakfast. They are a bad influence on each other, and Arman was laughing as she made them settle down. I was glad to see that—she does not often laugh. I wish that Mullein could stay with us."

"I told Sorrel I would watch over her," said Clovermead. "I want your daughter to be happy, but I have an obligation to him."

"And Mullein?" asked Fetterlock. "You have an obligation to her, too. Before you leave, ask her if she wants to stay." Clovermead's lips thinned angrily, and Fetterlock sighed. "Consider it, Demoiselle." He looked around at the crowded camp, and now he frowned. "I would like to talk with you privately. Will you walk with me?"

"I'm just as mulish by myself as I am in company, Horde Chief," said Clovermead. "You won't be able to persuade me any better."

Fetterlock laughed. "No doubt, Demoiselle. Come with me anyway." Clovermead nodded, and they strolled out of the White Star camp.

They walked up to a low rise above the river. From there they could look out over the hundreds of sprawling tents and thousands of horses that lay along the stream. The camp was full of constant motion, wonderfully bustling and thriving.

"There must be at least a thousand of you in the Horde!" Clovermead marveled. "We had more people in Timothy Vale, but they were spread out all along the

valley. Chandlefort has a lot more people, of course—
there must be ten thousand in the city—but you don't see
them all together like this."

"My Horde is beautiful," said Fetterlock. He glanced
at Clovermead. "I have told you some of my fears and
hopes, pretending to be only the warrior Fetterlock, and
everything I have told you is true. But I am the Horde
Chief as well, and that imposes far worse fears upon me.
I am responsible for every man, woman, and child you
see below. I do not think your Mother knows all her sub-
jects, but I know every one in the Horde, and I cherish
them more each day. If I fail in my responsibility to them,
I know the name of every one who will die."

"I don't know what to say to you, Horde Chief," said
Clovermead. She bit her lip in frustration. "I've been
practicing all sorts of speeches in my head about what to
say to the Horde Chief, but what's the good of saying
them to you? You know them already, and it sounds like
your wife's been a lot more eloquent that I ever could be.
She got you to come to Chandlefort in the first place!
Anyway, she said you wanted to take a look at
Chandlefort, and at Mother and me, so you could decide
if you wanted to ally with us or not. All right, you've seen
us. Do you trust us as allies against Lord Ursus?"

"I do not know," Fetterlock said slowly. "I know you
are brave and kind, Demoiselle, and I do not doubt your
good intentions. Those are powerful arguments in your
favor. But I worry about your steadiness. You let young
Sorrel leave us, so far as I could tell without a word of
complaint or a hint to him of punishment. I think perhaps your friendship with him has made you less stern
than a leader ought to be. And then you came down to
the ford last night. You did not free that bear, but you

125

came very close. Your heart is generous, but its impulses came close to bringing your mission here to ruin. I wonder what your heart will tell you to do next, and whether you will resist its promptings when necessary. Can you assure me of that?"

Clovermead looked south over the Steppes, toward distant, unseen Bryony Hill and Barleymill. Somewhere on the plains Snuff was digging his spurs into Boulderbash, somewhere Sorrel was riding to free his mother. She could not think of either of them without her heart leaping in her, and she could not answer Fetterlock to reassure him.

Fetterlock sighed. "And so I remain unsure whether to entrust the Horde to an alliance with Chandlefort."

"You told me that you had more hope when you saw Mullein and Sorrel were alive," said Clovermead. "Doesn't that mean anything now?"

"They give me hope that I might redeem myself before Our Lady," said Fetterlock. "But I cannot commit the Horde to war for so flimsy a cause." He touched the golden pendant at his chest. "My wife wears both Our Lady's crescent and the White Star, and that is good. But it is my duty to wear the White Star alone. I cannot be a servant to two masters."

"I understand," said Clovermead, but she couldn't help sounding bitter. *He's going to say no tonight. It will all have been a waste of time. The fortress will go up on Bryony Hill, Mother will march her army back to Chandlefort, and then we'll wait for Ursus' armies to come after us. All I've done out here is lose Sorrel as my friend.* "Is that all you had to say to me?"

"Not quite, Demoiselle," said Fetterlock. "My warriors have brought me some information that you may find useful. They tell me that the bear-priests have been bringing a great many carts of *hwanka-velika*, quicksilver, from Barleymill to their obsidian temple on Bryony Hill."

"That doesn't make sense," said Clovermead. She frowned. "There isn't any silver in Bryony Hill, is there? Why would they bother?"

"I do not know. But I offer you that information as a token of goodwill."

"I'd rather have your alliance," said Clovermead. Fetterlock shrugged. They stared at the Horde below them a minute longer, so vibrant and so fragile, and then Fetterlock led her back down to the camp in silence.

That evening Clovermead left the Yellowjackets in their tents and came alone to where the Elders were waiting. She was met by Mullein, who barreled over from Fetterlock's tent and jumped up into her arms. Her feet dangled in midair, she babbled in Tansyard, and then she said, "Calkin show me crayfish stream! We catch twelve!"

"I'm awfully glad," said Clovermead, laughing. "Was everyone nice to you?"

Mullein nodded vigorously. "Soft bed, honey eat, Bardelle sing sleep. Nice!"

Do you want to stay with them? Clovermead couldn't quite ask. She looked around at the gathering Tansyards. "You should go to bed now," she said to Mullein.

"No! I stay you! Not leave." She wrapped her arms around Clovermead's neck.

"All right! Mullein not leave! Mullein squeeze less tightly or Clovermead will choke. You understand choke?" Clovermead pantomimed clutching her neck, and Mullein loosened her hold and slid to the ground. Clovermead took Mullein's hand in hers, and walked with her into the center of the camp.

The Elders, both male and female, were waiting for them in front of the great circle of tents at the heart of the Horde. They sat down on intricately woven blankets all around the earthen clearing. They ranged in age from middle-aged to ancient; the younger ones helped prop up some of the feeblest. They wore an assortment of jewelry to match the warriors—some wore silver crescents, but almost as many wore obsidian teeth. Farther back from the circle of tents, standing in the shadows, young men and women watched in silence, waiting to hear Clovermead speak and to hear their Elders' decisions.

Fetterlock and Bardelle sat side by side in front of their tent, on high-piled blankets made of cloth-of-gold. Bardelle gave Clovermead the slightest glance of encouragement, then made her face immobile. Fetterlock smiled a little when he saw Mullein come with Clovermead into the open space among the Elders, then quickly stood up and strode forward to stand by their side.

"Elders!" he called out. "I will speak in common tongue, in courtesy to our guest." Some of the Elders began to whisper translations of his words to their fellows who knew only Tansyard. "The second ambassador has come to ask us for our aid. She is Cerelune Cindertallow, the Demoiselle of Chandlefort. Lord Ursus honored us by sending his great lieutenant of the northlands as his ambassador, and Lady Cindertallow honors us by sending her Heir Apparent. Let us hear her make the case for Chandlefort, as we have heard the bear-priest make the case for Ursus." Fetterlock bowed to Clovermead, and went back to sit by Bardelle's side on his golden blanket.

Clovermead looked around her at a hundred waiting Elders. Some stared back at her curiously, some with boredom, but none with friendship. She gulped, and she held more tightly to Mullein. *I must look awfully silly holding her hand,* she thought, *but it sure is a comfort.* Mullein squeezed her palm, and Clovermead began to speak.

"I think you all know why I'm here," Clovermead said. "We heard in Chandlefort that Ursus is building a fortress at Bryony Hill, and we knew we had to fight him before he finishes it. He's just about conquered the Thirty Towns, and he'll be able to launch an invasion of Linstock from the south and the east once he has his fortress walls up. He gets stronger every year, so we know we have to fight him now.

"We've come to ask the White Star Horde for help for two reasons. The first is that it looks to us like you wouldn't be too happy about the fortress yourself. Ursus will try to make himself lord of the Steppes once that fortress is built, and then you'll have to submit to him or fight him anyway. We think you'd have better odds fighting this summer, with an army of Yellowjackets at your side." Clovermead paused for breath. "The second reason we've come to ask you is that we're not fools. We want the best warriors in the world on our side, not on Ursus'."

There was a ripple of appreciative laughter among the Elders. *And they don't think it is flattery!* Clovermead realized. *Good heavens, they'd be insulted if I didn't tell them that once a day. They are a conceited bunch.*

She looked around the circle of Elders again and she saw that a fair number of the Elders were looking at her favorably. But when she looked closely, she saw that they all wore Our Lady's silver crescent. The Elders who wore obsidian bear-teeth, or no jewelry at all, looked at her as unfavorably as ever. *What do I say to convince them?*

Clovermead asked herself. *Look at them scowl at me! I don't think sweet reason and soft words is going to do it.* She glanced down at Mullein, wanting the comfort of her gaze—and her eyes caught on the scar on her own arm.

Gently she disentangled her arm from Mullein. She rolled up her sleeves, and the chill evening air prickled on her flesh. She held her arm up to the firelight and turned around, so every Elder could see the ugly, mottled flesh that ran from her shoulder to her palm. It was healed now, pale where it had once been livid, but it would never go away. Clovermead walked around the circle of Elders and showed it to every one of them. She stopped in front of a knot of Elders who wore Ursus' obsidian around their necks.

"Lord Ursus possessed me once," she said, and there was utter silence in the camp. "I put his tooth in my arm, and he drank my blood. I got this scar for my pains. I put his tooth in my jaw, and now I have a hole where my own tooth used to be." She touched the empty space in her upper jaw, still hollow and aching. "I had a choice, like you, about whether to fight Lord Ursus properly. I got it wrong the first time, and I surrendered to him. And I won't lie to you: I liked it. I liked hunting with Ursus. I liked seeing the world as my prey. I liked knowing what my master would do to the world."

Clovermead swung abruptly from the bear-tooth-wearing Elders to the ones who wore no jewelry. "I know what Ursus will do to the Steppes, Elders. What he did to Cyan Cross Horde, what he's done to Bryony Hill, he'll do to everyone and everything. He will set fires from one end of the grasslands to the other, and leave them in charred ruins. He will chop down every tree and poison every stream. He will send bear-priests into the Steppes to slaughter every horse of every Horde, for the sheer pleasure of watching you walk. And then he will hunt you down, one by one." She turned back to the Elders with the bear-teeth. "The only reward you can get is to help him hunt your brethren down. Whatever joy you get from that will be short-lived, for he will turn on you when the others are dead. In the end, you will die as they have died, with Ursus' gratitude as your only reward."

Clovermead walked back to the center of the circle, by the firelight. She let down her sleeve, so that it covered her scar. "I made the right choice the second time. I plucked out his tooth and now I fight for Our Lady. I don't know if we'll win. All I have is hope, and faith in Our Lady. But win or lose, at least we're fighting for a better world than the one Ursus will make, with something more than blood and killing. I liked hunting with Ursus, but I like fighting against him more. I won't die ashamed of myself. And neither will you, if you fight with us. My friend Sorrel would say, 'Our Lady will sing of our glory by her campfire.' *Noru Mari noru pakeyu sa le zilaya bi pajarat.*" Her throat was dry, and she paused to swallow. "I don't really have anything more to say."

There was silence for a long moment. Then the Elders whispered to one another in Tansyard. Clovermead tried to see their faces, to see how they had reacted, but they were too far away from the firelight. She couldn't tell.

Fetterlock stood up. "Do any of the Elders wish to question the ambassador?"

An Eldress with a bear-tooth stood up. "I do not wish to question her," she said scornfully. "I do not believe her. She brings us lies from Chandlefort. Ursus has promised us great things as his allies. It is not too late to accept his offer. At the worst, we should not make him angry. Let us stay neutral in this war." She spat at the ground. "Do not be swayed by this Chandlefort farmer-girl's stories."

"Not stories," said Mullein. She spoke suddenly, loudly, so all the Elders could hear her high voice. She took a step forward. "I know. I see bear-priests, in mines. All blood, all killing." She gulped and she looked around. "Why you leave us in mines?"

Fetterlock cast his head down, and Clovermead knew he was crying.

"You are Cyan Cross," said the Eldress with the bear-tooth. "We are White Star. Let Cyan Cross suffer. Let Cyan Cross die. They are no brothers of ours."

It took Mullein a moment to understand the Eldress. When she did, she retreated back to Clovermead. "Clovermead my sister," she said. "She care for me."

"She die with you," said the Eldress. She turned to the Elders around her. "But we should not. It is not in our interest to be destroyed as Cyan Cross was destroyed. Is that not true?" She was answered by silence, and she turned to Fetterlock. "What say you, Horde Chief? What is the interest of the Horde?"

"I cannot say," said Fetterlock. He touched his white-gold star uncertainly, and lifted his head. "Before tonight, I would have counseled you to vote against the Demoiselle's proposals. Now I do not know. My heart, my mind, my soul, whisper contrary things, and I am afraid I will deliver the Horde to destruction, no matter what I advise. Does anyone else have anything to say?" The Elders were silent. "Then vote, Elders. Shall we accept the alliance with Chandlefort against Lord Ursus? I will lead the Horde as you direct, no matter what course you choose."

Then all the Elders rose, some quickly, others shuffling slowly to their feet. They came forward one by one toward the campfire, where each shouted out "Yes" or "No." Those who wore silver crescents or obsidian teeth came to the campfire first, eager to make their votes. A few Elders who had worn bear-teeth cast them off, came to the campfire, and voted "Yes." They were crying as they came, and their former fellows scowled at them when they returned to their seats. Those without emblems of Our Lady or Ursus waited and said "Yes" or "No" unhappily, visibly uncertain as to whether they had made the right choice.

The very last votes were almost all "Yes." "Yes," "No," "Yes," "Yes," "Yes," they voted. When the last had returned to his seat, Fetterlock sighed. "Forty-nine have voted no. Fifty-six have voted yes. The Elders have spoken: We shall ally with Chandlefort, and we will fight against Lord Ursus. This I swear in all our names, and in the name of Our Lady. Let our honor and our souls be our pledges."

"This we swear," the Elders echoed. The words came with sour difficulty from the ones who wore bear-teeth, but they swore too. Then the onlooking warriors and women began to disperse, followed by the Elders.

Fetterlock came forward to Clovermead. "We are allies after all," he said heavily. "And you will have more allies. You need not go to the other Hordes yourself — I will send my warriors to the other Hordes, to tell them what you have said and what we have done. They will follow our lead and come with us into battle." He frowned. "But battle will be difficult. Barleymill's walls are too formidable for us to assault. We might take Bryony Hill, but the Hordes would remain in danger. So long as Ursus' army remains in Barleymill, he can always ravage the Steppes."

"Mother won't abandon you," said Clovermead. "We'll be sure to help you, no matter what happens. Speaking of Mother, where and when should she send her army to meet you? Should it go straight to Bryony Hill?"

"I do not think so," said Fetterlock. "They would go slowly through the Moors, and then some Harrowman spy in bear-priest pay could send warning to Bryony Hill. No, let them sail south of the Moors on the Whetstone River to Yarrow's Landing. It is only a day's march over the Farry Heights from there to Yarrow's Bowl, and we will meet them there, let us say in seven weeks, on Midsummer's Eve. That will give us time to gather the Hordes. We will march north from there to Bryony Hill. It is a little out of the way, but we will not lose much time. We will also be between Bryony Hill and Barleymill, and we will be able to keep bear-priest reinforcements from coming to Bryony Hill."

"What if Lord Ursus' army shows up?" asked Clovermead. "Won't we be awfully exposed down there?"

Fetterlock smiled. "If all the Hordes and the Yellowjackets are together, it is the bear-priests who will need to worry. We can only hope they will stumble across us."

"Then I'll send some Yellowjackets back to Low Branding," said Clovermead. "I'll have them tell Mother everything—not least the fact that you were the Horde Chief in disguise! She knew there was something not quite right in your story, but she couldn't tell what. But the important thing is that she's to be at Yarrow's Bowl at Midsummer's Eve."

Fetterlock unlooped his white-gold pendant, hesitated

a moment, then put it in Clovermead's hand. "Have your messengers give that to Lady Cindertallow. It is my pledge that the Hordes will meet her there."

Clovermead's eyes went wide. "You don't need to do this. I trust you."

"I have already played your mother false in the small matter of my true rank. She will be happy to have this token." He sighed. "Will you come with the Horde, Demoiselle? I would be glad to have your company the next few weeks."

"I'm free to do what I like? You don't need me for high politicking or anything?" Fetterlock shook his head. "I'd be glad to spend the time with you and Bardelle—"

Sorrel was riding south to Barleymill, alone. But he didn't have to be alone. *I can join him now,* Clovermead realized. *I've done what Mother wanted.* Sudden possibility swept over her. *Now I can make up for abandoning him, and I can help him save Roan after all. Maybe I can track down Boulderbash while I'm at it, and free her, too.*

Maybe Sorrel won't forgive me, she thought, and Clovermead's heart yawed inside her. *Maybe I've broken our friendship and it's too late to mend it. Oh, Lady, I've hurt him so badly, and I'm afraid to see him again. He'll look at me like I was the lowest thing on earth, I'll burst out crying, and he'll say I ought to cry. He'll say I'm trying to buy his friendship by making him grateful to me, and I'm not sure he'd be all wrong. I don't want to go join him, not really. He can't hurt me while I'm with the White Star Horde, and I can't disappoint him. I'd rather stay here.*

Of course you would, she thought she heard Boulderbash say. *Cowardly girl.*

Cowardly girl, she heard again, and now it was her own voice ringing in her ears.

135

Clovermead sighed. "Horde Chief, I'm afraid I'm going to decline your kind offer," she said out loud. "There's something else I have to do instead."

Fetterlock raised an eyebrow. "What, Demoiselle?"

"I need to go find Sorrel," said Clovermead. "He was riding toward Barleymill, to free his mother. He'll need my help."

Fetterlock whistled, long and low. "That sounds most imprudent, Demoiselle," he said. "Many go into Barleymill; few come out."

"It's the most foolish thing in the world," said Clovermead. "Really, I'd much rather remain with the White Star Horde. But Sorrel needs me, and I owe him—everything, really. I have to go. I'm not at all happy about riding after him, but I know this is right. If I'm still alive, I'll be at Yarrow's Bowl in seven weeks. And if I'm not—tell Mother this was my duty." Fetterlock nodded reluctantly. Clovermead grimaced. "I'd be grateful if you pointed out the quickest way to Barleymill for me tomorrow. If I'm going to be putting my head into the bear's mouth, I'd like to do it in time to be of some use."

Please, Lady, she thought, *let me get to Barleymill in time to save Roan. Please let me find Sorrel before he comes to hate me. I want Roan alive, and Boulderbash free, but I'm going off to Barleymill to get Sorrel's friendship back again. Forgive me, Lady, but when you get down to it, that's the truth.*

Chapter Ten

TANGLED DREAMS

CLOVERMEAD TOSSED IN HER SLEEP. *WHERE ARE YOU?* a voice called out. It was an old woman, very tired and very far away. *I can't find you, little one.*

I'm here, said Clovermead. She was sleeping inside her hide tent in the White Star encampment, but somehow she was above her body as well, watching herself snore in an appallingly graceless manner. *Look, I'm right here.*

She could feel fingers *riffling* through her, as if she were a book, and somewhere eyes were peering at her. *Not you,* the woman sighed. *Where is she? Lady, give me strength.* She let go of Clovermead, but Clovermead didn't return to her sleeping body. She was spinning through the darkness, untethered, and Clovermead was just opening her mouth to scream when —

She was sitting in a broad green meadow next to a Tansyard boy. He was no more than eight, and Clovermead was eight too, dressed like him in a shirt and short pants. Before them was a woman of fifty, dressed in white deerskins. Her black hair, pulled tight into a bun, had turned half-silver, her face was long and angular, and she glanced at the two children with a forbidding eye. She wore silver crescents at her neck, at her wrists, and

137

on the belt around her waist. She sat on a small stool of leather and wood, while Clovermead and the boy were seated cross-legged on the grass. It was autumn, and the woman held a yellow leaf in her hand.

What is this leaf? she asked. She spoke in Tansyard, but Clovermead understood her. The woman stroked its surface up and down. *It's common in the Harrow Moors.*

Elm, Shaman-Mother! the boy shouted out. He grinned with pleasure at the sound of his own voice. *Huge elms grow all over the Moors.* Behind the Shaman-Mother a grove of elms spurted out of the earth and rocketed upward until they were a thousand feet high and scraping the fluffy white clouds overhead.

No, Sorrel, said the Shaman-Mother severely. She waved a hand, and the elms plummeted back into the Steppes, to be swallowed once more by the grass. Clovermead gaped at the little boy. He was a tiny Sorrel, a chubby Sorrel, but unmistakably himself. *Elms grow on the slopes of the Reliquary Mountains,* said the Shaman-Mother. *What is this?* She rubbed the leaf again. Where she touched the plant, her fingers reddened. She turned to Clovermead. *Do you know?*

Clovermead looked close, and she gasped. *Poison sumac,* she said. *There's no end of it in the swampy ground behind Ladyrest Inn. Father said never to touch it. Shaman-Mother, let it go.* On either side of the meadow, the Reliquary Mountains suddenly loomed, and now they were in the narrow fields of Timothy Vale rather than the broad grasslands of the Steppes.

Shaman-Mother, let it go, Sorrel was saying at the same time. He looked at the mountains, shook his head in puzzlement, and frowned at Clovermead. *I was supposed to say that,* he said, and now his voice was a man's, the sound of the Sorrel she knew coming out of the boy. *Who are you? You look familiar.*

I can stand the pain, the Shaman-Mother said to Sorrel, said to Clovermead. But it wasn't a yellow leaf any longer, but a black viper that hissed and sank its fangs deep into the woman's flesh. Blood welled from her finger, a stream of scarlet and shining silver, the Shaman-Mother cried out in agony—and then the world was as it had been. The Shaman-Mother smiled, let the yellow leaf fall to the ground, and whispered a prayer. The rash faded from her fingers, until they were pink and smooth once more. *And I have learned healing arts from Our Lady. It is easy enough to heal myself.* Sorrel reached out a finger to touch the fallen leaf, and the Shaman-Mother intercepted his finger. *But harder to heal others, little Sorrel. Do you want me to itch for your sake?*

No, said Sorrel, wide-eyed. He spoke in a little boy's voice again.

Then keep your fingers to yourself! said the Shaman-Mother. The mountains disappeared into darkness, and they were in grasslands again. She tousled Sorrel's hair and laughed. *The Horde will suffer worse hurts than sumac. I need to make sure I am strong enough to cure them when they truly need me.* She looked up, and now wildflowers were bursting into bloom all around them. *Ah, here's your mother. I've kept you late. I'm sorry, Roan. He's an eager student, if a mischievous one, and I like teaching him. Quick, Sorrel, what town has rose walls?*

Chandlefort! said Sorrel. He turned to Roan, and she was young and beautiful, draped in a robe of marten, with chestnut hair that swung down to her waist thick- ened from bearing four children. *It sits in the heart of the*

*desert, they don't have any water, and I'll bet they stink there
because there aren't any streams to wash in.*

You see how well he studies? asked the Shaman-Mother.
*Already he knows more about Chandlefort than I do. I never knew
the Cindertallows don't bathe.*

When she said "Cindertallow," Sorrel jumped. He
looked at Clovermead again, and now he knew her.

The Shaman-Mother was an old woman bleeding silver in darkness. Roan, tired and haggard, stood in rags
that dripped from her flight through the Harrow Moors.

This hasn't happened yet, said Sorrel. He shook his head
violently, and the younger Shaman-Mother and Roan
reappeared, in the flower-filled meadow. Sorrel turned
his back on Clovermead and sidled away from her.

He's just hopeful, Shaman-Mother, said Roan. *You have no
idea how hard it is to get him under water. Dinner's waiting,
Sorrel,* said Roan, and she gathered Sorrel's hand in hers.
Good-bye, Shaman-Mother, said Roan, and Sorrel said,
Good-bye! I'll see you tomorrow! He turned away from her
smiling face, and behind him, the Shaman-Mother faded
from view. The meadow swirled into blackness.

Now they were in a tent, kind Roan and Sorrel's stern
father, Dapple, and all the children, Emlets and Clary
and Sorrel and baby Mullein. The pot in the center of the
tent was boiling, and Emlets was serving roast goat into
their bowls. Clary was tickling Mullein with a feather,
and a smile broke through Dapple's austere features as
he welcomed Roan and Sorrel.

I miss you so, said Sorrel, and it was grown-Sorrel's
voice again. *Lady, let me dream like this forever.* He turned to
Clovermead, and he frowned. *You don't belong here.*

Let me stay, Clovermead pleaded. *I miss you too.*

And I you, said Sorrel. Hesitantly he lifted his hand

toward Clovermead. Then he glanced at Roan, and he scowled. *You'd let her die. Go away.* He slipped out of Roan's embrace, rushed at Clovermead, and shoved her violently. *Leave me alone!* He pushed again, and Clovermead was howling and stumbling backward, out of the tent and into the darkness. The tent was a flicker of light falling behind her, and then she was alone in the night. She rushed through emptiness —

Now she walked with Waxmelt along the rose parapets of Chandlefort. In the distance she saw the cavalcade of Yellowjackets riding eastward to Low Branding. *There goes Milady after you, Clo,* said Waxmelt. He blinked at Clovermead in mild surprise, pinched himself, and sighed when he failed to flinch. *I knew you couldn't be real. I suppose I've fallen asleep on guard duty.*

I'm asleep out on the Steppes, Father, said Clovermead. *I've gotten unmoored somehow. I seem to be wandering into other people's dreams.*

Then I'm glad you came into mine, said Waxmelt. They walked through a doorway, and they were in the kitchen at Ladyrest. Waxmelt's armor was gone, and he was in his old, stained apron. Her father rolled up his sleeves, began rinsing a dirty dish in a pot of water, and smiled at Clovermead. *Do you know, your mother actually laughed at a joke of mine yesterday? The one about the goat, the cobbler, and the jaguar.* He handed the rinsed dish to Clovermead.

Clovermead found a rag, began to dry the dish, and wrinkled her nose. *That's such an old chestnut!*

True, said Waxmelt. He handed her a glistening spoon, and Clovermead began to dry that, too. *I expected her to just groan, but she'd never heard it before! She has quite a nice laugh. Like yours, but, um, more delicate. She doesn't snort.*

I do not snort! said Clovermead. Waxmelt raised an

eyebrow, and now they were in the barn behind Ladyrest bringing food to the trough as a half dozen pigs squealed ecstatically. Clovermead glowered at Waxmelt. *Ha-ha. I snort unbelievably delicately. I didn't know the two of you were getting along well enough to tell jokes.*

A pig nuzzled Waxmelt, and he scratched its ears absentmindedly. *We hadn't been, particularly, but we were working round the clock to get the Yellowjackets ready to depart and the servants ready to take their places, and we got punchy. Then we got giddy. She was making terrible puns while we were inspecting the Armory that last time. We—I quite enjoyed her company. She can be charming.* Waxmelt paused for a moment, then sighed. *It's another reason I wish I hadn't stolen you away from Milady. She must always hate me, in the cold light of day, and we can never be friends. I find myself wishing that we could be.* He smiled wryly, sadly. *But I suppose that is the stuff of dreams.* And they were back on the parapets of Chandlefort again. A cold wind blew in the night.

Clovermead shivered, and tried to smile. *Here I am, at least two hundred miles from Chandlefort, and I get to hear your voice. There's a dream come true for you, Father!*

There's a compliment from my daughter! The wind died down and Waxmelt chuckled and stopped walking, and turned to embrace Clovermead. *Ah, Clo, I do miss you so. Tell me, how are you doing out on the Steppes?*

We got to the White Star Horde safely, said Clovermead. *We had some scares along the way*—she saw Waxmelt frown—*but nothing too bad,* she added hastily.

What will you do now? asked Waxmelt.

And the words froze in Clovermead's throat. *I can't say, "I'm going to Barleymill,"* she thought. *I'd terrify him, and he'd tell me not to go, but I'm going anyway. All I'd do is make him feel miserable.*

We're heading to Yarrow's Bowl to meet Mother's army, she said. *There'll be no end of Tansyards coming to join up with us.*

I'm glad to hear that, said Waxmelt. Somewhere a bell tolled, and the walls of Chandlefort began to crumble. *Blast! I need to check on the sentries.* The bell tolled a second time, the metal gate shuddered into dust, and Waxmelt yawned again. *I'll be waking up now, whether I want to or not. Come wandering into my dreams again, Clo, whenever you like.*

As often as I can, Father, said Clovermead, and the bell tolled a third time. Waxmelt stretched—and faded from view. Chandlefort faded with him, melted into blackness, and now Clovermead could feel herself returning to the Steppes. Her body was coming nearer to her—

Nightmare waylaid her. She was in a meadow, and the corpses of the Cyan Cross Horde lay all around her. They were sprawled on crimson grass, their tents were burning rags, and the dead bodies stretched on forever on the Steppes. Bryony Hill rose above the plain of bodies, and it was covered with an obsidian skin. At the summit of the mount, Lucifer Snuff was hammering in an altar. The hill bled where the altar legs pierced its side.

Fetterlock stood by Clovermead's side. *I'm sorry,* he moaned. Corpses were piled about him, up to his knees. Their dead fingers clutched at him. *I didn't mean for this to happen. Lady, I know I should have warned them.*

You let this happen? asked someone on Clovermead's other side. She turned, and she saw Mullein. The little girl stood in a patch of open ground, and she stared at the bodies around her. Then she turned to Fetterlock in disbelief. *You were there?*

I should have spoken, said Fetterlock. He could not look Mullein in the face. Now the bodies were piled up to his

143

waist, and rising by the minute. *I hated Cyan Cross too much. I am sorry.*

You let me go to the mines? Mullein was weeping suddenly. *I thought you were a kind man. You did this?* And she was leaping at Fetterlock with outstretched nails, running over the dead bodies to rip his face and shred his flesh. She was snarling with anger and screaming with sorrow. Clovermead struggled after the little girl, waded through corpses, and pulled Mullein's hands away from unresisting Fetterlock's scratched cheeks. Mullein struggled in Clovermead's grip, her scream split the sky, and sent vast chunks of blue falling down to crush them all. Then the world shattered in darkness a final time, and Clovermead's heart was hammering as she woke up alone in her tent.

Chapter Eleven

VELIKA-GORA

FETTERLOCK AND A SCORE OF TANSYARD WARRIORS accompanied Clovermead, Mullein, and the rest of the Yellowjackets southward out of the encampment. "Just in case that bear-priest is waiting to ambush you," said Fetterlock. "He will think twice about attacking all of us." At noon, at the top of a rise from which one could see for miles, Fetterlock held up his hand and the Tansyards came to a halt. "There is nothing nearby," he said. "You will be safe for a while, Demoiselle." He looked uncomfortably to the south. "Normally I would tell you to circle wide around Bryony Hill, but Barleymill is more than four hundred miles away. You will need to hurry to catch up with your friend, and you must take the straight route. Still, be careful not to go too near Bryony Hill. Warriors who approach it seldom return."

"I'll be glad to stay away from it," said Clovermead. "Ugh! It sounds wretched."

"Once it was beautiful," said Fetterlock. "Once it was holy." He glanced at Mullein. "I wish you would let little Mullein stay with us. You are taking her into danger. I promise you, we would care for her as our own child."

"Do you want to stay?" Clovermead asked Mullein.

Her heart tightened within her. "It's true. We'll be riding to Barleymill. You can stay if you want." She looked at the little girl, and in her mind's eye Sorrel stared at her with accusing eyes. She wasn't sure if he would blame her more for bringing Mullein or for leaving her behind. "We would come and get you before winter."

"You want me stay?" Mullein looked at her with hurt eyes.

Clovermead shook her head. "No. But I don't want the bear-priests to recapture you either."

"Maybe I stay," said Mullein. "I scared, very much." She looked uncertainly at Fetterlock—then frowned. "You were there," she said suddenly. "I see in dream. You let Cyan Cross die." Fetterlock turned dead white, and Mullein's eyes widened. "Dream true, then." She glanced at Clovermead. "You there, yes? You also see?"

"I saw it also," Clovermead whispered. "Just for a moment. I don't know how we got into the same dream."

"It not matter," said Mullein. She glanced at Fetterlock for a moment, cold as ice, then turned back to Clovermead. "I stay with you. Fight bear-priests, find Sorrel, save Mother." She turned back to the Horde Chief. "You not care."

"It was just a dream," Fetterlock began, but then he fell silent. His head bowed. "Yes. We three shared a dream, by Our Lady's pleasure, and you saw what I would never have told you. But I do care for you, Mullein. Very much. I have changed—" But Mullein's scowl was fixed. "I also dreamed that you became my second granddaughter." Mullein trembled, but she would not look at him. He sighed. "But some dreams, alas, are not true. I am sorry, little one." He turned to Clovermead. "Lady watch over you all. Farewell,

Demoiselle. I will see you at Yarrow's Bowl in seven weeks." He wheeled his steed, cast a last glance back at Mullein, and led his warriors northward back to the camp.

Clovermead looked at the Yellowjackets. "I'm looking for Sorrel, and when I find him, we're going to go to Barleymill," she said loudly. Bergander made the crescent sign. "This isn't Chandlefort business anymore. If you don't want to come to Barleymill, just come forward now. I need at least a pair of messengers to ride to Low Branding now and tell Mother to bring her army to Yarrow's Bowl. You can all go as messengers, if you want."

The Yellowjackets looked at one another. Some of them looked very tempted to kick their horses toward her. Corporal Naquaire started to clench his knees against his horse—then, shamefaced, relaxed his legs. The rest settled back in their saddles.

"That's kind of you, Demoiselle," said Sergeant Algere, "but we'll be coming along with you anyway. Milady gave us fair warning back in Chandlefort. She said, 'I want volunteers to escort my daughter. If I know her, she's going to end up doing something horribly dangerous, and not at all what she's been told to do, and she'll need somebody to guard her, wherever she goes. So don't volunteer unless you're prepared to ride into the gates of Garum.'" Algere chuckled. "Milady had you pegged, right enough. Don't you worry about us, Demoiselle. We made our choice back in Chandlefort when we signed up as your escort."

"You can change your minds," said Clovermead. The Yellowjackets stared at her woodenly, and Clovermead smiled. "I don't much care for being mother-henned, and

I'm going to have words with Mother about that, but I'm glad to have your company. It'll be awfully dangerous riding to Barleymill."

"Not so dangerous as facing your mother, and telling her we left you out here on the Steppes," said Golion. The others laughed, and Clovermead laughed with them.

"I'll still need messengers," said Clovermead. "Sergeant, how many of the troopers have wives and children?"

"Corporal Naquaire," said Algere. The Corporal smiled in sudden relief. "Habick."

"Habick?" asked Clovermead. She looked dubiously at the redhead. "He can't even grow a proper beard!"

"He surprised us, too," rumbled Bergander. "Sneaked off to the chapel to get married without so much as a by-your-leave, with a girl no older than he is. And now they have a baby son!"

"I'm not asking to be sent back, Demoiselle!" Habick said hotly. "I'm no coward. The Sergeant has a wife and two daughters! Send him instead of me."

"Don't be a fool," Naquaire whispered to Habick with harsh urgency. "Take your ticket out of this madness."

"The Demoiselle can spare a trooper," said Algere. "She needs me to keep the lot of you in good discipline." Habick opened his mouth to protest again. "It's an order, Habick," said Algere, and the trooper sullenly acquiesced. "Give my goodwife my love, Habick," Algere said softly. The trooper gulped and nodded.

In a minute, Corporal Naquaire and Habick were riding west for Low Branding. Clovermead glanced at Algere. A melancholy look had settled onto his face. *I do need him*, thought Clovermead. *I think I'll need all of them if I'm to have any chance of getting out of this alive. Lady, I know they say they're volunteers, but I'm still the one who's decided to risk their lives. Please make this worthwhile. Don't let it be a madcap ride that ends with us all dead.* She made the sign of the crescent to seal her prayer, and then Clovermead turned to the south and set Auroche galloping. The remaining seven Yellowjackets rode after her.

They rode for days over endless grass. The Steppes shifted their appearance in trivial details constantly, but the landscape's monotony persisted from day to day. The sun wheeled overhead, and Clovermead was lost again, beyond what sense of direction the sun and the stars gave her. On rainy days she lost even that. She wouldn't have minded so much if the Yellowjackets had a better sense of direction than she did, but they were as disoriented as she was. After a while Clovermead realized they were following her. She hoped that she was going on more or less the right bearing.

Mullein's command of common tongue continued to improve. "The way you're going, by midsummer you'll be talking common tongue better than Sorrel," Clovermead said to her fondly one evening. They were huddled around the campfire: A damp wind from the Moors was cooling the Steppes. "He will be surprised to hear you!"

"I am glad," said Mullein carefully. She blew on her hands, still etched with quicksilver, and looked up at Clovermead. "What he like, Clovermead?"

"That's right, you were still a baby when he left the Steppes. You wouldn't know." Clovermead smiled. "He's a brave fighter—I've seen him kill two bear-priests in a single fight. He's a good friend. He's always helped me when I needed him. When I had just come to Chandlefort, and I didn't have a friend besides him, he never let me get lonely. He's always courteous to everybody and—well, he is a little vain, but he's got good reason. There isn't anyone handsomer in Chandlefort."

"Sound like good brother," said Mullein. She stared into the fire. "He knew mother alive? Knew me alive? In Barleymill?"

Clovermead shook her head. "He knew a few people from the tribe had survived, but he didn't know either of you had. He thought his family was all dead."

"He not abandoned us?"

"No!" said Clovermead. "Didn't you see how he rode after the bear-priests to rescue your mother? He'd have done that as soon as he knew you were alive." *As I should have done.*

Mullein nodded, satisfied. "He not like others. He better." Then she couldn't help but shiver. "In mines, slaves say, 'They come save us, someday. Our town send army. Our Horde raid mines. Husband come, father fight.' No one come. Then slaves die, lone in dark. Except Cyan Cross—Shaman-Mother keep us live." She looked up again, and she smiled tremulously. "Sorrel come for mother. No one like him in world."

"No one at all," Clovermead agreed.

Later that night, Bergander strummed a jolly tune on his lute, and sang, cheerfully off-key, of the Yellowjacket and the milkmaid, the Yellowjacket and the duchess, the Yellowjacket and the seamstress, and some other songs about Yellowjackets so shockingly bawdy that Clovermead blushed brick red and refused to help Mullein understand the lyrics. The next two days a hot wind came out of the south, and the Yellowjackets shucked their thick jackets in the summery warmth. The sun shone bright and friendly, and flocks of birds flew northward overhead. Spring flowers bloomed everywhere, and prairie dogs shot out of their holes to stare at the Yellowjackets pounding by. Now Clovermead felt like she could ride on the Steppes forever, and she knew how Sorrel could love this land so much.

That evening they saw a black streak on the plain. When they came closer, Clovermead saw that something had left a trail of charred black paw-prints along the Steppe as it loped southward.

"*Velika-gora,*" said Mullein. "Monster is here."

"It ran very fast," said Clovermead. "I don't think we'll catch up with it." She looked ahead. The blackened grass went on to the horizon.

The next afternoon they saw Bryony Hill on their right, far off to the southwest. It was a perfect cone that rose two thousand feet above the plain and could be seen dozens of miles away. A thread of a road ran up its smooth grass slopes, small dots traveled along the thread, and at the top was a large black square.

"They see us?" asked Mullein. She cowered from the distant fort.

"I shouldn't think so," said Clovermead—and they heard a distant howl floating from Bryony Hill. "But let's get behind the ridge here." They cantered farther east, and out of sight of the bear-priests' fort.

They continued to hear howls all day long. Mullein's face grew pale and drawn. *I must look just as scared,* thought Clovermead. *I hate that screaming.*

That night the air was hot and thick. It weighed heavily on Clovermead and made her skin tingle. Dark clouds rolled over the Steppes, and lightning flashed to the west, where Bryony Hill lay hidden behind the sheltering ridge. The bolts were suffused with silver and scarlet, mercury and blood; the night seemed to be dripping blood, and the lightning flashed again, brighter

151

than ever. A scream echoed through the Steppes, much louder and much nearer. There was terrible, racking pain in it and terrible hunger, the whimper of a serving dog and the growl of a wolf. It was the echo of nightmare.

"Monster," Mullein moaned. "Don't let eat me."

"Should we ride now, Demoiselle?" asked Sergeant Algere. His face was pasty white.

Thick raindrops began to fall. "No," said Clovermead. "We'd just slip and fall in this. I don't think I'd do much better if I turned into a bear again to lead you. We might as well get some rest—with our swords out. Will you take the first watch?" Algere nodded. "I'll take the second."

She slept for a while, then stood watch in a pelting rain that threatened to drench their campfire at every moment. There were more screams in the night, but they didn't come much closer. The monster seemed to be slowed down in the mud. The soldiers huddled as close as they could to the fire's warmth. Near dawn, Clovermead woke old Golion to have him take the third watch, then went to lie by Mullein. She took the little girl in her arms, so they could warm each other. Mullein clung to Clovermead, but tossed and turned with bad dreams. After a while Clovermead slept—

Three bear-priests were chasing Sorrel. He rode as fast as he could, but the bear-priests spurred their Phoenixians harder, and they came closer to Sorrel and Brown Barley. "How can I rescue myself?" he asked wearily.

"I'll help you," Clovermead cried out, but Sorrel couldn't hear her. She bounded back to the bear-priests and clawed at them — but she was a ghost, and her paws went through their flesh without them noticing. The Phoenixians galloped on.

"Help him," Clovermead heard someone say, but it wasn't her. Mullein stood by her in the dream, looking on at the bear-priests and Sorrel. "Save my brother."

152

"I am so tired," a different voice whispered in the darkness. "I hurt so much."

"I've helped you," Mullein said to the voice. "Help my brother."

"Help him," Clovermead repeated. She took Mullein's hand in hers and gripped it tightly. "Don't let Sorrel die."

"You don't know what you ask." The voice was familiar.

"Please," said Clovermead, and Mullein echoed her. "Save him," they said together.

"Lady, keep the pain from me," said the voice. Then silver lightning fell from the sky and struck the foremost bear-priest. He screamed and fell, and somewhere the unseen voice was screaming too. The other bear-priests reined up their horses, and jumped down to attend to their fallen comrade. He still breathed, but he was unconscious and his head and chest were terribly burned. Ahead, Sorrel disappeared from view.

"He won't live long," one bear-priest grunted to the other. "Let's bring him back to the temple. Tear out his heart on the altar while it's still beating. The master can always use warm blood."

The second bear-priest nodded, and they tossed their burned comrade roughly over the back of his Phoenixian. "Pity the Tansyard escaped," the second bear-priest said—

A scream woke Clovermead. It had stopped raining in the gray light of dawn, and the monster was much closer. It was still miles away, but it was terribly loud.

"Now we ride," said Clovermead to the Yellowjackets around her, and they scrambled to their horses. She paused for a moment, though, to stare curiously at Mullein. "You were in a dream of mine again."

Mullein nodded. "You in my dream. We save Sorrel." She smiled. "True dream, vision. He alive."

"That really happened?" asked Clovermead. Mullein nodded. "I know that woman's voice." Clovermead snapped her fingers. "That last night at the White Star encampment! I heard her voice just before I started wandering into other people's dreams." *Where are you?* the voice had said. *I can't find you, little one.* Clovermead's eyes went wide. "She was looking for you. Who is she?"

"Shaman-Mother," said Mullein. "She find me now, at last." She touched her chest. "She in here again, with me."

"What do you mean?" Clovermead asked, but then there was another scream, much closer. "Never mind. I'll ask again later, if there is a later. Now let's go."

They galloped due south in the early morning light. Their horses' hooves swished through the dew on the grass, and the sun rising on the eastern horizon stabbed Clovermead's eyes whenever she looked back to see what was chasing them. The screams came every few minutes, closer and closer. The horses whimpered with fear and bolted as fast as they could, now that there was light enough to see by. The thing came nearer still. It was running far faster than a galloping horse. Clovermead felt for her father's sword at her side and gulped. *I hope this thing can be fought, Lady,* she prayed.

They leaped over a tiny brook, past a row of poplars by the streambank, and then up a hill. The soil here was thick clay, and only supported a pale grass, less than half a foot tall. They reached the summit, and there was bare flatland ahead of them for another mile. Another scream tore through the poplar trees just behind them.

"Fight here," said Clovermead. "At least we'll have the advantage of height on it." She whirled around and drew her sword, and the Yellowjackets did likewise. Then the thing emerged from the trees and into the bare grass.

It glowed with a silver sheen, it loped on four legs, and it had long claws on each paw. It was as long as a bear, with fur like a bear, but it was far thinner than a bear, with a body of human thickness. Its face was almost human — flat and hairless, but with fanged jaws that protruded like a wolf's. It was a human being, Clovermead realized with a shock, but stretched all out of shape. Its bones had been pulled like taffy, stretched until it was ten feet long and more, and the misshapen thing howled its pain and its bloodlust. It ran at them with even greater speed. Where its paws touched the ground, the grass withered, blackened, and died.

Bergander spurred his horse, charged the creature, and swung his broadsword at it. The creature wrapped its great paws around the sword, let its edge dig into its flesh, and jerked the sword from the trooper's hands. The blade soared into the air, its surface corroded with acid, and then the creature swung backhanded at the Yellowjacket and smashed him off his horse. Bergander rolled twenty feet, and moaned on the grass as the creature moved on.

Clovermead charged the monster while the Yellowjackets galloped to surround it. The beast growled, pawed the ground — then flung itself toward the Yellowjackets behind it. It leaped onto old Golion before he could move his sword, grabbed his head, and broke his neck with a howl of delight. It dropped the dead soldier to the ground, and leaped for Algere, who shied out of its way. The beast's claws sliced through the Sergeant's chain mail, and opened up his arm from his shoulder to his elbow. Mullein whimpered, soldier and beast both shrieked, and then Clovermead reached the monster as Algere slumped to the ground.

Clovermead swung Firefly—and it blazed with light. The creature ducked beneath the arc of light, and then it was dancing to avoid Clovermead's blade, and its claws swung out all the time, so that Auroche jumped away from it and Clovermead's aim was wild as often as not. Clovermead pressed the monster close, the four unwounded Yellowjackets jabbed at it tentatively, and the beast, the *velika-gora,* kept them all at a distance. It was faster than any of them, stronger than any of them, and it *screamed,* never losing its breath, and each scream was a touch of nightmare that chilled and slowed down the Chandleforters.

The beast jumped suddenly toward a Yellowjacket behind him, cabbage-nosed Lewth. Lewth screamed and dropped his sword. The beast laughed—and in an instant leaped toward Quinch the lancer. With one motion it broke Quinch's wrist, with another it punched his jaw and sent him reeling, unconscious, to the grass. The beast turned in a flash and leaped toward Clovermead and Mullein. Clovermead screamed with terror and slashed at the beast with Firefly, whose light blazed brighter than ever as she sliced off the creature's paw.

The beast howled with shock and pain. Silvery blood bubbled out of its stump, and with a scream of pure hatred it swung its other paw with all its force at Clovermead. Auroche fell to one side as Clovermead tumbled to the ground with Mullein in her arms, and Firefly fell to the grass beside her. The beast prepared to leap—and the tip of a sword emerged from its chest. The beast looked down, whimpered, and then slid dead to the ground. Behind it stood Brown Barley, with Sorrel on her back, his sword drenched in silver from hilt to tip. The surface of his sword was melting from the beast's acid blood.

"You seem to need saving a lot, Demoiselle," Sorrel said quietly. Then he shook his head. "Ah, Clovermead, what would you do without me?"

"I never want to know," said Clovermead. On wobbly legs she got to her feet, then helped up Mullein. "I kept Mullein safe for you."

Sorrel smiled at Mullein, and Clovermead thanked Our Lady that she could see his smile again. *Even if it isn't for me. I was so afraid I would never see his smile again.* Sorrel swung down from Brown Barley, dropped his disintegrating sword to the ground, and ran to catch Mullein in his arms. They spoke to each other in Tansyard, hugged each other, and then Sorrel put her down. He looked at Clovermead again and she wanted to run to his arms, to hug him as tightly as he had hugged Mullein—but there was still a distance in his eyes, a coldness and a wariness, and she made herself stand still.

"I am glad to see you are safe," said Sorrel at last.

"I'm glad to *be* safe," said Clovermead. Then she couldn't help but look at the Yellowjackets. Bergander was still stunned, Quinch and Sergeant Algere were wounded, and Golion was dead. Clovermead made herself go to Golion's side and look down at his fresh-scarred face, at his neck so horribly awry. At his face twisted in pain and fear.

Not even Chandlefort business, she told herself, and her eyes were hot with tears. *My fault. And he's just the first.* She made the crescent sign over his body. *Lady, take his soul. Lady, don't let me get used to having people die for me.* Then she couldn't bear to look at the old trooper anymore, and she turned away from his body.

While Quinch's wrist and Sergeant Algere's arm were bandaged, Sorrel took Golion's sword to replace his melted blade. Clovermead looked with sudden dread at Firefly—and was relieved to see that the creature's blood had dripped off and left the metal unharmed. She wiped the blood on the grass, then sheathed her sword.

Sorrel was staring at the dead creature, and Clovermead went to join him. It still shone a ghastly black and silver. Fur like bristles covered leathery skin, which stretched over elongated, melted bones. It looked less of a monster in death: The scream and the snarl had faded, the pain was gone, and it was almost human. Still, its body burned the grass around it. The black poison had already spread three feet beyond the corpse.

"I saw him on Bryony Hill not two days ago," whispered Sorrel. "He was a bear-priest. Look, he had blue eyes and a scar on his left cheek. There they are." He pointed and Clovermead saw them. "He was made into a monster on Bryony Hill."

"Velika-gora," said Mullein solemnly. "Like others, in mines." She clung to Clovermead and looked up at Sorrel. "You rescued mother?"

Sorrel's face twisted in despair. "I tried. I cannot do it by myself. There were dozens of bear-priests guarding her, and they drove me away when I came too close."

"We came to help you," said Clovermead. She gestured awkwardly at the Yellowjackets, at Mullein, at herself. "We were riding to Barleymill to help you rescue your mother."

"You have given up your mission?" Sorrel stared at her wonderingly.

"No," Clovermead admitted. "I've finished it already." Quickly she told him what had happened at the White Star camp.

"Ah. You have done what policy demands, and now

you come to help me." For a moment Sorrel could not hide his disgust. With difficulty he wiped it from his face. "It does not matter. I am glad you have come." He looked back toward Bryony Hill. "We should ride quickly, before more such monsters come." Then Sorrel glanced down at his scuffed yellow jacket and trousers. "I know you gave me permission to depart, but let us not pretend that matters. Lady Cindertallow will say that I am a deserter from the Yellowjackets. I have not been able to change clothes yet, Clovermead, but I cannot be in the service of the Cindertallows anymore. I am simply a Tansyard riding with you."

"I'm sorry," said Clovermead. "I wish—"

"I am not sorry," said Sorrel brusquely. He strode off to mount Brown Barley.

Chapter Twelve

RIDING SOUTH

CLOVERMEAD HELPED THE YELLOWJACKETS BURY Golion, and then the party galloped south in a gray day where drizzle spattered down on them. No more monsters screamed. Toward evening they rode over the ridge and saw that Bryony Hill had almost disappeared behind them to the northwest. After dusk they made camp. Mullein and Sorrel separated from the others and talked for some hours. Then Mullein dragged Sorrel back to the fire where Clovermead and the Yellowjackets were huddled against the cold. She sat down and Sorrel sat down by her side.

"I hear you made quite a speech to the White Star Horde," said Sorrel in a low voice, so only Clovermead and Mullein could hear him. "Mullein says the stars came down from heaven to listen, and that every blade of grass on the Steppes will fight on our side against Ursus." Mullein blushed, and Sorrel smiled wryly at her. "I think my sister is fond of you."

"She like Shaman-Mother," said Mullein. "Never go from me."

Clovermead looked at Mullein curiously. "I never did get a chance to ask you about that. You said she was still

160

with you. And then—" She turned to Sorrel. "Did light-ning strike a bear-priest who was chasing after you?" Sorrel nodded. "I saw it in a dream. Mullein was there, and I heard a woman's voice, and Mullein and I asked her to help you. Then the lightning struck. Mullein, was that the Shaman-Mother?"

"Yes," said Mullein uncomfortably. "I ask her help Sorrel, she does." She tapped at her head and her heart. "Shaman-Mother in me. Never go." She held up her hands, and they were still lined with silver. "I help her. I carry *hwanka-velika*, take some her pain. Now she help me."

Clovermead took Mullein's hands in hers and exam-ined them in the firelight. The silver had faded for a while, but now it was as bright as ever. When she looked closely, it looked as if more threads of quicksilver were oozing into Mullein's flesh, coming from nowhere.

"How is this happening?" Sorrel asked angrily. "Why is she doing this to you? You are just a little girl."

"Not so bad," said Mullein. "I stand it. Shaman-Mother take lots pain, from me, from all, always. And I must. For now."

"How long?" asked Clovermead. She gingerly touched the line of silver in Mullein's palms once more. Now that she looked closely, she could see that Mullein was still thin, despite all the food she had been eating. A cobweb of quicksilver lined her body and ate into her. "Haven't you helped her enough?"

"Not yet," said Mullein. She cocked her head, listen-ing to something invisible. She nodded. "Shaman-Mother say, when you come Barleymill, I stop having pain. She say, 'Come quick.'" Mullein frowned. "I say, 'We come now.' She not hear me. She very weak. She not

161

help Cyan Cross much more. I think, we hurry." She looked up anxiously at Sorrel and Clovermead. "You save Shaman-Mother, too? She hurt so much, from helping us. Don't leave her in mines."

Sorrel swallowed hard. "We will save her also, Mullein. You do not need to worry."

"Good," said Mullein, and she smiled radiantly. "I sleep now," she added, and then she promptly leaned against Clovermead and did so.

Sorrel looked down at his sister, and he looked angry again. "I do not care how great the need was. The Shaman-Mother should not be using her like this."

"The Shaman-Mother saved your life," said Clovermead. "Doesn't that make a difference?"

"No," said Sorrel. Now he looked at Clovermead with smoldering anger. "You are always ready to have little ones pay prices for others. First my mother, now my sister. No, do not tell me how sorry and unhappy you are! In the end, you go ahead and let them suffer. For the, what is it called? The greater good." He grimaced. "From where did you get that habit?"

"My mother, I suppose," said Clovermead quietly. "I've been with her three years now, and I suppose some of her has rubbed off on me. I'm sorry you don't like me being that way, but I don't think I'm going to change. Somebody has to make the decision to say, 'You, you're going to fight against Lord Ursus, and you'll probably die in the battle.' 'You, I can't help you because there's a whole city full of people I have to save right now, and I don't have time to do both.' 'You, little girl, you have to do your part of the fighting too, even though you're just eight, because if you don't, a thousand other little girls are going to end up in the mines.'" *You, Golion, you're going to die at the hands of a monster, far away from home.* "I wouldn't have volunteered to make choices like that, but it turns out I'm Demoiselle and I have to. When I'm Lady Cindertallow, I'll have to make even more choices like that. I won't shuck that burden. I suppose it will get to be a habit, and I suppose it will be easy for me to tell other people to make sacrifices, and I'd hoped you'd be with me still, to tell me when I was doing something wrong." She wiped tears from her eyes. "Anyway, I wasn't thinking of any of that just now. I was glad you were alive, and I didn't care about anything else."

Sorrel opened his mouth, then shut it. He was silent for a long minute, then cleared his throat. "Thank you," he said. "I am glad to be alive too." For a moment Clovermead thought he might smile at her, give her his hand, say they were friends again—but he just looked away from her. He wasn't so hostile toward her, but he wasn't close to being friendly. Just civil. The same way he was with Saraband.

"Where have you been?" asked Clovermead hastily. She didn't want him to see how white her face was in the firelight, didn't want him to notice how much his cool indifference hurt her. "What did you do after you left?"

"It is a brief enough story," said Sorrel. "First I followed the bear-priests and my mother. They went through the Harrow Moors for a day, then out into the Steppes. Soon their tracks split—Snuff on that bear off into the Steppes, and the others south along the edge of the Moors. I did not know which of them had my mother, but I thought it more likely she was with the group heading south, toward Barleymill. So I went that way.

"I rode fast and I came within sight of them in three days. By then other bear-priests had joined them: I saw ten

163

bear-priests and a figure trussed up on a horse that I knew was my mother. I saw also that they watched the Steppes around them very carefully, that they kept good sentry-guard at night, and that I would not be able to sneak up to them and free my mother as I had hoped. Instead I had to follow them at a distance of some miles, not letting them out of my sight, but staying far enough away that they could not see me. So we went for several days.

"We came at last to Bryony Hill, which I had last seen as I fled from the camp of my slaughtered Horde. The bear-priests' fort and temple has grown huge since then: They squat upon the summit, there is a constant traffic of carts into the fort, and great bodies of bear-priests ride and march on the road they have slashed into the Steppe. The bear-priests led my mother into the fort and I knew I had waited too long. I knew I would have to try to rescue her that night—they would take her the next day to Barleymill in the middle of a regiment of bear-priests, and there would be no way to extricate her then.

"I tethered Brown Barley in a copse at the base of the hill and crept up in the darkness toward the fort. It was slow going: The road curls up Bryony Hill, and I had to curl too, to avoid the torches and the tramp of bear-priests. There were a great number of bear-priests marching up the road that night. I stopped once in the shadow of a boulder, by the side of the road, and watched the procession pass by me. At their lead was that bear-priest with the scar, the one that became a monster whom I killed this morning. He strode forward without a scimitar and the other bear-priests sang a harsh song of praise for him. He wore a dozen bear-teeth on his body, and he smiled in exultation. Behind him the bear-priests carried barrels of glowing liquid—*hwanka-velika*, quicksilver.

"They passed me by, marching toward the temple, and then I was past the half-built walls of the fortress and up to the wooden ramparts of their black fort. There was only one gate to the fort, and it was lashed tight in the darkness. I crept to the walls, staying out of sight of the sentries, and began to feel to see if there was some way to climb up them. The stones were rough, and I thought I could do it. I began to ascend.

"I came to the top and I saw a great barracks filling the fort. Torches lit the night, and I saw bars on the barracks windows. I thought perhaps my mother was imprisoned there, and I began to creep along the wall toward her. As I crept, I heard a wailing chant from the temple. It grew louder and louder, faster and faster—and then a crack of lightning broke from the heavens, scarlet and silver, and I heard a terrible scream from the temple's heart. The singing continued, loud and exulting, it shivered through me, and I stumbled as I crawled. My elbow cracked against the parapet, and a stone tumbled to the ground inside the fort.

"A bear-priest called out inside, and I knew I had been detected. I swore at myself for my clumsiness, and I took a last look into the temple. There I saw—ah, a terrible thing. The last part of the bear-priest to change was his head, and that was still human. The fur was thickening on his body, his claws were lengthening—not the way you change shape, Clovermead, but as if his body were a husk being consumed by fire. The line of fur crept up his neck and over his head—he screamed, and first it was a human scream, but then it was not. Part of him died while I watched, but something else, something monstrous, went on living. And that newborn *thing* looked at me in the darkness. It screamed again, with terrible joy.

165

"I ran from it, Clovermead. I scrambled down the outside wall, scraping my skin in my haste, and let myself fall the last ten feet. Inside I cried my regret to my mother, outside I ran as quickly as I could toward Brown Barley. When I was halfway down the slope of the hill, three bear-priests came out of the gates. At first they cast about, at random, but soon I was on Brown Barley and galloping away. When they heard the hoofbeats, they came after me. Then the lightning bolt came out of the sky, as you said, and I rode unpursued into the darkness. As I fled, I heard the screaming monster come in my direction. I hid in a stream in the underbrush, and thanked Our Lady very much when the beast turned out to be a very bad tracker and raced past my hiding place without detecting me. I slept the remainder of the night in the underbrush, for I was very tired.

"When I woke, I could hear it screaming still, and it came to me that it must be chasing someone else. I wondered if perhaps my mother had escaped again somehow, and I went chasing after its screams, most cautiously. I was surprised, very surprised, when I came over the ridge and saw it fighting the Yellowjackets, fighting you." He paused for a moment. "I confess, Clovermead, I was not sure at first whether I wanted to fight at your side. The monster was fearsome, and I have been very angry with you since we parted in the Moors. I hesitated. My anger whispered tempting words to me, telling me that I needed to ride away, to preserve myself from danger until I could save my mother."

"And then you remembered you had left your little sister with me," said Clovermead. "You rode forward to rescue her."

"No," said Sorrel. "I hesitated only for a moment. I

have not felt fond of you this last fortnight, but I could not stand aside with that monster coming after you. I am not—" He hesitated.

"Not like me?" asked Clovermead. For a moment resentment and anger burned in her, and she stifled them only with some effort. "Don't say it. I'll get mad at you, whether it's my fault or not, and I'll say things to hurt you back. Let it drop awhile. We need to work together long enough to get your mother out of Barleymill." Slowly, Sorrel nodded in agreement. "Good. And, Sorrel—I'm awfully glad you got away from Bryony Hill alive."

"We are agreed there," said Sorrel, with a ghost of a smile.

Clovermead laughed a little bit. Then she shivered. "You think Ursus *made* that bear-priest into a monster? How?"

"Bryony Hill is sacred. It has always been full of Our Lady's power, and we Tansyards came to it as a place of healing. Ursus must be perverting it somehow. It is a terrible recipe—combine quicksilver from Barleymill, that black altar on Bryony Hill, and the Bear's power, and those twisted beings are formed." He shuddered. "I think I know now why he slaughtered Cyan Cross. He wanted Bryony Hill to make monsters, and he could not have taken it while we were alive to defend the holy ground from him."

"How many of those things do you think there are?" asked Clovermead. She could not get those glowing silver bones out of her mind. "There must have been one in the Harrow Moors, that killed those poor people, and there were two chasing us as we rode to the White Star encampment. Snuff told me they were something new, but there could be hundreds, for all we know."

"The bear-priests used a great deal of quicksilver in their ceremony," said Sorrel. "It cannot be easy to bring it all the way from Barleymill. Besides, I saw very few tracks of blackened grass around Bryony Hill, and that seems to be an infallible sign of these monsters. I do not think Ursus has yet made many silver-bears."

"When next I see Mother, I'll tell her we really have to take Bryony Hill this summer. Once it's a proper fortress, there'll be no stopping Ursus from making silver-bears forever."

"If we could free the slaves from Barleymill," said Sorrel slowly, "that would also serve our purpose. No slaves, no quicksilver. No quicksilver, no monsters." He looked up at Clovermead and smiled sadly. "I have grown ambitious. I no longer wish to free just my mother, but to free whatever remains of Cyan Cross Horde, to free every slave in that ghastly pit. Would that not be lovely?"

"It would be wonderful," said Clovermead. "But how could we do it? There's just a handful of us."

"I do not know. But I can dream. And I will pray to Our Lady for ideas." Sorrel lay down by Mullein's side. "Enough talking for now. Good night, Clovermead."

"Good night, Sorrel," she said, and then she wrapped herself in a blanket and lay down. She let herself look at Sorrel for a moment—and saw his hurt and angry eyes still glittering at her in the firelight. He saw her looking at him, and abruptly turned his back on her. They were silent a long time. Clovermead's stomach hurt. After a while, Sorrel began to snore, but Clovermead couldn't get to sleep until late in the night.

They rode south the next weeks over ever more of the Steppes' grasses, poplars, and bluffs. They rode steadily, but not too quickly: Although the land was flat, it was roadless, and sufficiently uneven that the Chandleforters cantered more often than they galloped. Quinch's wrist and Sergeant Algere's arm healed slowly; in the meantime, both Yellowjackets practiced wielding their swords left-handed. Hordes passed them by in the distance, distant ants in the Steppes' immensity: Their warriors rode close enough to see that they were well-enough armed to defend themselves, then rode off again. The days grew warmer as they headed south, and spring turned into summer. The grass grew long and lush, watered by drenching thunderstorms that rolled through the Steppes every few days.

The Yellowjackets and Sorrel quickly returned to their old friendliness: He was half a deserter, but none of the soldiers could resent him for wanting to rescue his mother from the bear-priests. Clovermead and Sorrel remained civil, but nothing more. Sorrel much preferred to talk with Mullein than with Clovermead, trying to learn in a few short weeks everything of her lifetime apart, trying to share with her what he had done and seen since the destruction of the Cyan Cross Horde. Mullein was no less friendly to Clovermead, but it was only natural that she spent more time with her brother. They mostly talked with each other in Tansyard, and now Mullein's command of common tongue scarcely improved. Clovermead talked with the Yellowjackets during meals, and in the evenings she slipped into bear-shape and went running into the Steppes while Bergander entertained his comrades with his songs. She slipped back into pleasant memory while she ran—chopping firewood with Waxmelt at Ladyrest Inn while red maple leaves drifted down upon them, racing horseback with Lady Cindertallow in the ruddy sands of the Salt Heath, dancing a gavotte with Saraband in her cousin's room. Walking companionably with Sorrel through the streets of Chandlefort.

I'd rather be by myself, thought Clovermead. *At least out here I don't have to see Sorrel and not be able to talk with him, joke with him, laugh with him. It hurts less.*

The silver lines in Mullein grew thicker as they came closer to Barleymill, and she grew thinner, no matter how much she ate. She would not complain during the day, but during the night she moaned in pain and nightmare. She threw herself against Sorrel or Clovermead, and one or the other would cradle her feverish body for long hours during the night.

"I am not sure you should continue with us," said Sorrel one morning, frowning unhappily at Mullein. "I do not think you can stand much more of this."

"Worse for Shaman-Mother," Mullein gasped. It was a hot day, but she was wrapped in Clovermead's wool sweater. It was enormous on her small frame, yet she shivered. "I stand this. But, please, ride quick, Brother."

Far to the west, heading south along the horizon, the Farry Heights rose from the Heath. They were tall enough compared to the flat land of the Steppes, a few thousand feet high, but nowhere near as tall as the great peaks of the Reliquaries. Thick forests covered their slopes all the way to the top. Clouds lingered on the summits of the Heights. In the morning the sun lit their slopes the color of pink rubies; in the evening it silhouetted them as scarlet shadows.

"They look gentle enough," said Clovermead to Sorrel. "Why don't the Tansyards go raiding into Linstock over them instead of through the Harrow Moors?"

"They are much steeper when you get close to them. There are only a few decent passes through them—and the land on the other side of the Heights is almost a desert. There is nothing much to raid there, and then it is a long ride north to any place with horses worth stealing. It is easier to go through the Moors."

"Where's Barleymill?"

"There." Sorrel pointed far to the southwest. "It is in the crook of the Farry Heights, where the range turns east. We will see the southern range in a few days." He kicked his horse and they rode on.

The Farry Heights went on and on, always on their right hand. The hills grew nearer, grew taller, though never as high as the Reliquaries. After a while Clovermead saw the thin gray line of the southern Farry Heights on the horizon. They were very far away, and it took days for them to grow even a little.

Now they passed wagon ruts through the Steppes, and the black marks of silver-bears' paws running through the grass. Once they saw a broad, ebony swath through the grasslands, where a whole pack of them had run by. They heard screaming, here and there, scattered over the plains. The party rode along streambeds where they could, to hide their scent, and they turned from the straight route to Barleymill to ride along bluffs and through gulches. Mullein trembled every time she heard a scream.

One morning Clovermead woke to find that Lewth and Sergeant Algere had disappeared. They came back an hour after dawn, both sporting new bruises. "He tried to run away," Algere explained to Clovermead as they rode south that morning. "The screaming got to him. He won't try it again."

171

"He can go if he wants," said Clovermead. She looked at Lewth and his now-bloody cabbage-nose, and in her mind's eye she could see earth flying over his cold body. *Like Golion.* She shuddered. "I won't keep him here."

"I will," said Algere shortly. "That noodle-head would get caught by a bear-priest patrol inside of a day if he left us. They'd make him talk, and then they'd know who we are and where we are. And where we're going." He scowled at Clovermead. "We made a choice, Demoiselle. It's too dangerous to back out now. Unless we all do."

There was an invitation in those words. *I can't turn aside,* thought Clovermead. *I can't leave Sorrel to go to Barleymill by himself.* She rode on in silence, and that was answer enough. Algere sighed, and fell back from her to talk awhile with Bergander.

"What's your mother like?" Clovermead asked Sorrel one cloudy night, as they sat by the fire. "You never did say that much about her when we were in Chandlefort. I'd like to know."

Sorrel stared at her a second, then looked back at the fire. "I would prefer not to speak of her with you," he said.

"All right," said Clovermead. "I guess it isn't my business." She brought her knees up to her face, clasped her hands around her folded legs, and huddled behind them.

"I like know too," said Mullein. She had been asleep, but now she sat up. Her eyes glittered in the firelight as her blanket fell from her shoulders to pool in her lap. "All I know, Mother in mines. She take care me, feed me, protect me from bear-priests, but we not talk much. No time, we both too tired from digging. She tell me little bit, you and Father, Clary and Emlets, before we slaves. Not tell me of her." She glanced at Clovermead. "Tell us, Brother. Please."

Sorrel gazed at Mullein, then at Clovermead. Laughter bubbled out of him for a second. "Since you ask so prettily, little sister, how can I refuse?" He paused a moment to take a drink of water from the flask at his belt. "Mother was the finest hand with a needle in the Horde. She could embroider a wolf or a buffalo onto my clothes in no time at all, and she could patch a rip so expertly that you would never know there had ever been a tear. The Horde Chief himself came every year to our tent to ask her most politely to make him a new jacket, and in return he would give her a pure white foal of the finest pedigree. Father was a fine warrior, and an esteemed healer of horses, but Mother was the most respected woman of her age in the Horde.

"She sang when she baked or cooked, or when she washed our clothes in the stream. She never remembered the words to songs, but she had the melodies by heart. She warbled, and Emlets or I would sing the words for her. One time Father came back from a long raid against the Tawn Cross Horde with a half-grown beard, and when Mother saw it, she just started laughing and laughing, for it was a scraggly little thing, and then we were all laughing till we cried, and Father went off in a grump to scrape it from his chin. When we were sick, she would bake us a truly strange honey bread strewn with lumps of salt that she swore was medicinal. We all hated the taste, but it did seem to make us better. When I have fallen ill in Chandlefort, I have missed that bread's taste terribly.

"She was a little bossy, no gentle flower shy of offering her opinion, and once I had my warrior's tattoos I began to itch for a tent of my own, where I could manage my own affairs, no matter how badly. We quarreled from time to time, though never too severely. And when the

173

bear-priests came for the Horde, she kept her head when I was in a daze, while Dapple and Emlets and Clary were slaughtered, and she pulled and pushed me to freedom. I was not worthy of her sacrifice." He swallowed hard, and looked at Mullein. "May I stop?"

"For now," said Mullein. "Thank you, Brother." She smiled at Sorrel, winked at Clovermead, and lay down again. She pulled her blanket up, and in a minute she was asleep.

"You have made Mullein a pander for your curiosity," Sorrel said quietly. Bitterness laced his voice. "Are you satisfied?"

"Do you think I wanted to hurt you?" asked Clovermead. Her voice was breaking. "Do you think I didn't know how much you love Roan? I wanted to come with you—"

"And yet you didn't." Sorrel looked at her for a moment, then twisted away, as if his eyes burned. "I have thought about your arguments, Clovermead. I have tried to translate them into terms an ignorant Tansyard such as I can understand. A Horde Chief must sacrifice a straggling child, to keep the Horde safe from pursuing enemies, and I should understand that the Horde Chief may grieve even as he orders the Horde to abandon the weeping infant. I should be an adult who accepts these dark necessities, and not a child who wails his complaints. I know that here"—he tapped the side of his head—"but not here." He put his hand to his heart. "I am sure it is a failing of mine, that my mother is bigger to me than all the world, and that I would rather sacrifice it than her. I am cruel and stupid, seen with the Horde Chief's eyes, but I am so. I cannot change."

"You just seem stupid," said Clovermead, and she

wasn't sorry any longer, just angry. "You know, I said you could ride off after Roan yourself. I needed you with me, too—Chandlefort needed you—but I didn't force you to come. And I'd understand if you were just disappointed and hurt that I wouldn't come with you. But you've been angry at me, and blaming me, because I wouldn't drop everything and come after you. And that isn't fair of you. I have a responsibility as Demoiselle. And if I fail, everyone dies—including Mother and Father, and Saraband, and everyone I love, just as much as you love Roan. I know you abandoned your duty to help me save Father, and I'll always be grateful to you for that, but that doesn't give you the right to make me drop everything and come trotting whenever you call, or to be all self-satisfied about how much you despise me when I say no to you. I'm still sorry I couldn't come help you, but when you say 'I cannot change,' I know that just means you're determined to be petty and small-minded." She lifted up her chin, and stared at him in angry defiance.

Answering anger flickered in Sorrel's eyes. "How dare you," he began—and then his anger abruptly died down. He gazed at Clovermead for a long minute, and his face had become a mask. "I must think about what you have said, Clovermead," he said at last.

They lapsed into silence. Only a fire separated them, but it could have been a thousand miles. After a while Clovermead pulled her blanket over her and lay down on the grass. Quietly, without fuss, she cried herself to sleep.

When they were within a week of Barleymill, Clovermead looked toward the Heights, and now she could see their dense underbrush and sheer cliffs. *I see why the Tansyards don't go over them much,* she thought. *I'd hate to have to clamber over those rocks!* Then she lifted her nose, turned it into a snout, and sniffed at the Heights. *I smell bears up there!* she thought dreamily. *It's a good place for them. I think they must be free of Lord Ursus—they don't have his stench.* But she didn't call to them in her mind, in case she was wrong.

More days passed, and now hills on the southern Heights looked as high as the ones on the western Heights. Clovermead wrinkled her nose. *It smells acrid,* she thought. And then, as she looked around, she thought, *No wonder. Half the grass is charred black, and there's silver everywhere. I don't think I've seen a bird for miles.* A gust of wind blew a cloud of silver dust into her face, and she coughed, trying to hack the bitter grit out of her lungs.

"We are nearly there," Sorrel said that evening. He pointed ahead. "Those mark the borders of Barleymill."

Clovermead squinted. In the distance she saw city lights shining beyond a ridge, silhouetting the Heights in a silvery glow. Nearer she saw a single, straight post upon the Steppes. "What is that? Some sort of tree?"

"Some sort," said Sorrel grimly. "Take a look." They rode up to the post—and Clovermead gasped. It was a great cross, ten feet high, pounded into the plain. On the cross hung a crucified skeleton. Its clothing fell in strips from its bones.

"Who?"—Clovermead wanted to retch. Now she could hear the Yellowjackets murmuring behind her as they saw the hanging bones, with fear, disgust, and anger.

"Some slave. Or a wandering Tansyard who came too close without permission. Perhaps a merchant who charged the bear-priests too high a price for his wares." Sorrel shrugged helplessly. "There are so many reasons and so many dead. Look, you can see them all around

Barleymill." Clovermead looked to her right and left, and she saw a palisade of crosses, one every mile, stretching west to the Heights and in an arc to the southeast across the Steppes. "When we cross that barrier, we will be in Barleymill territory. No one may enter without permission. We are warned of the consequences of disobedience."

"I hate them," Clovermead said. Tears started in her eyes. "Every time I think I've seen the worst and most cruel thing they could do, they do something worse. I want them all dead." She clawed at the air with an arm grown huge and furry. "What they do is unforgivable."

"We do cruel things also," said Sorrel. He looked at Mullein. She was panting, and her face was gray. "See what the Shaman-Mother does to my little sister. Chooses to do. It is not enough to say that bear-priests make her be cruel." He tore his eyes away. "Let us reconnoiter."

Sorrel and Clovermead got down from their horses, left them with the Yellowjackets, and began to walk toward the hillcrest. Mullein came with them, her chest heaving, but with such a look of determination on her face that Clovermead could not tell her to stop. The three of them got onto their stomachs just before they reached the crest. They peeped over the top of the ridge, and there was the city of Barleymill.

Chapter Thirteen

BARLEYMILL

BARLEYMILL STOOD IN THE CROOK OF THE FARRY Heights, right where the southward-stretching hills turned to run eastward along the south end of the Tansy Steppes. Surrounding the city were the gray tailings of the mercury mines, piles of boulders and ash that rose seventy feet above the ground. A network of stone paths led through the tailings, with stone walls to either side of the roads to hold back the rubble. A hundred yards around the city walls there was only bare ground—an open space for the archers on the walls to fire upon, should any enemy come to the town. Within the city walls, Clovermead could see low, squat warehouses and barracks that stretched back toward the hills. Several dozen tunnel-mouths ate into the hillsides. From each tunnel-mouth, carts of shining ore came out, pulled by tiny, laboring figures. There were guards all around them, guards watching from wooden towers, bear-priests with savage whips who used them mercilessly. Beyond the mines the hills rose sharply in cliffs a thousand feet high.

"It will not be easy to enter the city," said Sorrel. "It will be harder to get out."

178

"I will get you in," said Mullein, but it wasn't entirely Mullein. A weary old woman spoke through her. Silver glowed in her half-shut eyes. "Wait until moon-set."

"Shaman-Mother?" asked Sorrel. "Is that you?"

Mullein nodded, and now the shadow of an old Tansyard woman's face glimmered over hers. "She has borne me so long," Mullein whispered, the Shaman-Mother whispered. "Searching for help. I told Roan, save the child no matter what. She did, she threw her to safety in the Moors. But I lost her there, she was so far away. I am so weak." Mullein swallowed. "Come tonight. We can rescue Cyan Cross together." Mullein turned with her silver eyes to Clovermead. "The bear-girl and you and Mullein can come. The others must wait outside. We will save the Horde."

"All of Cyan Cross? How?" asked Clovermead, but the silver was fading from Mullein's eyes, the old lady's visage wavered like moonlight and was gone. "Shaman-Mother? Are you there?"

"No," said Mullein. "Just me." She shivered in the cooling evening air. "I know what do. She tell me. Wait for moon-set." She looked back at the Yellowjackets. "Tell them, be ready. Horde come out, not can fight. Need soldiers, guard while run."

"Oh, Lady," Clovermead swore. "Sorrel, I know you talked about freeing lots of slaves, but I didn't really think we were going to do more than look for your mother and try to grab her on the sly if we could. Where do we take however-many-they-are slaves? The bear-priests are going to notice if a lot of slaves go missing."

"I would have us retreat along Yarrow's Way," said Sorrel. He pointed toward the line of darkness running northward beneath the Farry Heights. "It is narrow, and a handful of men can hold off an army, for a while. That is what Yarrow did, as he fought against the warriors of the Gray Bar Horde."

"Didn't he die in the end?"

"But gloriously." Sorrel laughed hollowly. "We will be retreating toward Yarrow's Bowl, and perhaps we will meet some Yellowjackets along the way, come foraging or scouting, and they will rescue us in the nick of time and carry us back to Chandlefort for a long rest in bed with sherbets to cool us after our hard exertions. Or perhaps the bear-priests will catch up with us and slaughter us. There is no certainty along Yarrow's Way, but I can think of no safer route from Barleymill."

"I'd like to be in Chandlefort already with the sherbets," said Clovermead. She swallowed hard. "I don't care about the glory. Try not to die if you can help it."

Sorrel's face cracked, softened, and he could not help but look at Clovermead with a flicker of friendship. "I want you to emerge from this adventure alive too. Let us watch each other's backs, so we need not worry."

"Agreed," said Clovermead, and her heart was singing. *We might be friends again. It's still possible. Thank you for letting me know that, Lady.*

They went back to where the Yellowjackets were waiting, and Clovermead told them her new plan.

Sergeant Algere scowled. "There's just six of us to back up you and Sorrel, Demoiselle, and two of us are wounded. You do realize that we're going to have every bear-priest in Barleymill after us?"

"You say that like that was a problem, Sergeant," Bergander drawled. Some of the other Yellowjackets laughed. Lewth and Quinch did not. "We made our choice to come to Barleymill, Demoiselle. It was always

180

going to be an adventure, no matter how many Tansyards we tried to rescue."

"I don't like this change of plan," said Lewth. "I agreed to do something foolish. I didn't agree to do something insane." He shook his head unhappily. "It was easier to be brave when we were far from Barleymill. I wish I'd gone off with Habick and the corporal."

"But you didn't," said Clovermead angrily, "and here we are. I'm sorry the plan got changed, but it did, and now we need you all to get us out of here alive. To get Sorrel's people out of here alive." She pointed at the cross standing near them in the darkness. "They're slaves of the torturers who did that. It's worth dying to try to free them." She stumbled into silence for a moment, then started again. "I'm the one saying it's worth dying, and it's your lives on the line. I know that. I've gotten you all into a mess, and I know I've just made it worse, but we've got a chance to get all of Cyan Cross Horde out of this slaughterhouse. We can't just leave them here."

"I would," said Lewth. He looked at the crucified bones, shivered, and made the sign of the crescent. "I'd leave now." He shrugged apologetically at Sorrel. "They're not my people."

"No. They are not." Sorrel looked at all his former comrades. "I join my voice to Clovermead's. I ask you to risk death for strangers, though I cannot make it a reasonable request. In Our Lady's name, I beg your aid."

Algere looked up again at the dark cross, then along the horizon at all the other crosses that formed Barleymill's borders. "I am afraid, Lady," the Sergeant muttered. Then he sighed. "I'll stay," he said more loudly. He looked around, and all the Yellowjackets save Lewth slowly nodded. Lewth only shrugged, with despair in his eyes. "We'll all stay, Demoiselle," Algere continued. "We'll help you rescue your Tansyards."

"Thank you," Clovermead began—but Algere held up his hand. There was despair as deep as Lewth's in his eyes, and an edge of bitter resentment. He turned abruptly from Clovermead, and shambled away.

Clovermead grabbed what rest she could, until Mullein stirred from her shallow sleep. The moon was gone, and there was only starlight in the sky. "It is time to go," she said to Clovermead and Sorrel, and the Shaman-Mother was speaking in her again. She stood up on short legs, with an aged face. "Bring the soldiers as far as the walls." Clovermead spoke to the Yellowjackets, and they came after her, still yawning. The band got onto their horses and began to pick their way slowly toward Barleymill.

They came over the ridge, their horses' hooves *clip-clopping* softly on the ground. Clovermead looked for the town walls—but they were invisible. Mullein chanted low words, and from the little girl's fingers black dust swirled into the air and formed a cloud that surrounded them, muffled all sounds from outside, and dimmed all light save the stars above. They were veiled from the world.

Mullein shook, and silvery tears fell from her eyes. "Are you all right?" Clovermead asked her anxiously.

"I sick," Mullein whimpered. "Hurry, please. Get Shaman-Mother out."

They quickened their pace, but then patrolling bear-priests came near to them. They stopped in their darkness until the bear-priests had gone, then threaded their way through the tailings to the rough, black walls of Barleymill.

"Go left," said Mullein, said the Shaman-Mother. "The tunnel is this way." They rode for two hundred feet, and aged Mullein raised her hand. "Here," she sighed. She waved her hand, and what had looked like a solid piece of ground wavered and crumpled away to reveal a narrow tunnel.

"Will the cloud stay here to hide the soldiers?" Clovermead asked Mullein. The little girl nodded and trembled. Her whole body was glowing silver. "You should stay here, Mullein. You're not well."

"I have to come," the old woman in Mullein gasped. "I have to show you the way. Quickly!"

The three of them got down from the horses, and Clovermead took a last look at cheerful Bergander, angry Sergeant Algere, despairing Lewth. Then Sorrel scrambled headfirst into the tunnel, Mullein followed him, and Clovermead came last. The tunnel curved down, five feet and more, and then it went flat for thirty feet. Clovermead could feel dirt above and below her, to either side, and there was very little room to spare. Twice she had to stop while Sorrel squeezed through a particularly tight spot. When they were under the wall itself, she could feel the rough stones pressing against her back. Then the three of them began to curve up again. By now the earth seemed to be pressing against her, tight as a coffin. She was short of breath and very hot. *Lady, help me*, she prayed. *Dear Lady, preserve me from fear.* She repeated the words as a mantra to keep terror away from her as she scrambled the last few feet. There was dim light ahead of her, she could see Mullein's feet, and then the little girl disappeared from sight. Sorrel's hand reached down and the Tansyard pulled Clovermead out of the tunnel and up into Barleymill.

183

They stood in a wide alley between two massive, low buildings. Tiny windows covered by thick metal bars pockmarked the dull beige, rough-hewn stone walls. The streets were made from the same rough stone. A musty smell that made Clovermead's stomach crawl filled the alleyway. Farther on, Clovermead could see more low buildings and the mountainside that rose behind them. Slag and rubble filled a valley rising toward the south, behind the nearest mines. The slag had an oily glow.

"How do we get to the mines from here?" Clovermead asked Mullein.

"I tired," said Mullein. She slumped to the ground.

"Mullein?" asked Clovermead. "Shaman-Mother?" She knelt by the little girl's side. Mullein was breathing rapidly and shallowly. "Sorrel, what do we do?"

Sorrel knelt by his sister's side. "Let her go," he said to the Shaman-Mother. "Enough of this game. Let me take her away from here!" He shook Mullein, and would have shaken her harder except that Clovermead tore his hands from the girl's shoulders.

"Let her be," said Clovermead. "You'll just hurt her worse."

"A curse upon the Shaman-Mother," said Sorrel. He crouched, picked up Mullein, and slung her over his back. Her arms curled around his chest. "I will carry Mullein. You look ahead and lead us through this town." He tried to smile. "Look for the big hole in the mountain, and there we are."

"Thank you so much." Clovermead rolled her eyes, then bit her lip. "I don't suppose you want to tell me the end of that story about the red fox?"

"For a while I did not think I would ever want to," said Sorrel. "But perhaps I was wrong. Not now." He smiled a little. "I am sure that Our Lady will not let you die until you hear it told, so I think it is better that I wait until we are out of the mines before I tell it to you. Does that make sense to you?"

"I'd rather hear the story," said Clovermead. Sorrel shook his head. "If I die without hearing it end, I'm never going to forgive you." She crept away from the tunnel and Sorrel came after, carrying Mullein.

They crept through the dark streets, slinking from shadow to shadow. They passed a few bear-priests, striding arrogantly along, but saw more slave-traders, silver merchants, and other people who traded in Barleymill. The people of Barleymill walked with a cautious, cringing air, but with the confidence that comes from usefulness. Most of the city-dwellers, however, were slaves. Some walked by themselves — with metal collars around their necks and metal cuffs that tied their hands together — and carried heavy loads of water and food from one part of the town to the other. Others, chained together in gangs, and guided by foremen with whips, lugged heavy timbers or carts filled with stones. Still others trudged along with pickaxes in their hands and no shackles — miners, too weary to think of escape, staggering at the end of their shifts back to barracks in the city.

The miners glowed. Silvery dust was ingrained in their ragged clothes and etched into the folds of their skin. Beneath the glow their flesh was oddly dark. All were emaciated, and the teeth of the thinner ones had fallen out.

"They look like Mother did when Mallow's venom was in her arm," whispered Clovermead, horrified. "Poisoned and dying."

"People do not last long in the mercury mines," said

Sorrel. He glanced over his shoulder at Mullein. She was not yet as emaciated as the miners, but she was not much better. "It is a miracle of Our Lady that she is still alive," he whispered.

"No miracle," Mullein whispered back. For a second she was awake. "Shaman-Mother." Her head drooped against Sorrel's back once more.

They walked on. Clovermead saw metal rings on every wall, where slaves could be tied. They passed a huge square where lines of people were being sold to the bear-priests, despite the late hour. These were still-healthy peasants from the Thirty Towns. The bear-priests bought them by the score, gathered up their chains, and jerked them toward the mines. A few bear-priests manned each entrance to the square: Great barricades stood by them, which could be lowered at a moment's notice. The whole city was a prison, divided into a honeycomb of smaller prisons.

Clovermead saw a bent-over slave loaded with a basket full of loaves of bread hurry toward them, then trip on a crack between two stones. He scrabbled on the ground for the fallen loaves. As he looked in the darkness, he saw Clovermead and Sorrel crouched, their knives drawn and ready to stab forward. He stared at them for a moment, then put his finger to his lips. His eyes dropped, and he finished tossing loaves back into his basket. Then he stood up and scrambled onward.

"I would not trust him," said Sorrel, as the slave scurried away. "Let us hurry, before he thinks to turn us in to the bear-priests." They pressed forward.

As they came closer to the mines, the buildings became a mixture of slave barracks and buildings whose insides glowed an ever brighter silver, a ghastly parody of moonlight. Here the mercury ore was refined into glistening pools of the pure liquid. In an open doorway Clovermead saw wooden caskets filled with the bright substance, waiting to have lids put on them. They hurried through the eerie half-light toward the mines.

The flat stones of the city streets ended, to be replaced by a rough trail up a shallow slope. Scattered barracks and buildings filled with mining equipment covered the broken land, but with large areas of open space between each of them, and a larger belt of flat ground before the entrance to the mines. Lone bear-priests loped through the open ground; more stood on high towers that overlooked the city, others guarded the tunnel-mouths. Chains of slaves trailed in and out of the mines. They were hollow-eyed skeletons.

"How long until dawn?" asked Clovermead.

Sorrel glanced at the sky. "At least five hours. I think we can get closer to the mine entrance. Do you see that little ridge of rock running toward that tower?" Clovermead nodded. "Follow me. If we go very slowly in its shadow, and keep our heads down, we should not be seen." Sorrel got onto his stomach and began to wriggle forward, his head down low by the ground and Mullein clinging to his back. Clovermead followed after him as they went agonizingly slowly from shadow to shadow, hugging the darker-colored patches of rock and coming closer to the towers that rose where the hills emerged abruptly from the plain. Sorrel circled around the nearest tower and led Clovermead to a patch of broken ground in the shadow of the towers. The main entrance to the mines gaped before them.

"Look," said Clovermead. She pointed at an empty cart that had stopped thirty feet away. The slaves around it had slumped to the ground while the two bear-priests guarding them argued with each other about something. Both bear-priests had turned their backs to Clovermead while they swore at each other. "They're going back to the mine. Quick, Sorrel, let's go. We'll never get a better chance than this." Sorrel nodded and they dashed toward the cart.

Some slaves stared at them with dead eyes. Clovermead made the sign of the crescent to them, put her fingers to her lips, then scrambled under the wagon with Sorrel and Mullein. After a while, the cart began to creak back toward the mine. Clovermead and Sorrel, bent double, walked on their hands and feet in the darkness under the cart, over the rough stones.

Quicksilver dust jounced through the boards above them, settled into Clovermead's hair, and burned against her scalp. More dust trickled down and worked its way under her shirt. Each granule slid greasily against her skin as it blazed its way down. Clovermead had to resist the urge first to itch, then to cry out. She leaned over to keep the dust away from her eyes, her nose, and her mouth. A few particles blew into them despite her best efforts: Tears ran from her eyes and she had to choke back a scream. *How can people endure this even one day?* Clovermead wondered.

They left the starlight behind and entered the mine, and silvery light flooded in on them from all sides. Farther in they could hear the distant crunch of pickaxes and shovels. Bear-priests yelled at the slaves, and the cart turned to the right. They left the main tunnel behind them and went a distance down a narrower side-spoke. The cart creaked to a halt, the bear-priests yelled again, and the slaves shuffled off. Clovermead waited for one of the slaves to say something, but they stayed silent. After a minute, the tunnel around them was quiet. Clovermead and Sorrel crept out from under the wagon. Mullein still clung to Sorrel's back, her face white, her chest barely moving.

A whole line of empty wagons filled the narrow tunnel. The tunnel walls and the quicksilver dust lining the carts reflected light at each other, and made a glow bright enough for Clovermead to see without squinting. They crept to the front of the tunnel, where the main passageway began. There they saw a constant stream of bearpriests and slaves in the shining light: There was no way to get past them unnoticed.

"Let me see what is at the back of this tunnel," said Sorrel. He crept backward, explored for a minute, then came back to Clovermead. "I have found another exit," he said. "Come, let us see where it leads."

They walked behind the last of the wagons, and then the tunnel narrowed abruptly. Two people could walk abreast, but no cart could get by. The ceiling became much lower too, barely higher than Clovermead. The edges were even rougher, with great outcroppings slicing into the corridor as it curved deeper into the hills. The tunnel twisted and intersected other, even narrower tunnels. Everywhere the same silvery light shone; everywhere the same dust itched and abraded Clovermead's flesh.

"Where are we going?" asked Clovermead.

Mullein raised her head at last. "Turn right," she whispered. "You are very close." Her eyes were blazing silver. The Shaman-Mother's voice was thick on her tongue. They swerved into another tunnel. "Right again. Then left." They followed her instructions and further whispers as they darted deeper into the labyrinth. Clovermead lost all sense of where she was going. Silver dust settled onto her and Sorrel. Their figures glowed in the dark and she began to itch worse than ever. She brushed away the dust from her arms, but more settled within seconds. Her eyes were burning.

They came around a last corner. "Here is the Cyan Cross Horde," said Mullein.

Chapter Fourteen

ESCAPE FROM THE MINES

A GREAT IRON GRILL TWENTY FEET BROAD AND SIX feet high rose before them. A double-bolted steel plate kept together the two halves of the grill. Behind the grill a cave stretched for fifty feet. In those thousand square feet was what remained of the Cyan Cross Horde. There were fifty of them—women and girls only. There were no old men, no warriors, no boys. The youngest was Mullein's age; the oldest were stooped, toothless women of seventy and more. A fair number were in their twenties and thirties—those strong enough to survive labor in the mines. All were wiry, with muscles born of long, hard labor. All wore ancient, tattered clothes. All glowed with the sheen of quicksilver.

In the center of the cave a cross had been erected. A woman had been strapped to the cross, and nails had been driven into her wrists and through her ankles to keep her pinned to the wood. She breathed with great, ragged gasps, her chest trying to support her weight and take in air at once.

"Mother!" Sorrel cried. He slung Mullein to the ground, rushed to the gates, and pulled at them vainly with all his might. Roan looked down from the cross, and smiled when she saw her son. The other women of Cyan Cross also gazed at him, with the barest spark of curiosity in their exhausted faces.

An old woman knelt by Roan and reached up her hand to touch her feet. She was barely strong enough to keep from collapsing utterly, she chanted beneath her breath, and a shadow of red pain coursed to her from Roan. With each flow of pain, wounds opened and closed upon the old woman's wrists and ankles. Her cheeks were tattooed with the Cyan Cross' crisscross pattern, but the lines were glowing, throbbing silver. Clovermead recognized the old woman's face: She had seen it shadowed on Mullein's. The Shaman-Mother bled and suffered so that Roan could survive her crucifixion.

"Let me," said Clovermead, and she padded toward the gate. She was growing into a bear and her head nearly scraped the top of the tunnel. She was angry, she was crying, and her arms were thick with bear-strength, strong with rage. The women of the Cyan Cross retreated from the gate as she wrapped her claws around the iron grill. She could see old blood running along the bars—long ago Ursus had interwoven a net of blood around the iron, to strengthen the shackles on his slaves. Clovermead pulled at the bars with all her anger. They creaked, but they would not break.

"I can't do this by myself," Clovermead half-cried, half-roared. "Sorrel, help me!" He came to her side and put his hands around the grillwork, pulling in tandem with Clovermead. *Lady, help me,* Clovermead cried inside. *Give me your light,* she begged, and in her mind she was swinging Firefly to snap the bloody bonds around the iron. She pulled against the gate once more, with Sorrel, and her paws were bright with moonlight. She had no time for anger now, only for concentration on the task in front of her. Sorrel's face was red, Clovermead's ribs ached with the strain, and the grill creaked, groaned, and pulled apart with a horrendous scream. The steel plate shattered, and blood trickled out of the broken iron and faded into air. A chunk of metal caromed off Clovermead's ribs and she felt a dull pain. Then she was lumbering through the broken gates toward the cross. With one paw she held up Roan, let Sorrel's mother rest against her weight, while with the other she plucked the spike out of the woman's right wrist. Roan's arm slumped over Clovermead's shoulder, bleeding, and Clovermead shifted to pull the spike from her left wrist. Then she held Roan while Sorrel ran and pulled the last spike from his mother's ankles. Free at last, Roan fell from the cross. Clovermead placed her gently on the floor, and Sorrel, weeping, tore strips of cloth from his yellow jacket to wind around his mother's wounds. Clovermead shrank to human, and as she did so she saw the Shaman-Mother slump to the floor by Roan's side. Her hand let go the crucified woman's foot, and the wounds faded from the Shaman-Mother's flesh. Clovermead knelt by her side and touched her hand—

She jerked away. A lash of pain scoured deep into Clovermead's flesh, so harsh that her muscles convulsed helplessly. Acid ate at her fingers where she had touched the Shaman-Mother, and burned away her fingerprints.

"I am sorry," the Shaman-Mother whispered. "I cannot control it any longer." Her hand fell against rock, and the rock softened at her touch. She smiled faintly. "You are here, bear-girl. I saw you in quicksilver, you and Sorrel. You will free us." She paused for breath, and her breath was very faint. Her face was more gray than silver now. "I saw the broken gate. I could not do it myself—Oh, Lady, I tried. I looked in a pool of quicksilver, and Our Lady sent a vision. Free Roan, free Mullein—that much I could do myself. Put a little of myself in Mullein to help you here, and you would come, Sorrel would come, and do what I could not. You are here at last." She lifted her hand, a frail twig, and gestured at the women and children around them. "Free them."

"You first," said Clovermead. She put her hands on the Shaman-Mother's shackles, making sure to keep from touching her flesh. "You deserve to be free."

The Shaman-Mother shook her head. "Save your strength, bear-girl. I am dying."

"Maybe you are and maybe you aren't," said Clovermead. "Even if you are, I'm not going to let you die in chains." She glanced back to where Mullein sat sprawled in the tunnel. "You're going to be free." She concentrated on the Shaman-Mother's shackles, and she could see a live thread of crimson blood curled around it, stronger and more vibrant than the blood in the gate had been. Clovermead concentrated hard. She had to untie the bond, and she fumbled at the slick red wire with her mind. It slithered out of her grip and she tried again. It was a little easier to catch hold of the blood-bond this time—and she had it! Her hands turned to paws, they glowed again with moonlight, and she cracked the Shaman-Mother's shackles in two. Blood dribbled from the sheared metal down to the silvery floor.

The women in the cave gaped as they saw the Shaman-Mother's shackles broken, then surged toward Clovermead with sudden hope, raised their own shackles to her, and babbled at her in Tansyard. "Get back!" Clovermead cried in sudden alarm. *They're going to suffocate me!* she thought, and she windmilled her paws in front of her. The women drew back. "One at a time," Clovermead growled. She went to the first slave.

She grabbed the chain with mind and paws, and now it took less time to grip it properly and break it. The freed girl cried softly in wonder. Then Clovermead went down the line of slaves, breaking each chain between her moonlit paws. The metal was hard and screamed as it broke. Slivers of iron dug into Clovermead's paws.

Soon the fifty slaves of the Cyan Cross Horde were free. "What now?" asked Clovermead, and she turned to the Shaman-Mother.

Mullein sat by the Shaman-Mother's side. "Don't die," she said through her tears. "Not now! We come, rescue you."

"Thank you," the Shaman-Mother whispered. "You have done more than enough." She lifted her hands an inch, so her broken shackles waved. "Here, little one, let me take your burden from you." She muttered a sentence, made the sign of the crescent, and a silvery shadow flew from Mullein to the Shaman-Mother. The silver faded from Mullein, and so did the lined weariness. She breathed fully and healthily for the first time in weeks. "I am sorry I asked so much of you," said the Shaman-Mother.

"Ask more," said Mullein. She was weeping harder. "Come with us."

"I cannot," said the Shaman-Mother. Then she gasped. "I hurt so much," she moaned. "Let it end, Lady. I have done enough."

"Don't hurt," said Mullein. She took the Shaman-Mother in her arms, and rocked her back and forth. Glowing silver crawled up her arms and flowed into her, and Mullein cried out in pain, but she didn't let go. "I hurt for you. I choose."

The Shaman-Mother relaxed. "It is not so bad now," she said. She smiled, at Mullein, at the unseen sky beyond the walls of the mine. "Thank you. You should not do this, but I am glad. There is no pain now."

A glowing crisscross tattoo, the pattern of the Cyan Cross and the color of quicksilver, was etching itself into Mullein's cheeks. "Don't worry, Shaman-Mother," she gasped. "I bear pain, awhile."

"Not too long," said the Shaman-Mother. "You are too little." She smiled. "Oh, Mullein, Our Lady was kind to send you to me." She closed her eyes, breathed out, and no inward breath followed. She was dead.

Mullein cried tears of quicksilver. The crisscross on her cheeks glowed, and all her body shone.

"We must come away, before the bear-priests find us," said Sorrel. He hoisted his mother onto his back. Her hands and feet had been bandaged in yellow cloth, and she had fallen unconscious. She was a dead weight on her son. "Mullein, we must leave the Shaman-Mother. She is with Our Lady now."

"She always here, for us," said Mullein. Her body trembled as liquid metal surged through her. "Everyone die, but us. She save us. What we do now?"

"Live as we can," said Sorrel. "But now we must hurry from here."

"More slaves next us," said Mullein. "Free them, too?"

"Some," said Clovermead. She went over to Mullein and scooped her onto her back. Even through her fur she could feel Mullein's mercury-drenched arms burn into her. "As many as we can before the alarm is raised." She ducked her head and squeezed through the broken bars, and then they were rushing into the tunnels again.

They staggered through the passageways, Mullein guided Clovermead, and they came to another cave. Here there were more Tansyards and men of Linstock, slaves from Selcouth and from the Thirty Towns. Clovermead broke another gate and broke more bonds. There were only thirty alive in this cave, and they were thinner, sicker, closer to poisoning and death. The women of the Cyan Cross Horde spoke to these new slaves in a harsh argot, a babble of Tansyard and common tongue, and the new slaves came shuffling after Cyan Cross. Clovermead's hands were raw and bleeding, with iron shards in every inch. They came to a third cave — here were forty! They came to a fourth cave, and only a dozen men, almost skeletons, came staggering to their feet. Another dozen lay dead in their chains, and Clovermead had come too late for them. She broke the living slaves' chains, she wanted to weep, but her eyes were burning with poison, and she could only blink them against the swirling silver dust. A trumpet echoed through the tunnels.

A Tansyard woman spoke to Sorrel. "She says guards are coming," he said. "It is the shift-change. We have to leave now." He spoke to the woman in Tansyard, and she replied quickly. "They patrol in pairs. I think we can deal with two, Clovermead." He shifted his mother to one side, drew his sword, then let her fall back upon his back.

"Yes," said Clovermead wearily. She adjusted Mullein's weight, and she followed after Sorrel.

They waited at a corner where an overhang of rock hid them in shadow, and peered down the corridor that shone deadly silver. Sorrel put his mother down to sit on the floor behind him, and Clovermead did the same with Mullein. Then two bear-priests came walking down the corridor. They carried short-swords and long whips with jagged nails at the end of coiled leather. They looked into a cave, where more slaves slept. Then they came down toward Sorrel and Clovermead.

Sorrel leaped out as the first came within reach. He rammed the bear-priest against the opposite wall, and smashed his head against the rock as hard as he could. With his other hand he stabbed underhand into the bear-priest's chest with his sword. The bear-priest barely had time to shriek before he died. Clovermead followed Sorrel a second later. Her claws raked the whip out of the second bear-priest's hand, then turned back and slapped the bear-priest's head with all her force. His head turned, twisted, and snapped, all in one dreadful instant. He hadn't even had time to see who had struck him.

Clovermead looked at her claws turned red with blood. Her stomach churned, her eyes burned, but not so badly as the first time she had killed a bear-priest. *I'm growing used to killing,* she whispered to herself. *I knew I would.* And she could not help asking Our Lady resentfully, *Why must I do this? It isn't fair of you to put this burden on me.*

"They will be missed soon," said Sorrel. "Let us get away from them quickly." He slung his mother over his back, and Clovermead picked up Mullein. The little girl had fallen unconscious again. Quicksilver surged through Mullein's flesh, and she moaned with nightmares. Her hands still trembled with pain.

"Do you remember the way out?" asked Clovermead. Sorrel shook his head, and she groaned. She wanted to give up, to let someone else save her—but there were more than a hundred shambling wretches waiting behind them. *My nose,* she thought suddenly. "I'll sniff for a breeze," she said out loud. "If I can find one, I'll follow it out." She let her nose grow into a bear-snout, and now she could smell a faint odor of fresh air. "This way," she said, and Clovermead began to lead them through the labyrinth.

They wove this way and that, up and down, through an endless length of silvery corridors. Half the time she had to bend double to progress. Now and then, they passed cells filled with other slaves, but they had no time to stop for them. Clovermead had bear-ears out for the sound of an alarm—she was sure it would come any minute. And when it came, there would be no way out. The bear-priests would shut the gates of Barleymill, and then they could round them up or just let them starve.

Help me, said Boulderbash. *I'm not far from you.* Her voice was loud inside Clovermead's head.

Where? asked Clovermead.

There are patches over my eyes, said Boulderbash. She roared—and Clovermead could hear her. She was only a corridor away, achingly near. *Free me, little cub.*

They came to a crossroads in the tunnels. One way Clovermead could smell the outside, nearer and fresher than ever. *I don't want to be caught down here,* Clovermead thought unhappily, but she kept her feet from rushing toward the way out. *Roar again,* she said to Boulderbash. Boulderbash obeyed, and her growl was just around the corner. Clovermead took a step toward her and she sent her mind questing for the blood-net that held Boulderbash. She could feel it! It was tight and intricate, but she could undo it. All she needed was a minute.

A horn blew, a terrible, echoing crescendo. The slaves moaned with dread.

I have to go, said Clovermead. *I'm sorry, Boulderbash. I don't have a choice.*

You always have a choice, said Boulderbash. *And it is never me.*

It never will be you, Mother, said Lord Ursus. His voice was great and terrible in the darkness. *She always will leave you behind. There is no hope for you. There is no light.* His voice, bloodstained and cruel, became seductive. *Will you believe me at last, Mother? Do you see that I have been right all along? Our Lady's servants have fine words, but nothing more.*

The boy Ambrosius freed me from the trap, said Boulderbash uncertainly. *He was kind to me.*

He is dead, said Lord Ursus. *His daughter does not measure up to him, and she never will. You are lost in darkness forever. Embrace it, Mother. Oh, Mother, I have missed your company for so long.*

You tortured me, said Boulderbash—and then she broke. *The golden cub has tortured me worse. You gave me hope, Clovermead, and you took it away. Son, I will join you.* She roared with a terrible anger. *I will be revenged on you, little cub. You have abandoned me for the last time.* Her growl filled the mines, and it was more terrible than anything Clovermead had ever heard. Even Ursus' growl seemed small compared to it.

No, said Clovermead. *Don't turn on Our Lady because of me. Please, don't.*

Welcome, Mother, Lord Ursus roared with delight. *I will have Snuff take off your eye-patches. Now you can see in my service.*

I have missed you, too, Son, said Boulderbash. She growled with a terrible hunger. *Run, changeling. I am coming for you.*

I'm sorry, said Clovermead, but Boulderbash only laughed with scorn. And howled. Then Clovermead did run toward the breeze before her, away from that scream that promised exquisite revenge. She ran with the most terrible fear in her as Boulderbash's roar filled the tunnel.

Mullein stirred on her back and muttered words in Tansyard, motioned with her hands. A thin cloud gathered around them, just enough to obscure their bodies as they fled out of the mines. There were bear-priests to either side of them, each with drawn scimitars, but they looked over and around the fleeing slaves, never at them. Sorrel and Clovermead waited at the tunnel entrance while the slaves came hobbling out. The horns blew again inside the mine, Boulderbash roared, and the guarding bear-priests looked curiously into the tunnel-mouth. The last of the slaves slipped by as the guards started to walk into the mines, shouting queries within. Then Sorrel and Clovermead were racing to the head of the line, to lead the slaves once more.

The ugly buildings of Barleymill were dark shadows before them. Far away there were trumpets and lights, but before them the way was dark. Clovermead smelled the breeze—yes, she remembered the way to the tunnel under the wall. "This way," she whispered urgently, and Sorrel and the slaves came after her. The city air was foul, but a fresh wind blew in the scent of grass from the Steppes. They left the charnel mines behind them. They went slowly: The slaves were weakened by long years underground. Tottering, one hundred slaves and more made their way through the dark town.

Long minutes passed, and they were coming close to the tunnel under the town walls. *I think we'll make our way out of here after all,* Clovermead thought hopefully. *Thank you, Lady.* Then a trumpet sounded once more, and this time it was in the city, not in the mines. The harsh scream of a silver-bear followed it, then another. *Or perhaps not,* thought Clovermead bleakly. But then they were by the tunnel.

"We'll send the slaves through first," she said to Sorrel. "The Yellowjackets will be waiting for them on the other side. We'll watch this side and bring up the rear guard."

"Agreed," said Sorrel. He put his mother down on the stones of the street, and asked her a question in Tansyard. She mumbled a broken answer. "She's too weak to go through by herself."

"I help her," said Mullein. She roused herself, and half-fell down from Clovermead. "I take mother through."

"You don't look like you can take yourself through," said Clovermead.

"I enough strong," said Mullein. She stumbled over to her mother. "Come, Mother," she said tenderly. "I take pain." She touched Roan, and it was as if life itself jerked through the Tansyard woman. The color came back to her cheeks, and the sparkle to her eye. The bandages on her hands and feet ceased to bleed.

Wounds gaped in Mullein's hands. The crisscross on her cheeks glowed brighter than ever. She trembled, but made herself stand. "You first, Mother," she said. Mullein waited while Roan fumbled her way on hands and feet into the tunnel. When she had disappeared, Mullein followed after her. Then there was a stream of slaves slipping into the tunnel while Sorrel and Clovermead stood guard, with drawn swords.

"I have been unjust," Sorrel said abruptly. He took a step toward Clovermead in the darkness, and his fingers touched her palms ravaged by the shards of a hundred shackles. "It is as you said. I have been so angry with you, and cherishing my rage, and I do see now that there was petulance at the root of it, because I whistled for you like a dog, then cursed you for a cur when you would not obey me. You have been angry with me for my treatment of you only once, and I deserved your anger a hundred times. Clovermead, I am sorry."

"I'm sorry I didn't come with you in the Moors. Every choice was the wrong choice." Clovermead clutched her palms around his fingers, though it drove a metal splinter deeper into her flesh. "I'd do the same thing again, Sorrel. I'm sorry. I've always wanted your good opinion, and maybe I don't deserve it."

"Perhaps I do not deserve yours," said Sorrel quietly. Somewhere bears were screaming and trumpets were blaring, but Clovermead wasn't paying attention to them. "It is not just that I have been unreasonable in my demands upon you. I understand, finally, what Saraband said to me. That I was a soldier, and that it was good for me to be a soldier, but that she had a different road to travel. You are a politician, sometimes, like your mother, and I am not. I will never think as you do, and I do not think I can ever abandon the person I see before me for the many far away. I am afraid you will again make me angry with you by the choices you make." He took a deep breath. "But not for more than a second. I will remember you are also the Clovermead who tore down that gate and took down my mother from the cross. And I think I see that you always have been that Clovermead, in the Harrow Moors as much as in Barleymill. I did not see your heart these last weeks—would not see your heart—but it is clear before me now, and I will never again let unhappy passion cloud that vision. I will take you as you are. I do not want to walk a separate path from yours. We may hurt each other again—people do that. But let us be friends again." Tears glittered in his eyes. "I do not deserve your friendship, but I ask it of you."

"I feel the same way," said Clovermead. She was crying too—and then the last of the slaves was slipping into the tunnel, and there was another blast of the horn. "I wish we had more time to talk. You go now. I'll come last." Sorrel began to protest—but the horn blew again, nearer than ever. He scrambled into the tunnel.

We are coming closer, said Lucifer Snuff in her mind. He was full of glee. *Where are you, girlie? Tell your old friend Lucifer. I'm so happy to find you in Barleymill! I never dreamed you'd take a jaunt this way. I can't wait to see you.*

Try to find me! said Clovermead defiantly. Sorrel was only in to his elbows; the rest of him stuck out on the street.

I know you're in the city, said Snuff. *Not by the gates, we have those guarded. You must have some other way through the walls—how else could you get in? Don't worry, girlie, we'll find you soon enough.* His laughter echoed in Clovermead's mind.

Clovermead looked anxiously back at the nearby buildings. She saw torches coming close, bobbing through the town streets.

She sees torches, Snuff, said Boulderbash.

Don't tell him, Boulderbash! cried Clovermead in horror.

You have abandoned me once too often, said Boulderbash. There was implacable anger in her voice. *Lucifer, she is standing by the city wall, next to a long, low building made of bricks.*

She's by the old granary, boys, cried Lucifer. *You and you, go after her!* Half a dozen torches suddenly shifted direction, and came at a run toward Clovermead. *The rest of you come with me. We'll ride down any slaves who escape beyond walls.* Several dozen more torches streamed toward the town gates.

Clovermead looked frantically at the tunnel, and Sorrel's feet shot out of sight. Clovermead dove down and followed hard after him. "Hurry!" she moaned at his boots ahead of her. How long was it to the other side of the wall? She couldn't remember. She scrambled in the darkness for one minute, two minutes. Far behind her, she could hear pattering feet coming close to the tunnel's entrance at last. Soon the bear-priests would start after her.

She came out to the other side. There was Sorrel on Brown Barley, and they had put Roan and Mullein on Auroche. The rest of the slaves were huddled in a mass on the bare ground, while the Yellowjackets guarded them in the fraying cloud of darkness.

"A few bear-priests will be coming through the tunnel in a few minutes," said Clovermead. "A lot more will be coming out the main gates, and I think they'll be on horseback. Sorrel, tell the slaves." He called out a few words in Tansyard, and pointed northward to the hills. The slaves jogged in that direction as quickly as they could, while the Yellowjackets formed a screen around them. Sergeant Algere rode up and down the line formed by his handful of soldiers, clapping their backs, giving orders, and whispering encouraging words. He looked down at the mass of Tansyards, he looked up at Clovermead, and he almost smiled. He shrugged, made the sign of the crescent, then turned to follow the fleeing slaves.

Sorrel drew his sword. "Accompany them, Clovermead. This time I will bring up the rear guard."

"We'll fight together," said Clovermead. She laughed. "Did you think you were going to get rid of me now?"

"I suppose not, hellion." He smiled and shrugged, and they turned to face the distant gates. "What precisely are we going to do?"

In the distance Boulderbash roared.

Chapter Fifteen

AVALANCHES

CLOVERMEAD LOOKED AROUND AT THE DESOLATE
landscape. Piles of rubble and ash loomed up in the darkness. Behind them the Yellowjackets and the slaves were
retreating up into the narrow opening of Yarrow's Way.
There were only three paths from Barleymill into the valley, each of them running between piles of slag. Great
boulders perched precariously on the summits of the
piles.

"I can go and knock down some rocks," said
Clovermead. "Those things look like they'll avalanche if
you look at them funny, and that would cut off the paths.
Can you delay the bear-priests until I get the boulders
down?"

"All by myself?" Sorrel rolled his eyes. "One of the
things I love about you is the way you ask me something that is patently impossible with such a thoughtful,
serious look. 'She is mad,' I tell myself, and then somehow I end up doing what you have asked."

"What else can we do?" asked Clovermead. "There's
just the two of us."

"I wish I came up with more ideas," said Sorrel. "I am
positive that some of them would be less dangerous." He

reached down and gripped Clovermead's hand in his, then released her. "Do hurry. I cannot keep the bear-priests away for long." Then he was galloping away toward the main gate of Barleymill.

"I'll be quick," said Clovermead, and then she was scrambling up the nearest ash hill. The surface was soft, and pebbles fell as she climbed. The stones were greasy with the stain of quicksilver. Her hands and feet, already abraded, itched worse as they rubbed the rough ore.

Clovermead came to the top and she looked back at the Barleymill gates. Sorrel was pounding toward the town gates in the darkness, howling as he came to the torches of the gates, with his sword drawn. The gates were just opening, and Sorrel stabbed the first bear-priest through the chest before the surprised man could draw his own scimitar. The bear-priest fell back with a scream, and his body slammed into the bear-priest behind him, and knocked him off his horse. The riderless horse stumbled and fell onto the ground between the opening gates, and his limbs entangled in the swinging metal. The bear-priests behind cried out in frustration, and swung down from their horses to clear the gates while Sorrel rode into the darkness again, crying out his triumph.

Silver-bears screamed behind the gates. They were anxious to be hunting.

Clovermead transformed, grew, let fur and muscles, claws and fangs, come to her. Her paws still ached, and the iron slivers went deep into her tender flesh. She stood up on two legs, and leaned and pushed against the nearest boulder. It was a rough cube, perhaps twelve feet across on each side. It groaned and creaked under the pressure of her paws, dug mulishly into its bed—and sprang out! Grumbling, rolling, biting up pebbles behind it, it rolled down toward the valley below. Half of the loose slope came with it, from sand and pebbles to rocks half the size of the boulder. Clovermead stumbled to a boulder almost as large as the first one and sent it plummeting after the first one. Now even more of the slope crashed down, and Clovermead was caught in the slippage. She struggled to keep her balance as she half-fell, half-ran down the slope of collapsing ash. A rock the size of her fist banged hard into her shoulder; she roared in pain, but had no time to focus on the bruise. Then she was down at the bottom of the gulch. Fifty feet of it was covered with rubble ten feet high, and no horse could ride over it. Clovermead growled with satisfaction, turned human, and began to scramble up the next slope.

Sorrel was conducting a desperate fighting retreat between two ash hills on the far side of the Barleymill gates. Fooled, the bear-priests and silver-bears came after him, and ignored the slaves' actual route of retreat. The silver-bears came so fast that Sorrel had to gallop pell-mell in the darkness. Clovermead prayed that Brown Barley wouldn't trip and fall. The silver-bears' screams were more eager than ever as they inched closer to Sorrel. A bear-priest fired an arrow into the darkness—and it hit Sorrel! Clovermead felt her heart turn to ice, but it had just grazed his arm and she could breathe again.

Boulderbash bounded out of the gates of Barleymill. Lucifer Snuff rode on her back, but this time he had no bit and no reins, no eye-patches to blind her. She rode free of control, but listened to Snuff as he whispered instructions to her. They were a terrible centaur, with strength, intelligence, and malice combined in their fused figure. Boulderbash snuffled at the darkness—and raced toward Clovermead. Snuff yelled, and the silver-bears and bear-priests turned away from Sorrel to follow Boulderbash.

"Lady's wimple," Clovermead cursed. "By her knotted belt!" She was up the second slope by now, and she pushed at more boulders with frantic haste. There were no boulders bigger than six feet across here, and none produced so satisfying an avalanche as the last one had. She had to push four, five, six, before the whole scree collapsed in a slow but powerful wave. Clovermead came down in a surge of dust, a constant undertow that threatened to suck her beneath the flow of ash and rock. Clovermead's arms and legs grew sore as she struggled not to slip, and then the second path was blocked. The ash was only six feet deep here, but it covered a hundred feet of the path with a morass almost as treacherous as quicksand. *Just one path left*, thought Clovermead. She toiled up the third slope, and her lungs and ribs were aching and weary.

Sorrel galloped toward her, struggling to catch up with Boulderbash. He raced the silver-bears and bear-priests that had turned to follow Snuff, struggled to overtake them, and squeezed such speed from Brown Barley that she outpaced the fastest Phoenixian any bear-priest rode. Even the silver-bears fell behind her. Bear-priests sent crossbow bolts whipping through the night toward Sorrel. Sorrel crouched low over Brown Barley as bolts ripped open the clothes on his back and sliced through his hair.

Clovermead was at the top of the third hill, and here was the obvious boulder to create a great avalanche, a monster twenty feet across and made of squat, hard granite that would scoop out a hill full of ash as it rolled. *It's so big*, thought Clovermead. *And I'm so tired. Lady, help me.* She set herself up against it, and began to push once more.

The iron shards pushed even deeper into her paws, and she howled. The boulder creaked, but so did her spine and her ribs, and the bones in her arms and legs. *I'm strong*, Clovermead told herself desparately. *There isn't a human on earth who could even move this stone. This is why I have the bear-strength, the bear-shape. It's so I can do something impossible, and stop the bear-priests and keep the slaves free. You made me strong, Lady. Make me strong enough to move this stone.* She pushed harder and the stone creaked some more—and then creaked again as it fell back into its resting place.

Sorrel had passed the silver-bears and caught up with Snuff. The two of them were coming up fast to the valley before her. Snuff swung out with his scimitar, and Boulderbash clawed at Brown Barley even as she charged ahead. Sorrel swerved—and a crossbow bolt chunked through his calf. Clovermead heard him scream, saw him sway on Brown Barley's back. The tip had come through the front of his trouser-leg. The ash hills shone their poisonous light, and Clovermead could see blood spurting down his leg. Sorrel screamed again, but still he made himself ride, still he struck at Snuff. He grazed Snuff's elbow.

No! Clovermead howled. Then all words dissolved from her roars, and she pushed at the boulder with all the strength of terrible grief. This time the boulder *moved* when she pushed. It ground rocks beneath it to powder, the boulder groaned as low and terrible as an earthquake, and it began to roll downhill. It moved slowly and ponderously at first, but then it gained speed. The whole hill followed it, and this time Clovermead simply let the rocks carry her down. She rode the collapsing slope toward the oncoming silver-bears and bear-priests. They were all there in the valley, Sorrel and Snuff and Boulderbash, the four snarling silver-bears, and the first score of bear-priests. The wall of rocks came down toward them, and Clovermead could see Snuff turn toward the slope with amazement in his eyes and yell at Boulderbash to run faster. Sorrel grinned with delight as he saw the avalanche, and he squeezed Brown Barley with his knees. She, too, raced toward the land beyond the avalanche. Behind them the silver-bears and the bear-priests turned back, but they were too late. The rocks came crashing down on bears and bear-priests, on Snuff and Boulderbash, on Sorrel and Clovermead.

Clovermead fought free from a foot of pebbles and ash. When she emerged, the dust that had risen from the avalanche had settled down, and the sky was clear again. *Praise Our Lady,* she thought. *It's a miracle I didn't get crushed or suffocated.* She stumbled forward and then she heard Sorrel crying "Clovermead! Clovermead!" as she stumbled into the valley beyond. There was no one but the two of them. The rocks behind them had blocked the valley, buried their pursuers, and no bear-priests would come through there until daybreak at least.

Clovermead turned human as she stumbled onto the packed flat ground, and there was Sorrel. He brought Brown Barley to a halt, but he couldn't get down from her. The bolt in his calf was in the way. Clovermead lifted up a furred arm to break the awful thing, but Sorrel said, "No, Clovermead! It might break in me. Leave it for a Yellowjacket. They know how to remove such things smoothly."

"You're still bleeding," Clovermead said numbly. "Oh, Sorrel, I'm so sorry."

"We are both alive," said Sorrel. He laughed, almost hysterically. "I thought I had done well tonight. I have killed at least three bear-priests and wounded another five, and only have some arrow-shot to pay for it. But you have buried twenty at once, and silver-bears, too, as you played ninepins with mountain-slopes. Not even Yarrow did the like." His hand came down to clap her admiringly on the back.

"I killed them, didn't I?" said Clovermead bleakly. Her heart barely twinged. *I've grown used to murder,* she thought. She wanted to cry, but she couldn't. *Why am I the one who has to do this?* Then she barked with cold laughter. *I choose to do this. To kill. I won't forget that, and I won't make excuses. It's always my choice.*

"I'm awfully tired," she said. "Can I ride Brown Barley with you?"

"I think that is possible," said Sorrel. "We can ride up to the Yellowjackets and the slaves, and tell them what we have done. It should be dawn when we arrive. Yes, let us go now." He reached down to lift up Clovermead.

Not so fast, little cub, Clovermead heard in her mind, and the rocks shifted behind them. She turned to see a boulder three feet across fly out of the avalanche. Another boulder soared into the air, and then Boulderbash emerged from the heart of the rubble. Snuff was on her back, and they *swam* out of the cinders. They were covered with silvery ash, and they looked more like

213

one beast than ever, almost adhered together. All four of their eyes glowed red. Lord Ursus' blood-power was thick in them. *You can't stop us that easily,* Boulderbash growled. *You'll have to drop a bigger mountain on us.*

Sorrel drew his sword, but Clovermead saw him shake with weakness, saw blood drip from his leg. "Run," she said. "Catch up with the soldiers. I'll distract Snuff."

"I can't leave you," said Sorrel. "We'll fight them together again—"

"You'll bleed to death if you stay," Clovermead almost screamed. "Go to your family. They need protecting." Sorrel still looked irresolute, Boulderbash was getting free of the rubble, and Clovermead didn't have time to argue. "Good-bye, Sorrel," she said. "I don't have any better ideas." Then her mouth was lengthening into a snout, and she roared, so Brown Barley neighed in panic and galloped off, and Sorrel didn't have a choice anymore. As Brown Barley fled into the darkness, Clovermead was turning into a bear. She readied herself to fight, and then Snuff and Boulderbash leaped at her.

Boulderbash's great paws buffeted Clovermead, and Snuff's sword slashed along her side. Boulderbash bit savagely into Clovermead's fur, and pulled out a tuft of fur six inches across. Clovermead was able to scratch her claws along Boulderbash's left forepaw, but that was all. Clovermead was big in bear-shape, but Boulderbash was huge. *I can't fight her,* thought Clovermead. *She'll kill me.* Boulderbash bit at Clovermead's neck, just missed her, and Clovermead's remaining courage fled from her. She turned in helpless fear, and she ran. Boulderbash came after her, she and Snuff howled with the joy of the chase, and Clovermead was their prey. Only the slight limp Clovermead had just given Boulderbash kept the great bear from catching up with her at once.

Clovermead ran in darkness with Boulderbash's breath hot on her heels. Once, Clovermead had dreamed Lord Ursus was chasing her through northern woods, and this was like that, but it was real. She heard no thoughts from Snuff and Boulderbash now, only felt their murderous rage. She had no idea if she was running after the slaves or in a different direction. She fled through the wilderness of ash hills, and tried to ignore the pain in her ribs. It was a flame inside her and she ran slower with every minute.

The slope beneath them began to rise, and Clovermead felt stubbly grass beneath her feet once more. They were some miles from Barleymill, and they had left behind the poisoned earth and piles of rubble at last. Boulderbash still came after her, *But at least I'll die on clean ground*, thought Clovermead. *That'll be a relief.* And it wouldn't be long now. She could feel the last of her energy giving way.

Boulderbash was coming nearer, and Snuff cried out at last in triumph. They were only a few feet behind Clovermead, she heard Boulderbash leap at her in mid-air, and there was nothing Clovermead could do. Her legs kept on going mechanically—

But there was no ground underneath her. She was falling, Boulderbash's claws missed her in midair, and then the bear was yowling in surprise. Clovermead bounced against a small tree, then against a rock, and she was plummeting with Boulderbash and Snuff down the side of a gorge. All three of them fell at once, Snuff still screaming in shock, but Clovermead had no breath left in her to scream. She simply rolled and fell, and it was a relief not to have to move or to think anymore. *It doesn't take any effort at all to fall,* thought Clovermead. *Frankly, I wouldn't mind more falling and less fighting.*

Then Clovermead's head knocked hard against a rock, and the world went black.

Chapter Sixteen

IN THE GORGE

CLOVERMEAD WOKE WITH HER LEFT FORELEG CLAMORING
its unhappiness at her. She groaned and opened her eyes.
It was late in the morning, and the sun was shining
directly down the steep, rocky walls of the chasm. She
was lying in a heap at the bottom, and she could feel
the bruises from every rock that had hit her on the
way down. *Good thing I didn't break my neck,* thought
Clovermead. But her left foreleg was sticking out at a
funny angle, and she howled softly when she tried to
move it. *But that's broken. Oh, Lady, I'd better not try to walk
on that.* She turned human, and now it was only her left
arm that was hanging awkwardly. Her clothes were cut
and torn, and she was scraped and bruised all over. She
staggered to her feet.

She was in a narrow V of a gorge, one hundred feet
tall and no more than twenty feet wide at the bottom. The
slopes were gentle enough that she had bounced down
rather than plummeting, steep enough that the fall had
not been gentle. The chasm continued for several hundred feet in either direction before curving out of sight.
In the center of the chasm a shallow stream trickled
northeastward over a white stone streambed, from the

217

unseen Farry Heights to the equally invisible Steppes. To either side of the stream, tufts of grass sprouted in the rocky soil. The slopes were blazingly white chalk mixed with swirls of creamy limestone and gray granite, punctuated here and there with further tufts of grass, wherever a cup of earth had built up in the crevices. The day was cloudy and cold.

Fifteen feet away Boulderbash lay on the ground, slumped on her side and breathing shallowly. Two of her legs lay at awkward angles, and a long gash had opened up her stomach. Clovermead had an awful feeling that her guts had been punctured. Her tongue lolled out, and her eyes were glazed and unseeing. The great bear was dying.

"Are you up at last, girlie?" Snuff's voice snapped through the air, and Clovermead couldn't help jumping back in fear. He laughed with bubbling, mocking delight, and now Clovermead could see him as he lay on the grass with his leg caught and twisted beneath Boulderbash's bulk. His face was gray and drawn, but the horrid spirit in him was as strong as ever. "I wondered if you were going to wake up."

"Sorry to disappoint you." Clovermead looked him over. He had a sword, but she couldn't see any daggers on him. She approached a little closer, but stayed carefully out of reach. "I see you've learned why you shouldn't ride bears."

"Thank you for the expression of kind concern." Snuff touched his thigh, and grimaced. "A horse can crush your leg just as easily." His eyes darted to Clovermead's arm. "I see you have not come out of this unscathed either. Good, good."

"Shut up," said Clovermead. *Can you hear me, Boulderbash?* she asked with her mind. *Please wake up.*

So cold, Clovermead heard faintly, and then there was only incoherent, fading growling in her mind.

She'll die soon enough, Snuff said in her mind. Then he said out loud, "Me too, girlie. The way my leg's crushed, I must have gangrene by now. But not you! The sky-crone blesses you. You fall off a mountain, and all you do is dislocate your arm."

"I think it's broken," said Clovermead mechanically.

"Dislocated," said Snuff. He gazed dispassionately at her shoulder, like a butcher at a cut of beef, and nodded. "I know wounds. I've made a good deal of them." He laughed feverishly. "Would you bring me a drink of water? I'm awfully thirsty."

"For you?" Clovermead almost screamed. "You dare ask me for anything? You're a murderer, a monster, a—"

"A thirsty man, Demoiselle." Snuff clacked his filed teeth together. "Pretty please, girlie? Fill your hands with water, and give it to me to slurp up like a dog. I promise I won't bite." He gasped in sudden pain. "I thought the sky-crone said we're all supposed to be merciful, girlie. Show mercy to me."

"If Boulderbash fell on me, you'd kill me in a flash. I don't have to be nice to someone like you."

"I beg you, Demoiselle," said Snuff. "Give me a drink." He swallowed painfully. "Sky-crone didn't say anything about being merciful only to nice people. I remember the nuns were strong on that, back in Queensmart. 'Nobody's nice, when you get right down to it,' old Abbess Spurge said. 'You have to be nice, even to the nasty ones. Our Lady doesn't have to be nice to a nasty lot like us, and we should be nice like her, even to the worst villain on earth.'"

"You sure have some gall," said Clovermead. "You

spend your whole life trying to kill nuns, and now you start quoting them."

"I'm thirsty," said Snuff. "A drink, for pity's sake."

Clovermead hesitated. "Throw away your sword," she said at last.

"Of course, of course," said Snuff. He fumbled at his belt, untied his scabbard, and slung it out of reach. "Hurry, girlie."

"Demoiselle to you," Clovermead snapped. More laughter bubbled out of Snuff, and Clovermead hurried away from his voice to the stream. First she drank herself, gratefully lapping up cool water, then she put her still-bruised, still-lacerated hands into the water, brought them tightly together, and brought up a handful. Walking slowly and carefully, she brought the water to Snuff and knelt down so that her hands were under his mouth. He bent over and snuffled it up. His sharp teeth grazed the raw skin of her palm, but he didn't try to bite, to slash, to hurt her in any way.

"Ah, that's good," he gasped. "Would you bring me some more, Demoiselle?"

"Boulderbash first," said Clovermead. She walked back to the stream, and brought a handful that she trickled into Boulderbash's jaws. The bear didn't wake up, but she swallowed the water.

"You're wasting your time," said Snuff. "She's dying."

"You're dying too," said Clovermead. "I'll bother for her as much as for you." Then she went to bring Snuff another mouthful of water. She went back and forth a dozen times, bringing water for both bear-priest and bear.

Boulderbash groaned happily. *I knew you'd rescue me again, Ambrosius.*

"He's dead," Clovermead whispered. She stood up, and turned her back on the bear. "I brought you water, not him," she said angrily.

"Hard to measure up to your father, Demoiselle?" asked Snuff. "That must be exasperating. You extract thorn after thorn from her paw and all she thinks is 'Ambrosius, Ambrosius!' But you haven't done that much for her, now that I think of it. Just brought her some water and left her a prisoner. Left her a prisoner three times, I think it is? She isn't happy with you," he added conversationally.

"Shut up," said Clovermead. "Take it for granted you should always shut up."

"Why should I? I've got water in my throat, and now I can speak until I die. Let me tell you, girlie—"

Clovermead's unhurt arm lashed out against Snuff's jaw, but now her hand was a bear's paw. Her claws raked against the stubble on his jawbone, and rattled his mouth. He spat blood, and a razor-sharp tooth came out too. "Shut up!" Clovermead almost screamed. "Or I'll keep on hitting you. Shut up!"

"That's my girl," said Snuff. He grinned at her, then shut his bloody mouth as Clovermead raised her paw again. He looked at her with ironic expectancy.

"I ought to kill you," said Clovermead. But with an effort she brought down her arm and turned her hand human. She turned to Boulderbash. "Good-bye," she said quietly, and she patted the dying bear's bulk. "I hope you rot," she said to Snuff, and then she was hobbling as fast as she could to the walls of the gorge.

She started to climb the walls. It was difficult, with only one arm to grab at rocks, and both legs unsteady. Soon it became impossible. A third of the way up the cliff on either side of the chasm was a ten-foot high stretch of near-vertical chalk, too smooth for her hand to grasp at for support. She slid back down to the valley floor and hiked up and down the chasm, looking for some gentler route, but the sheer chalk stratum girdled the chasm. High-piled fallen boulders blocked the way both upstream and downstream: The stream wended through crevices between the stones, but there was no way Clovermead could walk out of the gorge.

I could climb up if I were a bear, thought Clovermead. She transformed, grew taller, and now the tops of her paws could scrabble at the ledge above. She tried to pull herself up with her one good foreleg—but her body was far too heavy, and her leg felt as if it were pulling out of her body. She dropped with a gasp, and collapsed on the scree. She sighed, turned back to human, and went back to the stream for another drink.

"I could push that arm back into shape," said Snuff. "It would hurt. Oh, yes it would." He giggled. "But then you could put some weight on that limb. You could climb out of here, girlie." He chuckled. "If you help me."

"What do you want?" asked Clovermead.

"My leg might heal if you can shove that lump of flesh off of me," Snuff gasped. "Move her. And promise you'll carry me out of this gulch."

"I'd rather die," Clovermead spat.

"Then you will, brat," said Snuff. He giggled again. "My offer's good whenever you care to accept it. I'm not going anywhere."

"You'll die there," said Clovermead, and she flung herself away again, looking feverishly for a route out of the canyon. She sniffed for a route in bear-form, peered for one in human form, searched relentlessly, but without

In the Gorge

luck. She spent hours, until the sun had passed the gorge walls, and dusk was approaching. It was growing colder.

"Light a fire for me, girlie," said Snuff. "I'm cold— agk, ice is creeping up my leg. Fire, girl. And more water."

"Don't you even know how to be polite?" asked Clovermead.

"But of course," said Snuff. Suddenly his entire face and voice changed, and he was a courteous nobleman through and through. "Would the Demoiselle be so kind as to succor me with fire and water? I would not bother you, kind lady, but for the dire necessity that drives me to this request. Grant this boon, and I will be grateful all my life. I beg it of you in Our Lady's name." The nobleman vanished, and Snuff spat out a curse. "I had enough of that idiocy in Queensmart. Get me water, girlie. Make me a fire. I hurt!"

"Beast," said Clovermead. Snuff shrugged. "I don't even have tinder."

"I do," said Snuff. He fumbled at a pouch at his side, and drew out the tinder. "Bring me the kindling, girlie, and we'll be nice and comfortable."

"Us and Boulderbash," said Clovermead. "We'll have the fire near her."

"Be careful the sparks don't light her up," said Snuff. "I don't mind roast bear meat, but roast Snuff I don't care for."

"Don't tempt me," said Clovermead. She went to gather kindling, and brought them back to a few feet from Boulderbash and Snuff. She brought a stick to Snuff, and he lit it with his tinder. Clovermead brought the stick back and lit the fire. Soon they had a roaring fire to keep them warm as dusk approached.

223

Clovermead brought back more water for Snuff and Boulderbash.

How kind you are, little boy, thought Boulderbash. *I have waited for you so long, Ambrosius. I always knew you would free me. I was waiting for you.* Clovermead averted her face from Snuff, so that he wouldn't see her cry.

Her stomach rumbled, and Snuff rubbed his own belly. "I'm hungry too. You'd think I'd be too busy dying to bother about hunger, but my stomach doesn't care about my leg. It wants food, no matter what. You wouldn't have any food on you, girlie?" Clovermead shook her head. "Pity. Well, when we get down to gnawing our limbs off, I'll have sharper teeth. Do you want me to relocate your arm?" Clovermead shook her head. "See how you feel when you get hungrier."

"Once you're free, you'd come after Sorrel and the slaves in no time with your silver-bears and bear-priests. I'd rather stay here than let you out."

"They're hunting the runaways already, girlie. Do you think they're wasting their time looking for me?"

Clovermead studied Snuff over the fire. She smiled. "Yes, I do. Fetterlock called you Ursus' 'great lieutenant of the northlands,' and that sounds pretty important to me. I bet they're trying to find out where you are. Anyway, even if they are chasing after the slaves, I'll bet they go off in the wrong direction. Sorrel would have had them fooled for a good long time last night if you and Boulderbash hadn't come out of the gates. I'll bet he can fool them again, if you aren't around to detect his stratagems."

"You flatter me," said Snuff. Then he scowled. "They are numbskulls. Without me—" He gazed back at Clovermead. "There were only four silver-bears in

Barleymill, and you killed them. The others aren't any nearer than Bryony Hill. You needn't worry too much if you let me go."

"I'm not entirely reassured," said Clovermead. "If I let you go, will you swear never to hunt down the slaves we freed, and to let them live their lives in freedom?"

Snuff laughed, long and low. "No, girlie. Lord Ursus would be most displeased if I made any such agreement. I'll take my chances here."

"Then you can die," said Clovermead, almost happily. "Suits me."

"Lord Ursus will preserve me. I am his loyal servant, and I have faith in him." Snuff smiled. "His growl is always with me. It is—"

"A comfort. I remember." Lord Ursus had possessed her, and she had never wanted him to leave her. She had rejected him, but the desire for his companionship still haunted her. "And you love your bloody master. Even though he cast you aside for me. Do you remember that, Snuff?"

"I do." For a moment, there was the most anguished loneliness on Snuff's face. Then he wiped it away, and put his jaunty smirk back on. "He will not do it again. He has tested me, and found I am not wanting. You failed that test, not me. I am his, and he is with me, until the end of the world."

"Why?" asked Clovermead. She turned to look straight at Snuff. "I mean, I know how tempting he can be. I know it in my heart. But he is . . . repulsive. All he offers is killing and blood. Why do you stay with him?"

"Why?" Snuff's face spread in a glorious smile of infinite hunger endlessly sated. "Oh, girlie . . . Well, now, there I was, your age, or a little bit more, down in

225

Queensmart. I was in the greatest city in all Our Lady's lands, glorious even in its decay, and I was what they call 'a promising lad.' I was the pride of the rhetoricians — I could make an oration that called a hundred men to the recruiting office, or set a hundred women to tears. I was handy enough with my sword that I was tapped for lieutenant in the First Legion when I came of age. My father had promised me that I would be a member of the Senate by the time I was twenty-five, and high office would be mine as soon as I proved myself worthy of it. I had no doubt that I could achieve it soon enough.

"Yet somehow all those prospects didn't glitter so brightly. If Queensmart were the Empire of old, where I could command a legion as it conquered a dozen cities — if I could compose a code of law that would last a thousand years — why, even if I could build temples to Our Lady in strange lands that never knew her, and bring distant peoples to worship her, I thought even that might be something worth doing. But what could I look forward to in Queensmart's dotage? Petty wars in the Thirty Towns that could at best delay the retreat of our Empire a few years more. Squabbles among Senators, all bribed by our neighbors, about which temporizing policies our child Empress should adopt. What part could I play? At best I could have risen to be the iron man who fights a few vain years to save a dying city — Lucifer Snuff, tyrant, who abolished the Senate, deposed the Empress, and revived the power of Queensmart for a generation, before it vanished forever. Ah, no. I had read enough history books already. Those men are loved or hated while they live, and forgotten, save by scholars, as soon as the earth covers their coffins."

"It's always worth fighting for Our Lady," said

Clovermead. "It doesn't matter who remembers you on earth. She'll know."

"So the nuns told me," said Snuff. "It's a funny thing, girlie. About the same time I realized that I didn't want to serve a dying Empire, I realized that I'd never believed in Our Lady. I'd mouthed the words the nuns told me, I'd done the things they told me, but I didn't feel her in my heart. I saw the glitter in her temples, but I knew that glitter was much tarnished since the temples had been built by glorious Empresses three centuries ago. I saw the Abbess in her glorious robes that had grown thread-bare of late. I saw the charity of the nuns, and I saw poor men curse the nuns once they had received their bread and soup. I saw them flourish stone bear-teeth when the nuns weren't looking, and I heard them say, 'One day we won't need your charity. One day Ursus will come, and then we'll take what we want.' Those words struck a flame in me." Snuff groaned with pain and he massaged his thigh, right by Boulderbash's heavy flesh.

After a moment he continued. "Garum isn't far from Queensmart. I slipped out of the city, and I rode to my master's capital. I saw his armies spreading out and conquering. I saw his temples rising, huge and black. I saw the slave codes read out to new gangs of laborers, and I knew they would last for centuries. Oh, there was scope for glory in Lord Ursus' service. And I saw sacrifice and murder. I knew it should horrify me, but it didn't. I hungered to join the killers. And then I did." He smiled. "Lord Ursus came into my soul. He was my friend, my guide, my master, everything terrible and everything I could ever want to love. He said, 'We will kill together, and you will live a glorious life. You will be great in my service, and your name will ring down the centuries.' I did not return to Queensmart. I filed my teeth, and I put on the furs of a bear-priest. I gave all my talents, all my service, all my heart to Lord Ursus."

"I still don't understand," Clovermead said in a low voice. "Ursus came to me, too. He said all the same things. But I was in despair. I'd learned that Father wasn't really my father, and that he had lied to me all my life. It was such a treachery that I couldn't bear it. I wouldn't have turned to Ursus for anything less than that. And you were just ambitious?"

It was dark now. Snuff's eyes glittered. "I prayed to Our Lady, girlie. I sat there in Garum, watching the sacrifices, and I felt the urge to join the bear-priests come over me. I said, 'Save me, Lady. You know what I want. You know it is evil. Just give me a word. Show me your light. I've heard tell of it all my life, I've seen it painted on the walls of your temples, but you've never let me see it myself. Show your glory to me, and I won't commit these sins. One speck of light, and I'll fight against Ursus all my life.'" Snuff laughed, and there was a hint of old and terrible sorrow in his laugh. "I saw no light. I was left to myself and left to Lord Ursus. I knew then that the nuns were liars. Our Lady never was—or if she was, she was long gone. I was happy to join Lord Ursus after that. I'm glad to extirpate that lie."

"I've seen her light," said Clovermead. "She's talked to me—"

"Lies," hissed Snuff. "Hallucinations and dreams. There is only darkness. There is only Ursus. If she's there, why did she abandon me?" He clacked his teeth at Clovermead. "Shut up, or I'll bite out your lying tongue." He coughed. "Is your curiosity satisfied, girlie? Then be quiet. Let me sleep. Ah, Ursus' teeth, my leg hurts."

They both lapsed into silence, and then Snuff fell into labored, moaning sleep. In the silent night Boulderbash's thoughts grew louder. *Ambrosius,* she cried. *Ambrosius, where are you? I'm dying, Ambrosius.*

He's dead, said Clovermead. *I'm here. Me, Clovermead, his daughter. Please, tell me what I can do to ease your pain.*

Clovermead? She abandoned me to darkness. Boulderbash growled. *I don't want her. I want Ambrosius.*

He's dead! Clovermead repeated. *There's only me.*

Then I want to die, said Boulderbash. Her breathing was shallower than ever. *I want to be with Ambrosius. This world is so dark and there is no hope. Let me die and be with him. He was kind to me.*

"Don't die, Boulderbash," said Clovermead out loud. She was weeping now. "Oh, Lady, don't let her die. I've abandoned her so often. Let her live."

And there was only terrible silence and terrible darkness.

"You see?" said Snuff. He was awake again. "You call, and she doesn't come."

"We're not just supposed to wait for her all the time," said Clovermead angrily, desperately. "Sometimes we're supposed to do something."

"What?" asked Snuff. "What are you going to do, girlie?" He laughed. "Use your father's precious sword? Lord Ursus told me about that little trick of yours. Free her from Lord Ursus, for all the good that'll do. Then she'll be free and dead."

"The sword just helps me think how to use the power properly," said Clovermead. "I can free bears from Ursus by myself." She drew Firefly from its scabbard, and looked at the medallions her father had carved. There the boy Ambrosius freed Boulderbash

229

from the steel trap. There the man lifted his sword up to the moon.

"Is that it, Lady?" asked Clovermead. She got onto one knee and lifted up the naked blade. "You showed me how it happened. You gave Father and me the power to turn into bears, the power to free all the bears, because Boulderbash asked you to reward him for saving her from the trap. Oh, Lady, I love being a bear, and I want so much to free all the other bears, but I'd give up all the power you've ever given me if she could just live. Sorrel said I keep on choosing to let people suffer for the greater good, and he's right, I have. Not this time, Lady. I offer you my father's sword. I offer you back the gifts you've given me. Lady, maybe the bears will be enslaved to Ursus forever, but I can't ask Boulderbash to pay that price again. Take my power and let her live."

Nothing happened. The moon shone on, the stars twinkled, and Boulderbash was still dying. There was a deafening silence from the sky.

"I told you," said Snuff. Clovermead looked up, and he was crying. "Hallucinations and dreams. There is only darkness."

Clovermead cried too, as pity for Snuff swept through her. "I hate you so," she said. "Why are you weeping?" She pounded her fist against the ground, and she let her sword fall. "I loathe you. I despise you." She took a great, shuddering breath, and yelled up to the sky. "Heal him, too, Lady! Let him live. He's evil, and he'll destroy the world for Lord Ursus if he can, but let him live." She sobbed. "Take my power for him. Show him there's something more than darkness and make him stop crying."

A great roar echoed through the gorge, and

Clovermead *felt* light burst from her. It streamed from her, streamed from Firefly, and flew to Boulderbash and Snuff. Boulderbash jerked, and her eyes flew open. The gash along her stomach closed, and became a faded scar in seconds. Her bones reknit. With a glad roar she surged to her feet. Beneath her, Snuff screamed as light straightened his leg and uncrushed his flesh. Both of them were healthy and whole, and Clovermead's light was drained from her.

She tried to turn large and furry, but she couldn't. She was small and human and nothing more, and she was very tired. She couldn't lift Firefly if her life depended on it.

You saved me, Boulderbash rumbled incredulously. She ran a claw lightly over her healed flesh. *After all the times you've abandoned me, you rescue me now.* The white bear was laughing, crying, and furious, all at once. *Am I supposed to thank you?* She shook her head uncertainly, and slowly she padded a few feet toward Clovermead. *Am I supposed to forgive—* And she couldn't finish the question. The uncertainty, the shadow of gentleness, drained from her face. Boulderbash snarled at Clovermead with uncontrollable hostility. *I don't care if I owe you my life. I'll kill you anyway.*

"No," said Snuff. His face was pale in the firelight. Slowly he got to his feet and put his weight on his once-crushed leg. It supported him easily. "Don't you do that, steed of mine. You be grateful to the girlie. And I've still got your son's blood-net, don't you forget that. Try to bite her, and I'll rein you in."

Let me kill her, Boulderbash roared. *We are healthy now. We are cured. Kill the treacherous girl. She deserves it. Please, Snuff. Why are you being merciful now?*

"I have a sense of honor, she-bear," he said. "I did not abandon it when I entered Lord Ursus' service." Boulderbash growled unhappily, and drew back from Clovermead. Snuff swallowed hard. "Such light. Why wasn't there such light for me?"

"I don't know," said Clovermead numbly. "I don't understand Our Lady either. She wouldn't take my power for Boulderbash, but she took it for you. It doesn't make any sense."

"She is a fool," said Snuff. He looked at Clovermead, and his hands shook. "She depends on my gratitude. I can feel that dribbling out of me already. I could wring your neck so easily. Lord Ursus would be grateful to me."

"Do what you like," Clovermead whispered. "But do it quickly. I want to sleep."

Kill her, Boulderbash repeated. *Nothing can make up for the evil she's done me.*

"I should," said Snuff. "I owe Lord Ursus her death." He strode toward Clovermead with his hands out, long nails by her throat—and then he trembled, and his hands moved. He seized her shoulder, and he wrenched it. Clovermead screamed as it popped back into its socket. "I owe you my life," he said. "Now we're quits. You should be able to clamber out of the gorge now."

Snuff lifted up his head to the dark sky. "Sky-Crone!" he called out. "I've seen your light at last, but it's too late. I'm one of your enemy's servants, now and forever. I will die for Lord Ursus, whatever happens, and my soul will follow his for all eternity. You know what I am, and I ask a boon of you. Give the girlie her powers back. I won't give you anything if you do. Nothing at all." He swallowed hard. "Just the satisfaction that you know I asked."

There was another great roar, and Clovermead felt strength return to her. For a moment her hands became paws, her mouth a snout, her ears long and tufted, and then she was human again. But she could change into a bear again, she could free bears again, and she would have wept with gratitude if she were strong enough.

"Let's go, Boulderbash," said Snuff. He patted the white bear companionably, and he grabbed a burning stick from the fire, to become a torch in his hand. "Let's climb out of this gorge. Back to Barleymill to gather the bear-priests and send for silver-bears from Bryony Hill, and then we'll come after the slaves and butcher them all for Lord Ursus. There'll be no defiance of him if I have anything to say about it."

Kill her, said Boulderbash implacably.

"I will the next time I see her," said Snuff amiably. His glittering eyes caught Clovermead's. "I shan't chase you too quickly, girlie. Leave the slaves and run. I'll give you time to get away." He smiled, so his teeth gleamed. "We're quits now, debts all paid, so this is a small kindness from your old friend Snuff. Take advantage. I don't plan on making a habit of mercy."

"I won't run," said Clovermead. "You know that."

Snuff shrugged. "Maybe you'll change your mind. Run before I meet you again in battle, girlie. I'll have no mercy for you then."

Clovermead laughed softly and bemusedly. "Will Lord Ursus forgive you?"

"He doesn't have a better servant than me," said Snuff, with a bubbling laugh. "He knows that well enough. And he knows I won't slack in his service again."

"Thank you," said Clovermead.

Snuff shrugged. "It's amusing," he said. "Whatever

happiness you get out of being a bear from now on—
whatever you do with that bear-strength of yours, however many bears you free—that'll be thanks to me. And
whatever I do will be thanks to you. What do you think
of that, girlie?" He turned up to the dark sky. "What
about you, Sky-Crone? What do you say to that?"

He beckoned Boulderbash, and turned away from
the fire. Laughing, brand in hand, he stalked off with the
white bear into the darkness, back toward Barleymill.
Clovermead could hear his laughter long after he had
disappeared from sight.

Then Clovermead slept.

Chapter Seventeen

CONSEQUENCES

CLOVERMEAD HAD BEEN ASLEEP, BUT NOW SHE WALKED in a barren, flat land under a scorching, brazen sun. The burned skeletons of trees dotted the landscape, and dry streambeds cracked the land. Rubble that once had been houses sprouted here and there. Rats scurried behind walls, and cawing crows hopped from tree to tree. Far off, vultures were eating the carcass of some carrion that Clovermead didn't want to look at too closely.

Lucifer Snuff walked by her side. He whistled happily as he walked, and he mopped sweat from his bald forehead with a handkerchief. His sweat was blood, and it stained the thin cloth a brilliant crimson. "Isn't this a fine place?" asked Snuff. "It took me a long time to perfect it, but a garden has to be made just right. Do you like it?" He grinned at Clovermead, and blinding sunlight glinted off his bronzed teeth.

"It's loathsome," said Clovermead. "Where are we? Garum?"

"No, no, this is Chandlefort. Don't you know your own home?" Snuff leaned down, picked up a chunk of masonry, and tossed it to Clovermead. It was rose-pink, and Clovermead recognized a piece of Chandlefort's walls with

235

horror. She looked around again, and now she could see the trace of Chandlefort's streets under the blowing dust. "Ah, I see you do! It took a long time to uproot the trees and get rid of the people, but my garden's done at last. It is lovely, girlie. I'm so glad you could help me make it."

"I never did," said Clovermead. "I never would. What do you mean?"

"You helped me out of the gorge," said Lucifer amiably. "That made all the difference. After that I led the bear-priests into battle, we drove the Tansyards from the Steppes, and then it was on to Chandlefort! Really, the war was won that summer, and there was nothing much left to do. Except for the killing. You don't want to hurry that too much." He giggled. "Thank you, girlie. I couldn't have done it without you."

"I'm not responsible," said Clovermead, horrified. "I didn't want this to happen."

"But it did," said Snuff tranquilly. "Will you come with me to the Castle? I have such a lovely collection of skeletons there. You'll recognize some of them."

"No!" cried Clovermead, and she ran away from Snuff as his laughter rose to an insane, joyful shriek. She raced over shifting sand, there was a forest ahead, and she took refuge in its shade from the terrible sun. The wind moaned oddly in the trees.

Boulderbash paced back and forth in the dark center of the forest. Her white fur was matted brown with blood. *Thank you for curing me,* she roared. *I have hunted well since then. I could never have been so magnificent without you.* She laughed. *To think I spent so long enslaved to my son! Now I am freely his, forever, thanks to you.*

I wanted to free you, said Clovermead. *Things just turned out wrong.*

They turned out right, said Boulderbash with satisfaction. She licked her lips. Her jaws were red. *I have treated humans as they deserve for a long time now. The little traitors are mine forever.*

How? asked Clovermead. *There's nothing living in the forest.*

Look up, said Boulderbash. Against her will, Clovermead did. The trees were not trees, but crosses, extending as far as she could see. It was not the wind moaning, but people, crucified, and the forest was nothing but a giant larder for Boulderbash.

"Lady curse you, Demoiselle," Clovermead heard the nearest piece of flesh moan. The words repeated, louder and louder, all through the forest of crucified men. "You did this. Lady's curse upon your head!"

You abandoned me, said Boulderbash, and she cried tears of blood. *You made me what I am. I will never forgive you.* She leaped at Clovermead—

Clovermead was in a marshland. A ragged, hobbling figure led a troop of bear-priests in the dawn light toward a hole from which smoke rose. He was a whipped cur, and he leaped to obey every barked order the bear-priests gave him. "Here they are," he said. "Don't hurt me. Hurt them instead. Leave me alone." He lifted a quavering finger to the mud hut, then stepped aside as the bear-priests leaped howling toward the door.

Lady Cindertallow came out of the hut. Her hair was white, her face lined with age, and she wore inch-thick spectacles on her nose. She still swung her sword agilely, though, and she slew two bear-priests in seconds. Then there were four bear-priests all around her, jabbing at her, and her sudden strength ebbed from her. She was an old woman fighting hopelessly. Clovermead wanted to

237

leap forward to help her, but she could not move, could not speak, was stuck behind glass to scream silently. A bear-priest clawed her mother's glasses from her face, and Lady Cindertallow was left to blink blindly in the marsh. She swung her sword at shadows. The bear-priests guffawed at her, and then one lunged forward and stuck his sword through Clovermead's mother's guts. Clovermead screamed so loudly that she couldn't hear her mother cry, and then her mother was falling, dying, dead.

Saraband came out of the hut. She had silver in her hair, and she was still a beautiful woman. "I am the last," she said calmly. "Do as you will. I will not fight you." Then she turned to the lurking figure, and her face twisted in shock, in bitterness, and finally forgiveness. "Never mind," she sighed at last. "Lady bless you." A bear-priest screamed a curse to hear Our Lady's name, and in a horrible instant his sword had lopped off Saraband's head. Clovermead averted her eyes and saw the hobbling figure face on —

It was Waxmelt. Her own father. He turned from the dead bodies, and he saw Clovermead, *saw her*, and wretched shame filled his face. "I'm sorry, Clovermead," he said. "I should have been stronger. Please forgive me." Ursus' laughter rolled through the sky like thunder, and a black cloud followed his hilarity and covered all the earth.

The marsh was gone, and Clovermead stood on a dark and moonless plain. Once the grass had stood head-high everywhere, but now it all had been burned and withered black by quicksilver. She walked amid the ashes of the Steppes. Ahead there was a lone campfire. Clovermead walked toward it, the only comforting light in the world.

Sorrel sat by the campfire—also older, with silver strands like Saraband's lining his hair. There was a terrible sadness in him. He looked up and he saw Clovermead.

His face twisted in loathing. "You," he said. "How dare you come to me again."

"Please," said Clovermead. "Don't turn on me too. I need a friend. I need you."

Sorrel snarled with black laughter. "You let this happen. Look at the Steppes—gone, destroyed, all because you let those monsters live. What idiocy was in you?"

"I couldn't kill them," said Clovermead. "Did you want me to just let them die?"

Sorrel drew his sword. "Yes, Clovermead. Most assuredly, yes. Look at what you have done." He stood up, and Clovermead saw two bodies by the fire. One was Mullein and one was Roan. They were emaciated with hunger. Clovermead knelt by them and touched them. They were cold, and the fire would never warm them again.

"Our Lady gave me my family back, beyond all hope, and now they are dead again," said Sorrel. "You did this. You!" He drew his sword, and there was pure and deadly hatred on his face. She could not move, and his sword lifted high—

He let it drop. The hatred drained from his face. All that was left was icy indifference, and that was far worse. He had ceased to care about her.

"I'm sorry," said Clovermead, but the words fluttered away in the darkness.

"Say your apologies to the dead," said Sorrel. He turned from her, left her forever, and walked into darkness.

The Steppes were gone, so was Sorrel, and so were the two bodies. There was no earth beneath her feet and no sky above her head. Clovermead stood alone in darkness.

In the emptiness, Our Lady whispered to her. *Why did you let them live?*

"Boulderbash was dying," said Clovermead. "Snuff, too. And he was crying for your light, Lady. I couldn't let him die in darkness." She wept helplessly. "I didn't know what would happen, Lady. How could I?"

You do not have that excuse now, said the whisper. *You know what your ill-timed mercy may lead to. Do you regret it?*

"*May?*" asked Clovermead in sudden hope. *It doesn't have to end like this?*

It doesn't have to, said Our Lady sadly. *But chances are it will.* There was a pause for a moment. *If you want, Clovermead, I can undo some hours that have passed, and you can make another choice. Shall I grant you that wish?*

"Yes!" said Clovermead instantly. She saw Snuff smiling in his garden of delight, blood-smeared Boulderbash in her final corruption, her father a traitor again, her mother and Saraband murdered, Roan's and Mullein's starved corpses on the wasted Steppes, and Sorrel with his back turned on her forever. She wept, and she opened her mouth to say "Yes!" again with all her heart.

But she could not quite. She saw Boulderbash lying still as death before her, saw vicious Snuff cry in wretched darkness, and she couldn't be the person who turned away from them and let them die in the night. Sorrel turned his back, and his heart was dead to her, but she could not let Snuff weep with such terrible sorrow.

"I've done enough cruel things for the greater good, Lady," said Clovermead. "I suppose I will again. Not this time. Snuff saw you, and I won't take that away from him." Her heart was bleak, and icy tears trickled down her cheeks.

You know what may happen, said Our Lady. *Are you sure?*

Clovermead sighed. "Even if I knew for certain, I wouldn't change what I've done. I'm a fool, Lady, but let the world go on. I'll fight for you as best I can."

Very well, said Our Lady, and then Clovermead felt fingers gently stroke the cold tears from her cheeks. *I am a fool too. I would choose as you have done.*

Then Clovermead was weeping helplessly, and Our Lady was weeping with her. Their tears mingled. "Oh, Lady, please don't let Sorrel stop caring. Anything but that."

I will do what I can, said Our Lady. *And you do what you can, and perhaps the world will turn out all right in the end.*

"Perhaps?" asked Clovermead.

I cannot offer you certainty, Clovermead. All I can give you on earth is hope.

"I guess that will have to do," said Clovermead. And then she couldn't help but ask, "Why didn't you show yourself to Snuff when he called to you in Garum?"

I did, said Our Lady sadly. *He did not see me.* Then she caressed Clovermead a last time. *He saw me at last tonight. You have done that for him.*

"I still hate him," Clovermead whispered, and then once more she fell asleep.

Chapter Eighteen

THE LONG RETREAT

THE NEXT MORNING CLOVERMEAD TURNED TO BEAR-
shape and scrambled up the north slope of the gorge. Her
foreleg still complained, but she was able to put weight
on it and climb. She paused for breath when she had
reached the top, then after a few minutes she began to
lope northward, sniffing for the scent of the fleeing
slaves. She ran along Yarrow's Way. To the left the Farry
Heights lifted high in an impenetrable maze of rock,
scrub, and pine forests, while to the right was a low scarp
thinly covered with a forest of oak, elm, and beech.
Humans could scramble over that ridge, though horses
could not. Yarrow's Way itself was a long and gentle
upland valley that had become richly green in the late
spring, dotted with white-flowering apple trees and azal-
eas blooming bright and pink. Wildflowers sprouted in
the grass. The valley was half grassland and half garden.

Soon Clovermead caught the smell of the slaves.
They're two days ahead of me, she thought. She snuffled
again. *Sorrel's only one day ahead. Oh, Lady, I can still smell
his blood on the grass. Don't let anything happen to him. Don't
let him die.* She whimpered and tried to go faster, but she
was too tired, and the shards in her paws ached. She

went no faster than the slaves that day, and lost ground against Sorrel on his swift horse. That night she rested by a stream and gulped a meal of grass and fish. *Don't let him die, Lady,* Clovermead repeated before she went to sleep.

She followed the slaves for the next three days. Crumpled rock slopes regularly interrupted the valley from the second day on, and slowed her to a crawl at human speed. At the end of the second day, Clovermead smelled that Sorrel had caught up with the slaves. After that she couldn't smell his blood any longer. *Thank you, Lady,* she said, and she yipped with happiness and relief. As she recovered her strength, she came a little nearer to the slaves each day. She ate more grass and fish, and even once an unwary prairie dog to sate her hunger. Her paws hurt constantly from the iron slivers in them.

On the third night she heard hunting horns behind her. The bear-priests were giving chase at last.

Clovermead dreamed again. She couldn't remember her dream in the morning, but she knew that Lucifer Snuff had been in it, and that she had woken up with her throat raw from screaming.

On the fourth day the valley turned into a straightaway of grass again, and Clovermead raced to catch up with the slaves. She could smell them nearer and nearer in front of her, and at dusk she finally caught up with them as they camped by a streambank. The slaves had woven grass into crude nets, and caught fish for their dinner. Three of the Yellowjackets rode sentry around their camp, while the other three sat exhausted on the ground. Bergander, on sentry-duty, raised his sword when he saw Clovermead, then lowered it when he recognized her golden fur. Lewth cursed when he saw her;

Sergeant Algere only nodded recognition. Clovermead staggered into the camp, and sniffed for Sorrel's scent. She found him at a campfire with Roan and Mullein, turned human, and collapsed by their side.

"Clovermead!" Sorrel cried out. He crawled over to her, reached out his hand to hers—and Clovermead gasped as he touched her palm. Sorrel instantly drew back his hand and looked at her scraped flesh. "Have you been running on these, Clovermead?"

"I'm afraid so," said Clovermead. "How do they look?"

"Awful," said Sorrel. He tried to smile at her. "You do not have any luck at avoiding wounds."

"You should speak," said Clovermead. "But I heal quickly. It's one of the nice things that come with the bear-shape." Clovermead looked around the fire for a moment. Mullein huddled in a tattered blanket, her flesh glowed silver wherever it was open to the air, and the crisscross on her cheeks were as bright as the moon in the sky. Her feet were so much pulped flesh. Roan sat by her side, and crooned a lullaby to her in Tansyard that distracted Mullein a little from her pain. Roan's hands and feet were still bandaged, but she looked much healthier than she had been. Sorrel was the healthiest of the three: All he had was a wounded calf. Clovermead gestured at his leg. "Can you ride?"

"Slowly," said Sorrel—and he hopped between Mullein and Clovermead. Mullein had thrown off her blanket, and had begun to crawl toward Clovermead. "No, Mullein!" he said. "Not her."

"Clovermead need help," Mullein said between chattering teeth. "I Shaman-Mother. I heal her."

"You are a very sick girl," said Sorrel firmly, and he

blocked Mullein's arm as she reached for Clovermead. "Other people can help her." He shouted out in Tansyard, and there was a rustle of movement at a nearby campfire. "See? A lady who knows doctoring will come to take care of her hands. Mullein, you must stop doing this."

"This what Shaman-Mother does," said Mullein, but she sat back and let Roan put her blanket on her shoulders once more. "No one else can." She looked round at the campfires dotting the night. "Cyan Cross die, without me. You know, Brother."

"I know," Sorrel whispered, then he cleared his throat. "Rest for now." He spoke a sentence to Roan in Tansyard, she nodded, and she started to sing again. Mullein lay down on the grass by her mother's side, and closed her eyes. Roan stroked her hair, still singing, and after a while Mullein fell asleep.

A Tansyard woman came to the campfire, sat down by Clovermead's side, and examined her palms. Then she put her thumb and forefinger together, and began to extract the iron filings one by one with her short, sharp fingernails. Clovermead cried out as the shards pulled free from her flesh, and Sorrel reached out to hold her forearm steady, to give her what comfort he could. After an hour the woman with sharp fingernails let go of her hands. Another Tansyard woman who had come up to the campfire bathed Clovermead's hands in a bowl of stream-water and bandaged them in soft cloth.

Roan looked at Clovermead and spoke to her. "She says you are very brave," said Sorrel. "She says she is grateful to you for saving her life. She had thought she would fear bears forever, but now she will always think of you when she sees one. She thanks you in Our Lady's name." Roan made the crescent sign, bobbed her head to Clovermead—then turned once more to Mullein. She looked at her daughter with terrible worry, and began to sing for her again. In her sleep, Mullein smiled.

The bear-priests' horns blew in the darkness behind them. Sorrel frowned. "This slave-break was not, perhaps, the best idea in the world. They will catch up with us."

"Don't give up yet," said Clovermead. "Maybe something will turn up."

"I hope so," said Sorrel, but there was no hope in his voice. "We both should rest. Shall we sleep?"

"Yes," said Clovermead. She slid down onto the grass, utterly exhausted. "Good night," she said. Then she closed her eyes and fell into a dreamless sleep.

The next day Clovermead and Sorrel were both put astride Brown Barley, Sorrel in front and Clovermead in back, and they rode among the slaves while the Yellowjackets formed a loose screen behind them. Mullein, wrapped tightly in blankets, rode with Roan on Auroche's back. The slaves walked slowly along the valley. Every now and then one would stumble over to Mullein, and hold out her hand for Mullein to touch. Each time the slave recovered some of her color and her health, and walked on with a new spring in her step; each time Mullein grew more drawn, and her silver crisscross grew brighter still. The slaves, still shedding quicksilver dust, left a trail of trampled grass behind them as they fled, whose blades were speckled with silver, and withering here and there to black. The bear-priests would have no trouble following their trail.

At noon Clovermead heard a rumble in the north, and then a hundred horsemen shouting greetings in

Tansyard came galloping toward them. They streamed among the slaves and the Yellowjackets, and Clovermead saw that Sergeant Algere's eyes were as bright with relief as hers. Lewth wept openly, and even Bergander was croaking prayers of thanks to Our Lady.

"Which Horde are they?" Clovermead asked Sorrel.

"The Green Spike Horde," said Sorrel. "Do you remember how I disguised you as one of them as we sneaked into the Army of Low Branding? See, they are as dark-complected as I said. Also they wear small drums at their sides—there, that warrior is beating his drum to send a message to his brethren—and their hair curls like peppercorns."

"An awful lot of the people in the White Star Horde wore bear-teeth," said Clovermead worriedly. She scanned the Green Spike warriors, but every one wore a silver crescent. "I don't think any of these do."

Sorrel smiled. "The Green Spike Horde has always been especially devoted to Our Lady, ever since they wandered north into the Steppes. They say they are the newest Tansyard Horde, but that they are the best Horde, because they love her so well. I do not know that they are superior to Cyan Cross, but they are a worthy nation. Sit up, Clovermead. Here comes their leader to talk to you." He slipped off Brown Barley, supporting himself on his way down with his arms, then rested on his good leg. "I will be a translator-on-foot. The Demoiselle of Chandlefort should ride by herself when she talks with a Horde Chief."

The Green Spike Horde Chief rode up to Clovermead, respectfully put his hand to his chest, and spoke several long sentences in Tansyard. "He greets the Demoiselle of Chandlefort, whom he recognizes by her yellow hair," Sorrel translated. "He says that a messenger from the White Star Horde has come in Chandlefort's name to request the Green Spike Horde to join them at Yarrow's Bowl in a war against Lord Ursus, and that the Green Spike Horde has accepted the invitation. He says the Horde was camped not far from Barleymill when the messenger came from the White Star Horde, and that as they rode north they saw the bear-priests marching north along Yarrow's Way, hurrying as if in some wild pursuit. He wondered what they chased, and came to take a look. Now that he knows what they are chasing, he offers us the assistance of the Green Spike Horde."

"Tell him I will pray to Our Lady to bless him forever," said Clovermead. "Tell him Chandlefort will always be grateful to his Horde, and that we accept his kind offer." Sorrel spoke in Tansyard, and the Horde Chief nodded gravely. "Ask him if he can send his warriors to cover our rear against the bear-priests. The valley's narrow enough that a hundred of them ought to be able to slow down a thousand bear-priests."

The Horde Chief listened to Sorrel, then spoke again. "He says they can hold against two thousand bear-priests, because they are Green Spike warriors, and because they are fighting for Our Lady," said Sorrel. Then the Horde Chief smiled a little, and spoke again. "But they are not foolhardy either. With your permission, they will send a few warriors on to Yarrow's Bowl and out into the Steppes, to see if they can bring back any other Hordes as reinforcements. He says Our Lady is no lover of bravado."

"Tell him that sounds sensible to me," said Clovermead. The Horde Chief nodded, put his hand to his chest again, then rode off. "Does that mean I can stop worrying for a while now?"

"I believe so," said Sorrel. "The Green Spike Horde has solid warriors. They do not scare easily, and they are difficult to kill." He remounted Brown Barley.

"Good," said Clovermead. "Wake me up in a fortnight." The sun was bright in the cloudless sky, but she closed her eyes, and she promptly fell asleep. When next she woke, it was evening, and they had traveled another ten miles to the north.

The next week Clovermead, Sorrel, and the Yellowjackets spent recuperating among the slaves while the Green Spike warriors kept the line against the advancing bear-priests. The bear-priests were still out of sight, several hours march behind them, but their horns blew constantly. The Green Spike warriors had concentrated in the valley behind them, though a few rode along the ridge lines to make sure no bear-priests sneaked by to flank them. A steady trickle of wounded Green Spike warriors rode back to the camp to have their wounds bandaged. Each night they sang a funeral chant for the warriors who had fallen during the day.

Mullein let the Green Spike warriors live and die on their own. She saved what strength she had to keep the slaves alive and on their feet. She grew thinner by the day. Roan spent what time she could talking with the son she had not seen for so many years, had thought was dead, but she was busy watching after her daughter racked with pain.

"Green Spike's warriors fight well, but I think the bear-priests are leisurely in their pursuit," said Sorrel by another campfire at the end of the week. It was still brisk at night, though the days had become hot and long. "I wonder why."

Snuff is being kind to me, thought Clovermead. *He's giving me a chance to run away.* "I think I can join the Green Spike warriors tomorrow," she said out loud. She held up the new pink skin of her palms. "They're still tender, but I think I could walk on them, as a bear."

"I'm also ready to fight," said Sergeant Algere. He looked at the Yellowjackets around him. All of them nodded, even Lewth. Algere smiled lopsidedly. "After all, this isn't suicide any longer. It's just folly." Bergander laughed.

"My wound is healed enough," said Sorrel. Gingerly, he touched the ugly, raw scab where the arrow had gone into his calf, winced, and sighed. "I, too, will go into battle with you."

The next day Clovermead, Sorrel, and the Yellowjackets joined the line of Green Spike warriors. Clovermead gasped when she saw the bear-priests at last: Fifteen hundred soldiers, marching in columns, came tramping steadily along the valley after the slaves and the Tansyards. A few cavalry on the outskirts probed along the ridgetops, but it was overwhelmingly an army of infantry. They came in silence, save for the sigh of dust rising from the grass beneath them and the tramp of their feet.

In the middle of them, Clovermead thought she saw a white bear. She cast out her mind, but the distance was too great.

Flee, Demoiselle, she thought she heard Snuff say. *Go while you still can.* But the words were very faint in her mind, and then they were gone.

I can't, Clovermead called out to the silence. *I won't.* Then she turned into a bear and moved to the center of the Tansyard line, opposite to where the bear-priests were thickest and came the fastest. The front row of bear-priests paused a moment when they saw her, then came on more slowly. More bear-priests shuffled to the middle of the valley.

That afternoon the bear-priests suddenly attacked on the right edge of the line, toward the Farry Heights. A hundred of them broke into a run, and a cloud of arrows rose from just behind the running mass of bear-priests, aimed at the nearest Tansyards. Half a dozen Tansyards were hit, three fell from their horses, and then the bear-priests were on them to hack at their fallen bodies. Clovermead stayed where she was, snarling at the bear-priests opposite her to keep them from advancing, but Tansyards from all along the line came riding at once, shooting their own arrows and concentrating on the right bulge, and the bear-priests fell back, leaving a few wounded and dead of their own. The Tansyards swiftly fell back another hundred yards from the bear-priests, and thinned their line as they sent newly wounded warriors to join the slaves. The bear-priests crept forward to occupy the terrain the Tansyards had abandoned. More Tansyards arrived from among the slaves, healed enough to take the place of the warriors who had gone. Still, there were fewer Tansyards than before.

That night fifty warriors of the Red Spiral Horde arrived in the camp. "We need more, don't we?" asked Clovermead.

Sorrel shrugged wearily. "Normally I would think so, but the bear-priests are coming slowly. We may even make it to Yarrow's Bowl, where, Lady willing, an army of Yellowjackets and Tansyards will be waiting for us."

I doubt it, thought Clovermead. *Snuff won't be that kind to me.* She looked at Sorrel's face, and she saw he had no hope for the future either.

251

The next day the bear-priests charged Clovermead's
section of the line. There was no time to prepare — suddenly
there were bear-priests charging toward her with drawn
scimitars, and arrows whistling all around her, and
Clovermead charged the bear-priests not because she was
brave, but to get out of the way of the arrows. There was a
bear-priest right in front of her, and she struck out with a
claw, raked his sword-arm, and smashed him to the ground.
A scimitar sliced through a corner of her ear, and
Clovermead hit back, bit she didn't know who, and more
scimitars were scraping along her fur. Then the bear-priests
were retreating from her, followed by pursuing Tansyard
arrows, and there were another two Tansyards and four
bear-priests dead on the ground.

"Still alive, Clovermead?" asked Sorrel. He had been
slashed along the back of his hand. "Me too. I think I am
even well enough to stay on the line. And you?"
Clovermead twitched her ear — the cut was shallow, and
nothing else had done more than score her skin. She
growled agreement. "Not to worry. I think we have
bloodied them enough that they will stay away from us
the rest of the day."

What about tomorrow? Clovermead asked herself, and
then she turned to keep an eye on the bear-priests. They
advanced inexorably.

The next few days were a blur. Somewhere in them
Clovermead must have eaten and slept, but she seemed
always to be pacing back and forth, and growling at bear-
priests who came on, despite her growls. Sometimes there
was sudden combat, the whir of arrows, the clash of
swords, but it ended as quickly as it started. Snuff was
somewhere among the bear-priests, and it was because of
his kindness that they weren't dead. Oh, Lady, he was still

waiting for her to run, and every day Clovermead was more and more tempted to take up his offer. Every arrow that whipped past her strained her nerves a little more. And now there were screams in the eastern distance, silver-bears coming closer from the Steppes. Soon they would join the bear-priests, and Snuff surely couldn't delay anymore after that. The bear-priests would, at last, attack with all their might.

A bear-priest struck Lewth through the guts with a scimitar, and he died. Dunnock, a silent trooper who had never exchanged two words with Clovermead that summer, died from an arrow that pierced his skull. *Two,* thought Clovermead. *Three.* She couldn't quite remember what she was counting, but she made sure to keep track.

Day after day they went, and then one day she heard the sound of trumpets ahead of her as they bugled out a Yellowjacket marching song. Then came the trumpet call of Low Branding and the chanting of Tansyards, and Clovermead felt tears trickling down her cheeks. She looked up and down the line. Once there had been more than one hundred and fifty Tansyards and Yellowjackets, but only seventy warriors remained, and half of them were wounded. In front of them the bear-priests looked uneasy for a moment at the sounds of trumpets and chants, but then a few horsed officers among them rode up and down their lines, barking encouraging words. The bear-priests continued their advance.

I don't care, thought Clovermead. *We've made it, and I didn't run. Oh, Lady, thank you.*

The valley widened out to a circle a mile in diameter, backed by sheer cliffs rising into the Farry Heights, and they had come to Yarrow's Bowl at last. From the west the soldiers of Chandlefort and Low Branding were still coming into the Bowl from a pass that cut across the Heights toward the Whetstone River. There were almost a thousand of them, half Yellowjackets and half Low Branding soldiers. From the east, two thousand Tansyards streamed into the Bowl from the Tansy Steppes. Minute by minute, Yarrow's Bowl was filling up with friendly soldiers.

The slaves staggered behind the oncoming soldiers, and collapsed onto the grass at the edge of the cliffs. Roan hobbled down from Auroche, took glowing, trembling Mullein in her arms, and pulled her to the ground. Sorrel collapsed by his mother and sister, Clovermead turned human, and she was helplessly smiling as the soldiers rode up to her. There was her mother and Fetterlock, there were Yellowjackets and Low Branding mercenaries, and there were Tansyards in a rainbow riot of different tattoos.

"Clovermead!" Lady Cindertallow cried out, and she swung down from her horse and ran to embrace her daughter. They held each other tightly for a long minute, and then Lady Cindertallow drew back a second to look her daughter up and down. "What happened to you? Never mind, you can tell me later. I should have known you'd be in trouble of some sort. I thought you were coming straight to Yarrow's Bowl."

"With a small detour to Barleymill," said Clovermead, and she almost laughed to see her mother's face turn pale. "I'm alive. And I brought some bear-priests after me." She let go of her mother, and turned to Fetterlock. "You said you wanted a chance to catch the bear-priests' army? I've brought them here for you. Two thousand of them, maybe more."

Fetterlock glanced at the south end of the Bowl, where the bear-priests were beginning to march into the valley, and he turned a little pale. "I did not expect you to be quite so eager to carry out my wishes. Next time I will express a mild hope that Ursus can be conveyed to us bound and trussed, and wait for you to deliver him." He looked back at the oncoming Hordes, then at the soldiers of Chandlefort and Low Branding, and he looked a little more confident. "The odds are as good as we shall ever have. We might as well have our battle here."

"I agree," said Lady Cindertallow. She turned to Fetterlock. "Horde Chief—I understand from the messengers Clovermead sent that you are the Horde Chief?"

"Truly," said Fetterlock. "I apologize for the small deception, Milady."

"Lady grant that you never practice a large one," said Lady Cindertallow drily. "At least not on me. But there was no harm done by your trickery, so let us forget it." Then she unlooped a white-gold star from her neck, and held it out to Fetterlock. "I believe this belongs to you, Horde Chief?"

"So it does," said Fetterlock, and he tied the pendant around his neck once more. "And I am here at midsummer, as I promised you." He looked around the Linstocker army. "Is the Mayor of Low Branding also here?"

"He sailed down the Whetstone with me, but he stayed with a regiment to guard the boats. His feet are too gouty for him to ride anymore." Lady Cindertallow nodded at a Low Branding patrician a little ways behind her. "General Spinel leads the Low Brandingmen." Now she turned to look south. "Those bear-priests look too tired to attack right away, and I know my soldiers need a rest, to recover from their long march. I think our battle will be tomorrow morning. I'll have my soldiers get as much sleep as possible before then. I'll set up pickets halfway up the Bowl. Will you have some Tansyards join them?" Fetterlock nodded. "We can make more plans later this evening. Let's get ourselves settled down first."

"Agreed," said Fetterlock. "I will give the warriors their instructions." He bowed to Lady Cindertallow, then to Clovermead, and he rode back to the Hordes.

Lady Cindertallow saw Clovermead was wobbling on her feet. Smiling, she pushed her daughter down to the grass. "You, rest. You're not needed for a while."

"Thank you," said Clovermead. Her mother rode off, and then Clovermead just let herself rest on the green meadow.

Sergeant Algere sat down beside her. "I wonder if Habick and Corporal Naquaire are here," he said. "It seems like years since I saw them."

"Just seven weeks," said Clovermead. She shook her head in wonder. "Thank you, Sergeant."

"I wasn't fighting for you, after we reached Barleymill," said Algere. "Or for Milady. It was for that skeleton on the cross. And those slaves." He sighed. "Poor Lewth. I should have let him go." He staggered to his feet. "I need to find a pallet," he mumbled, and he wandered off.

For a while Clovermead watched her mother putting the allied armies into order and preparing them for the oncoming battle. Then she fell asleep.

Chapter Nineteen

THE BATTLE AT YARROW'S BOWL

CLOVERMEAD WOKE AT DAWN TO THE SCREAM OF silver-bears and the sound of horns. The bear-priests brayed derisively at their foes and Clovermead leaped up—

"They are not attacking yet," said Sorrel. He sat by her side, calmly heating a pot of oatmeal over a fire. "They are merely making sure we don't sleep in. Look, they are not assembled for an attack yet. I think they will have breakfast first, to see that they are well fed." It was true. The bear-priests were taking rations from their packs and gulping them down. They kept their scimitars close to them, but they were not going to attack just yet. "So we have time to eat too," Sorrel continued. He put his palm over the steaming pot, nodded with satisfaction, and ladled oatmeal into two wooden bowls. "You have spent fifteen hours or so asleep. Are you well rested?"

Clovermead yawned. "I guess so," she said. "But you shouldn't have let me sleep! You've done just as much as I have—"

"And I have slept a mere thirteen hours." Sorrel blew on his oatmeal. "Do not worry, Clovermead. Neither of us has been needed."

"Where's Mother?" asked Clovermead. She shoveled a small bit of oatmeal into her mouth. It scalded her throat, but it tasted wonderful.

"Over on that little hill," said Sorrel. He gestured to a knoll a hundred yards away, where Lady Cindertallow sat on horseback. He looked at Lady Cindertallow, then down at his yellow uniform. "I wonder if your mother has been informed yet that I am no longer a Yellowjacket in good standing?"

"Don't worry. If she yells at you, I'll yell back, and louder."

"Then indeed I should have no fears," said Sorrel. "I have faith in your lungs." For a moment they smiled at each other.

They finished their breakfast, and then they rode over to join Lady Cindertallow and Fetterlock. "Good morning, Clovermead," her mother greeted her. "You always seem to have trouble getting up in the morning."

"I got up at daybreak!" Clovermead protested—and then she saw her mother was smiling. "That's me. Late for the morning hunt at home, late for the morning battle abroad. I hope I haven't delayed you."

"I think you've showed up in time." Lady Cindertallow's eyes strayed to the bear-priests opposite, then returned to Clovermead. "I'm sorry we didn't talk last night. I came to see you, but you were deep asleep. I thought it better to let you rest."

"I'm sorry too, Mother," said Clovermead. She swallowed, and kneed Auroche a little closer to Lady Cindertallow. "I can't remember," she said in a low voice. "Is the Lady Cindertallow supposed to direct her soldiers from behind, or lead them into battle?"

"Opinions vary. My advisers always suggest the

former. I find the latter is essential for my self-respect."
She saw Clovermead was about to speak, and she shook
her head. "I don't think the Demoiselle's counsel will
make me change my mind."

"Pity."

"True. It's the funniest coincidence, though. I was
about to suggest that the Demoiselle could stay behind
the lines and guard those slaves she brought out of
Barleymill. By all accounts, she's already done enough
fighting these last few weeks."

Oh, Lady, I'm tired of fighting, thought Clovermead, but
somehow the thoughts had turned into words and
blurted out of her mouth. She couldn't help but laugh.
"And just plain tired. Thank you, Mother, but the
Demoiselle will decline your kind offer. Can't you just
imagine what I'd say back in Chandlefort? 'Sorry, I mis-
placed my mother.' 'Where did you leave her?' 'Oh, I left
her on the front lines at Yarrow's Bowl.'" Clovermead
shook her head. "They wouldn't think much of me. I
don't think I'd think much of myself either."

"This search for self-respect will be the death of all of
us." Lady Cindertallow treated her daughter to a mordant
grimace. "I like the sound of that. Put that on my tomb-
stone." Lady Cindertallow brought her horse back a step
from Clovermead, put on her spectacles, and squinted
through them at the solid mass of bear-priests at the south
end of Yarrow's Bowl. The bear-priests had hoisted up
their scarlet flag with the great black bear. The allied
armies had formed a solid line opposite the bear-priests,
along the north end of the Bowl. Behind them sat the
slaves, too exhausted to do more than sit and wait for the
result of the battle. The allies had scores of flags —
Chandlefort's burning bee, Low Branding's sapphire

pike, and all the different Tansyard flags. "I hear you've been fighting off these bear-priests for a week now," Lady Cindertallow continued more loudly, so their companions could hear her too. "How on earth did so few of you do that?"

Gratitude, thought Clovermead. *Mercy*. She shrugged awkwardly. "I think they were waiting for reinforcements," she said. "The silver-bears, those screaming monsters, had to come from Bryony Hill. The bear-priests didn't want to attack until they had arrived."

"That was a mistake," said Lady Cindertallow. "We've given them a surprise, all right, showing up like this!"

"Be careful, Milady," said Fetterlock. "The silver-bears are formidable."

"We'll still win the day," said Lady Cindertallow.

"I hope so." Fetterlock made the sign of the crescent. "Lady have mercy on us."

Lady Cindertallow ignored him. She took off her glasses, raised her hand high, and waved her arm. Behind her a Yellowjacket herald raised an enormous golden flag with a silver crescent gleaming in the center. "There's a flag for all of us," she cried out to her audience of soldiers. She smiled with sudden enjoyment of her role as centerpiece of the martial spectacle. "Chandleforter, Low Brandingman, and Tansyard can fight for Our Lady together. Trumpeters, play!" She let her arm fall, and a chorus of horns burst out in glorious defiance.

The horns of the bear-priests brayed in response, and their front line opened up. Boulderbash ran through it, toward the allies, with Snuff on her back. He carried a white flag of truce, and waved it in the clear air. The sun shone brightly on them, and Clovermead gasped to see how handsome Snuff was. For a moment she saw the young noble of Queensmart riding toward her—and then a cloud crossed the sun, and his beauty faded. He was only sharp-toothed, bloody Lucifer Snuff.

Snuff brought Boulderbash to a halt fifty feet away. The Yellowjackets near Lady Cindertallow raised their swords, to warn him from getting too close. "Greetings, prey," Snuff said cheerfully. "Are you ready to surrender?"

"You are overconfident," said Lady Cindertallow. She looked at the bear-priests opposite them. "I grant your soldiers are formidable, Snuff, but there are more of us. Your men cannot frighten us."

"I do not intend to frighten you with my men," said Snuff. "That is what Lord Ursus' other servants are for. It has taken a certain amount of time to gather them, but here they are. Look at them." He lifted his own horn, and blew it sharply three times.

There was another stirring among the bear-priests. Their lines opened again, and silver-bears padded through the front lines, here, there, and everywhere. There were a dozen of the monsters, a score, and finally thirty of the beasts stood scrabbling in the grass. One howled, and each in turn took up the cry. The screams traveled up and down the line. Ten feet tall, misshapen, jaws snapping, they looked eagerly at the army opposite them.

"We cannot trust our bears, thanks to your brat," said Snuff to Lady Cindertallow. "But these are still more man than bear, and she cannot affect them. Besides, they serve my lord from choice. I advise you to surrender."

"I came here to fight, bear-priest," said Lady Cindertallow. "Save your breath." But she had grown more uncertain now that the silver-bears had come to the fore.

"You came to die, Milady," said Snuff sweetly. "And you, Horde Chief," he said, turning to Fetterlock. "The Hordes will lament if you fight—of that I assure you."

"I know it already," said the Horde Chief. His voice throbbed with sorrow. "I tell you frankly, Bear-Priest, I do not want to see tomorrow."

"I will attempt to satisfy your desire," said Snuff. He flashed his bronzed teeth at Fetterlock, then grinned at them all. "A fight, then." He raised his voice. "This is your last chance for quarter! Any man who fights on will be killed. You are warned." He waited, but the allied soldiers kept in place. Snuff shrugged, and he and Boulderbash rode back toward the bear-priests. His white flag lowered and disappeared.

Run, girlie, he thought at Clovermead. *You won't be pursued.*

Thank you for the offer, said Clovermead. *I won't.*

No quarter for you, either, said Snuff. *I am my master's loyal servant, now and forever.* He disappeared behind the bear-priests' lines.

The bear-priests came rushing across the valley. The silver-bears loped ahead of their companions, screaming, and bear-priest horns blared. The Yellowjackets and Low Brandingmen answered with a yell, and charged at the silver-bears and bear-priests while the Tansyards came galloping in on both flanks. There was a great clash of swords against swords, and the battle began.

A silver-bear came howling at Clovermead and Auroche. She swung her sword in defense, and it was a flame of silver light. She slashed along its ribs, but its burning paws smashed against her and swiped her off Auroche. Her stirrups snapped and she went flying onto the ground. She turned bearish as she flew, so she could absorb the impact. She tried to keep her hand tight around her sword, but it flew from her hand.

She turned back human, scrabbled for her sword, but she had no time: The terrible beast was leaping at her, screaming. She rolled away and its claws sank three inches into the dirt beside her. The grass charred beneath the silver-bear. It turned at once and leaped toward her again, and its screaming rang in Clovermead's ears and made her dizzy and confused. The world spun and she didn't know which way to run. She darted to the left, but it was the wrong direction, and the monster was coming down on top of her—

Fetterlock ran from behind her and slashed the silver-bear with his broadsword. Its edge crumpled the creature's rib cage, but the sword rotted and cracked with the impact. Fetterlock didn't give the silver-bear time to recover, but hammered at its broken ribs with the stump of his sword. It howled, ribs snapped one after another, but the metal was sloughing from Fetterlock's hands and the creature still hadn't fallen. He kept on pounding, and now Clovermead saw tears start from his eyes. The last of his blade had fallen away, and he was punching the creature with his bare hands. His skin was turning red, as acid ate into it, and he was bleeding—soon the quicksilver oozing from the silver-bear would eat into his flesh and bone—and at last the monster collapsed onto the ground. Fetterlock dodged to one side of the dying silver-bear and came rolling toward Clovermead.

"My hands hurt," Fetterlock moaned. He rubbed his hands against his shirt and gasped as the flecks of acid oozed into the cloth. He tore two strips of cloth from his shirt, and bound them around his burned hands.

"Thank you," Clovermead gasped.

"Tell Bardelle I fought hard for Our Lady," said Fetterlock. He fumbled behind his neck, and drew another sword from a scabbard slung over his back. "I must be fighting again, Demoiselle," he said, and he charged back into the battle.

Clovermead recovered her sword from the ground, swung up onto Auroche, and galloped after Fetterlock. He hadn't gone far: A line of bear-priests and White Star warriors fought with each other fifty feet away, and Fetterlock and Clovermead joined in the fray. There were more Tansyards than bear-priests, but each bear-priest fought with more than human savagery. Still, Clovermead's sword parted their mail like soft cloth, and Fetterlock's sword splintered their armor. Clovermead felt half a dozen slashes on her arms and legs, and one blade sliced down her side like searing flame. The ground around her was thick with the bodies of bear-priests and Tansyards.

Clovermead had a moment's respite, and she looked up to see silver-bears scythe through the battlefield. One a hundred yards away mowed its way through dozens of Tansyards, burning them, biting them, and smashing them to the ground. Tansyard after Tansyard rushed at it to throw a lance, fire an arrow from horseback, or strike at the monster with a sword. The beast howled its insatiable bloodlust, its pleasure at killing, and it struck down another half dozen Tansyards in seconds. Another score of Tansyard warriors came at the silver-bear. Now, at last, it howled in pain and disappointment, and fell dying to the ground. The remaining Tansyards had no time to rest, but moved on to fight the nearest bear-priests. Thirty Tansyards, dead or wounded, lay around the fallen silver-bear.

The sun rose high in the sky. The armies fought each other in intimate embrace along the middle of Yarrow's Bowl. The first eagerness that had galvanized both sides seeped out, and now they fought among the fallen with weary endurance. Soldiers sweated as much as they bled, and the grass had grown slippery underfoot. More than half the silver-bears lay dead on the field, but the remainder still ravened among the allied soldiery. Clovermead had lost sight of her mother hours before, she was barely aware of the battle around her, and she fought among dismounted Yellowjackets against a knot of bear-priests. Bergander was by her side, and so was Sergeant Algere. Habick and Corporal Naquaire were on Algere's other side. Clovermead's arm rose and fell, rose and fell, and Firefly had become nothing more than a hacking butcher's knife. Bergander was singing some song, and then a scimitar sliced open his lungs. He fell, he died, with a look of surprise on his face. *Four,* thought Clovermead. Algere also fell, wounded in the thigh. Clovermead crushed the fingers of the bear-priest who had stabbed Algere, slew another bear-priest, raged forward, and left Habick and Naquaire and Algere far behind her. She fought alone, and then for a moment there was no bear-priest to face.

Snuff came riding by on Boulderbash. He held a sword in either hand and he slew two Low Branding patricians as she watched. Boulderbash roared with terrible fury, and her great claws killed as many men as Lucifer's swords. They moved in deadly harmony through the battlefield, more deadly than any silver-bear, and no soldiers dared oppose them. They simply fled whenever the fatal pair came close. Snuff caught sight of the slaves huddled behind a screen of Tansyard warriors, and he chortled with joy. He said something to Boulderbash, and she began to race toward the slaves.

Wait, Snuff, Clovermead cried out in her mind. *Don't you want to fight me, Boulderbash? Here I am.*

I do, said Boulderbash. *Turn around, Lucifer.*

As you wish, Snuff said amiably. He whirled around and faced Clovermead with his two swords high. Then Clovermead brought out Firefly, and swung it at him. Boulderbash's paws swiped at her, and Clovermead parried swords and paws as quickly as she could. Snuff pressed forward, Boulderbash lunged toward her, and Clovermead fell backward. Firefly was a blur in her hands.

"Not bad," Snuff gasped out loud. He drew back Boulderbash for a moment and rested. "You're a proper fighter now. You were just an amateur the last time we dueled, girlie." There was admiration in his eyes.

"You're better too," said Clovermead. "You had Ursus in you last time to help you fight. This time it's just you."

"Any Queensmarter should be the match of a dozen Linstockers," said Snuff. He grinned. "I don't need his help to finish you off." He raised his swords, gave Clovermead a second to prepare herself, then came galloping at her once more. His swords were a blur, and the left blade missed Clovermead's neck by a finger's width. Clovermead stumbled away from Snuff, and he drew back his swords again as Boulderbash reared high onto her hind legs —

Sorrel's sword sent Snuff's first blade twirling into the air, and then he smashed Snuff's second sword to the ground as it swung toward Clovermead. He was galloping in front of Boulderbash on Brown Barley, the bear's paws barely missed Brown Barley's rump, and then Sorrel was whirling around Boulderbash. He grinned at Clovermead from behind the bear. "You know, Clovermead, saving your life is becoming a habit. Bear-priest, butterfingers, can't you even keep hold of your swords?"

"Stupid whelp," Snuff snapped. "Stop interfering." In an instant he drew a dagger from his belt, turned, and threw it with deadly accuracy at Sorrel—and as Sorrel drew up Brown Barley to avoid the whirring blade, Snuff pushed himself up into a crouch and leaped from Boulderbash's back into midair. He slammed into Sorrel before the Tansyard could bring up his sword to defend himself, and the two of them tumbled off of Brown Barley to the ground. Sorrel's sword spun into the dust, and the two of them, unarmed, gouged and kicked at each other as they rolled on the grass—

Boulderbash roared and leaped at Clovermead. Clovermead struck at her with Firefly, and Boulderbash didn't try to avoid the stroke, but took the sword in her paw and swept it out of Clovermead's hands. Only the side of her paw struck Clovermead, but the force of her blow sent Clovermead flying to the ground. Clovermead was turning into a bear, and then Boulderbash was on her, snapping at Clovermead with her teeth and clawing at her.

Did you know I killed your Horde, Tansyard? Clovermead heard Snuff say in her mind, heard him say out loud to Sorrel however many feet away they were. Clovermead clawed at Boulderbash's front legs, but barely scratched her skin. *I convinced the Mayor to send his soldiers over the Moors. I summoned the bears and bear-priests. I led them all into your Horde that night.* Boulderbash's claws scoured

Clovermead's legs, and her fangs bit deep into Clovermead's side. Clovermead screamed, rolled away from Boulderbash, and banged her paw against Boulderbash's snout. The white bear recoiled for a second.

You had a father, Sorrel? Snuff asked. *He's dead because of me. I pounded the nails into your mother's hands myself—rank has its privileges.* Boulderbash stalked toward Clovermead, and Clovermead scrambled onto all four feet as the bear approached her. She was twice Clovermead's bear-size, and she wasn't even tired. Clovermead's ribs ached from the effort of breathing. *I'll kill you, too, Tansyard, and tie up the last loose end of the Cyan Cross Horde. But first you'll see me entertain myself with the deaths of your mother and sister—*

Sorrel screamed. He flailed at Snuff like a madman, like a beast, and all his self-control was gone. Cool and collected, Snuff easily dodged Sorrel's blows. He clawed and punched the Tansyard with dispassionate precision, but Sorrel didn't even realize how badly he was being hurt. He fought berserk, and Snuff was going to kill him. Boulderbash was coming toward Clovermead, and Clovermead had to turn and fight her, or she'd die too, but she couldn't let Sorrel die. She ran toward Snuff and Sorrel, ignored Boulderbash's oncoming fangs, and she leaped at Snuff. He cursed as he saw her coming, jerked away from her oncoming bulk, and Sorrel's windmilling fist caught him square in the jaw. Snuff slumped to the ground—

—And then Boulderbash caught the scruff of Clovermead's neck in her mouth. Effortlessly she shook Clovermead, tossed her from side to side as if she were a rag doll. Clovermead bit at midair, scraped Boulderbash's fur with her claws, but the white bear boxed Clovermead in the ear, and the blow shivered through Clovermead. She couldn't move, could barely see, and she hung limp from Boulderbash's jaws. Contemptuously, Boulderbash let her go, and Clovermead slumped helplessly to the ground.

Boulderbash stood over her, panting. She looked at Clovermead with grief and rage greater than anything Clovermead had ever seen. Tears fell from the old bear's eyes, blood dripped from her mouth, and her fangs were close to Clovermead's throat. *You deserve to die*, she growled, with all the anguish in her heart. *Torturer.*

Clovermead rolled her eyes away from the oncoming jaws, to Sorrel. Snuff lay unconscious on the grass, and Sorrel knelt above him. He had drawn a knife from his belt, and held it over the bear-priest's chest. His face was a mask of hatred and grief. He cursed the unconscious bear-priest in Tansyard. His knife slashed toward Snuff's shirt—bounced off a button and skidded to the grass. A drop of blood ran down Snuff's chest.

Boulderbash lowered her jaws. Her teeth were grazing Clovermead's neck. *You sacrificed me so as to save him, changeling? You left me in darkness for his sake? He's nothing but a killer.* She laughed through her tears. *Look, he doesn't even care about you. He'll let you die, just so he gets the pleasure of his kill.*

Clovermead turned back to Boulderbash. Half the world was the old bear's great jaws. *I didn't expect anything back from him when I rescued him*, Clovermead said fiercely. *I don't love him any less. He isn't so nice now, but he's not in his right mind. He* will *be kind Sorrel again, and brave Sorrel again, and everything that's worth loving.*

You're wrong, said Boulderbash. Her teeth tightened on Clovermead's neck. *You look at him and you feel sure the cub you knew will return, but he never does. He kills once, he kills twice, and he acquires a taste for it. All that's good in him leaches out, day by day. And all the sacrifices you've made for his sake turn to ashes. You let other bears be slaves for his sake, you let him abandon you without complaint, but there's never any reward. It doesn't turn out right in the end. He wallows in darkness, darkens all the world, and all that's left is the shell of my little Ursus.* Tears fell from her eyes onto Clovermead's fur, blood stained Clovermead's golden fur red. *Better to kill you now, changeling, before you learn how your love has been wasted.*

"No!" Clovermead heard, and the words seemed to ring through the battlefield. She heard running footsteps. Boulderbash's jaws snapped, as if to break Clovermead's neck then and there, but somehow she didn't. She turned to see who it was, and Clovermead turned too.

It was Sorrel, running toward her. In his haste, he had left Snuff behind, left him alive. The bear-priest still breathed, with the Tansyard's knife lying by his side. "Don't kill her," he said. He stood in front of Boulderbash and Clovermead. He showed his open hands to Boulderbash. Boulderbash raised her head, and listened to the sound of his voice. "Please," said Sorrel. "Not her, too. I have lost nearly everyone I loved. Don't kill her." Boulderbash snarled at him, and made a half leap at him, to scare him away. Sorrel stood firm. "Kill me if you want," he said tremblingly. "Spare her."

You came back, said Boulderbash. She swung her head from Sorrel to Clovermead, from Clovermead back to Sorrel. *Why for her? She doesn't deserve it.*

"You see, she makes me a better person," said Sorrel. It was as if he understood Boulderbash. "Sometimes I have been a coward, and she has given me courage. Sometimes I have been melancholy, and she reminded me that the world still contains joy. I have been a childish fool of late, and she endured my spleen with the patience of a nun. She does good so easily, and I have learned from her how I should behave. She is sometimes thoughtless and foolish, too, and only a few weeks ago she almost broke my heart, yet I find that what I cherish in her far outweighs the parts of her that have pained me. You will tear out my heart if you kill her." He lifted his neck to Boulderbash's jaws. "If you will not let her live, kill me first. I could not endure to see her dead."

Boulderbash lifted her paw to strike at Sorrel—and Clovermead helplessly whimpered. The white bear turned back toward Clovermead—and Sorrel tried to dart between them. Boulderbash looked at Clovermead with hatred, with envy. *You are blessed to have each other,* she said. *You are blessed to deserve each other's love.* She lowered her paw. Her eyes were dry now. *I cannot kill either one of you.* Snuff groaned in the grass, and Boulderbash looked around her. The silver-bears had all fallen by now. The bear-priests still fought stiffly, but the allied soldiers had surrounded them and driven them into tiny pockets. The bear-priests asked for no quarter and were granted none.

I will take Snuff back to my son, said Boulderbash. She went over to him and picked him up carefully in her jaws, like a newborn cub. *I will beg for his life too, to balance the one I have given you. Otherwise Ursus might take it: He does not care for servants who fail him.* Boulderbash laughed. *I will let him ride me still—he knows how to ride bear-back now, and I would hate to train a new rider.* Then she roared so the echoes bounced off the mountainsides. *Lady, I cannot stop loving*

271

my Ursus, and so I must serve him forever. He loved me once. Give me back my son who loved me. Please, Lady, I beg you. And she was bounding toward the warriors and the slaves ahead, Snuff dangling from her mouth. The Tansyards scattered, so did the slaves, and then she was riding through their lines and toward the Farry Heights beyond.

Clovermead shrank back to human. She was bleeding from a dozen wounds. Sorrel knelt by her side, and dabbed at her broken skin with his shirtsleeves. He smiled at her, but with great worry in his eyes. "How badly are you hurt?"

"I'll live," Clovermead whispered. She smiled tremulously. "Thank you."

"And I must thank you. Turnabout is fair play, and so we save each other's lives. Ah, Clovermead, what would we do without each other?"

"You'll never find out, if I have anything to say about the matter," said Clovermead. She frowned a little. "I hope I won't be hearing too much of that thoughtless-and-foolish line from you, though. That could get annoying."

"I will say it no more than you deserve, and I trust that will be very rarely indeed," said Sorrel. With all the strength Clovermead could muster, she punched him in the shoulder. Sorrel laughed. "I suppose I deserve that," he said. "But this is not the time to talk of such things. Now we should rest. When the battle is done we will talk."

"When the battle is done," Clovermead agreed. Then Sorrel helped Clovermead stand up, and whistled for Auroche and Brown Barley. The battle had wandered far away from them. Far-off dolls slew one another. Sorrel helped Clovermead up onto Auroche, swung up onto

Brown Barley, and then he was leading her toward the rear of the battle, toward the doctors who would bandage her wounds, as the men of Linstock and the Steppes finished their terrible, bloody victory over the bear-priests.

Chapter Twenty

THE RED FOX

HALF OF THE ALLIED ARMIES HAD DIED. THE SURVIVING soldiers spent days gathering the bodies of the dead and burying them. The Low Brandingmen and the Chandleforters scoured the slopes of the hills, and gathered wood, carved markers with the names of each of the dead, and put them each by the proper grave. Lady Cindertallow had her officers make copies of the names. "I'll have a stone monument carved in Chandlefort with the date of the battle, the nature and number of our enemies, and all our fallen soldiers' names," she said. "We'll bring it here when it's done, so no one will ever forget the fallen. I'll have the stonemasons carve the letters so deep that their names will be read a thousand years from now." She turned to Fetterlock. "Give me the names of your warriors, and I'll have them written down with ours."

"That is not our way," said Fetterlock. His face had been a mask of grief ever since the battle. "We remember our dead in our songs. If ever they are so forgotten that their names must be read to be known, then they may sink into oblivion on this earth. Our Lady will remember them forever." He paused a moment. "Write only that the

274

victory could not have been won without the Tansy Hordes, and that we lost the flower of our youth in this terrible spot." He glanced at Lady Cindertallow. "Tell me truly, Milady, do you think this victory was worth the sacrifice of our dead?"

"What can I tell you, Horde Chief? If Ursus had conquered us, we would all have been slaves forever. All our victory does is buy us time. If we use it wisely, we may yet find a way to defeat the Bear once and for all." Lady Cindertallow shrugged wearily. "Our dead have bought us hope." Then Lady Cindertallow gazed at the dug-up valley floor, filled with the bodies of the dead, and she was crying. "My poor Yellowjackets. Oh, Lady, let some of my soldiers survive these wars."

"And bring us an end to these wars quickly, Lady," said Fetterlock. "One way or the other, let it be soon."

That evening the Tansyards gathered their dead in a mass in the center of Yarrow's Bowl. Then they pulled up a circle of grass all around the bodies, and set a fire on the inside of the circle. The flames swept in to consume the dead bodies in a great pyre while the surviving warriors, all around, chanted a song of grief and farewell.

The freed slaves had recovered enough strength to sing too, to shout in harsh dissonance, to mourn. The remnants of Cyan Cross sang of their vanished nation. The other freed slaves, Tansyards and stray captives from the Thirty Towns and Linstock, sang in harsh argot of the years stolen away from their families, amid the torture of the mines. They had been given new clothes from the Yellowjackets' commissary, and each slave solemnly cast their Barleymill rags into the fire. But they were scarred still. They all had calluses on their wrists where their shackles had lain. Each of them bore on his or her skin etched with mercury the ineradicable tattoo of bondage.

Mullein sat in the center of the freed slaves, and Clovermead, Sorrel, and Roan sat around her, to hold her up. She glowed bright silver through the blankets around her, her flesh nearly as bright as the silver criss-cross on her cheeks. She sat and shivered in the heat of a midsummer night, with a blazing bonfire only a dozen feet away. She had not spoken since the battle. She trembled and burned in silence. She barely seemed to notice the singing.

Fetterlock sat down next to them. "How are you, Shaman-Mother?" he asked.

Mullein only sighed.

"She is no better," said Sorrel.

"I got her to take a drink of water this afternoon," said Clovermead. "She won't eat. Roan and Sorrel have begged her, but she won't open her mouth. She —" Clovermead gestured at Mullein's wasted body, to let Fetterlock know the obvious. Mullein was dying. "There isn't anything we can do."

"I am sorry," said Fetterlock. He smiled sadly at Mullein. "I wish you had stayed with us, Mullein. Calkin loved playing with you. Arman and Bardelle — I think they loved you as much as I do."

Mullein turned her head toward Fetterlock. Her neck moved slowly, as if she were an aged woman. She pointed at Fetterlock's tattoos. "White Star," she whispered. Roan gasped to hear her daughter speak. Then she pointed at her own cheeks. "Cyan Cross." Her voice was faint and rasping. "No love. Never."

Fetterlock sighed. "Not in the past. And I have been as unloving as any." He touched the white stars on his cheeks, scratched at them with his fingers as if to claw them off. He let his fingers drop. "I cannot remove my tattoos, Mullein. Nor can any of my Horde. But I swear to you that you will always be welcome in the White Star Horde. So will all of Cyan Cross Horde. There will be no more enmity between us."

"Words," said Mullein. Silver tears leaked from her eyes. "We gone now. No more hatred?" She shuddered. "Too late. Nothing left, but pain." She turned away from Fetterlock to look back at the fire.

"Then let me share it with you," said Fetterlock. He held out his great arm to Mullein, and he trembled with fear. "I was silent once, and I let terrible things happen to you, to all of Cyan Cross. The pain should be mine, too. There are parts of me that should be burned clean." Mullein turned toward him again. Silver fire flickered around her flesh, and Fetterlock gulped. Still his hand remained extended. "You should not bear it all."

"You cannot," said Mullein. "You are not strong enough."

"Nor can you," said Fetterlock. "Nor can anyone." He made the crescent sign with his left hand. "I will pray to Our Lady to help me to bear it. If we share the pain, perhaps we both may live."

For a moment, hope lit Mullein's eyes. Then Clovermead saw it fade in recrudescent suspicion, saw the little girl's mouth clamp shut. Fetterlock had run out of words, and no one else spoke. Mullein was dying in the silence.

"Mullein," said Clovermead, and the Tansyard turned to look at her. "Do you remember what I said to the Elders of the White Star Horde?" Mullein shook her head. "We can all make the right choice the second time.

But we have to be given a chance." She glanced at Sorrel, and she had to blink away sudden tears. "I think I have an idea of how hard it is to forgive someone who's hurt you. I know how wonderful it is to be forgiven. When you don't deserve it at all, it's the most amazing gift in the world. Please, Mullein. Give Fetterlock a chance."

"All dead," said Mullein, and tears were streaming down her cheeks. "Because of him. I saw them. Unforgivable." A ragged sob broke out of her lungs. "If I forgive him, I break faith with dead. Who forgive me? No one."

"I would," said Roan. They were the first words in common tongue Clovermead had heard her speak. Roan reached out her still-scarred hands to Fetterlock, and gripped his hand for a moment. Startled, he almost jumped away from her, then stayed with his huge fingers trembling in her grip. The firelight shown on her healing wounds. "Enough death already," said Roan. She brought Fetterlock's hand toward Mullein's. "Please, Mullein. Live with me."

"Dead scream at me," said Mullein. "I know it." She sobbed again, a great racking howl that twisted her tiny frame. But when it had escaped her, it was as if a shadow had flown away. Hesitantly, she let herself look at Fetterlock with wistful hope. "I can play with Calkin?" For a moment the weary age had lifted from her, and she was only a little girl. "We can be friends? You promise?"

"I promise," said Fetterlock. "In Our Lady's name I swear it, now and forever." And as Roan let her own hand fall away from Fetterlock's, Mullein lifted her hand to touch his.

Silver fire flared through the night. It lit up Fetterlock, joined him and Mullein in one blaze. Quicksilver surged from Mullein's veins, across the bridge of flesh, and into his. Fetterlock jerked as fire and liquid burned into him — but he did not scream. He kept his mouth clenched shut and his fingers tight around Mullein's. His skin was turning pink where it touched Mullein, but he would not let go. The fire crackled, and a wisp of white flame touched Sorrel, touched Roan, touched Clovermead —

Clovermead hacked at ore with a pickax, silver grit struck her eyes and slipped into her lungs. Her arms ached, her throat was dry, and her stomach yammered for food. She burned, she withered, she was dying. Fifty women dug by her side, and each of them was dying too. She passed from one to another, touched them and took their pain from them, into her. She was on fire —

The stray flame passed and Clovermead was weeping. *How can either of them stand it?* she asked. *It's unbearable. Oh, Lady, take the pain from them.* She could see Sorrel and Roan weeping and praying too. She gulped and reached out her own hand. *I'll take some too, Lady. Just keep them from hurting so.*

No need, Clovermead heard, deep in her mind, up in the heavens, far underground. The silver fire suddenly rose from Fetterlock and Mullein, and arced high into the sky. It raced as an arrow toward the moon, and when it struck it, Clovermead heard Our Lady cry in anguish. *Oh, Mullein,* Clovermead heard her cry, in pain and pity. *Oh, Fetterlock.* And there were other names — all the dead of Cyan Cross Horde, Boulderbash with her helpless love for her unworthy son, Snuff weeping in darkness, every slave in Barleymill, everyone in the world. Our Lady knew them all and she took pain from each of them, and her scream echoed through the night as Fetterlock and Mullein fell apart, crumpling to the ground. A silver crisscross tattoo had etched itself into Fetterlock's cheeks, overlaying his white star. The tattoo was twice as long and twice as deep as Mullein's.

Mullein's silver and gray complexion was gone. She was terribly thin, but her face was pink with health. She struggled out of her blankets and smiled. "I not hurt now," she said. She took Fetterlock's hands in hers. He winced a little, his hands still pink, but the silver had gone from him, save the crisscross on his cheeks. "Thank you," she said.

"It was the least I could do," said Fetterlock. Then, gravely, he folded Mullein in his arms. She hugged him back. It took Fetterlock a long minute to let her go. He smiled at her. "Are we friends, little Shaman-Mother?"

"We are," said Mullein. Her stomach growled. "I eat? I very hungry."

"Of course," said Sorrel. And, laughing, he hoisted Mullein onto his shoulders and took her jogging toward where a sheep lay roasting. Roan, Clovermead, and Fetterlock came after him.

Sergeant Algere's leg was healing, Habick had lost a finger, and both Quinch and Corporal Naquaire had survived unscathed. Clovermead came to say good-bye to them, but then she didn't know what to say. "Golion, Dunnock, Lewth, and Bergander," she said at last. "They weren't all at Yarrow's Bowl, but I asked Mother to make sure all their names will be on the monument she's putting up. They won't be forgotten."

"That's good," said Algere.

"Very good," said Habick, with cheery indifference. Naquaire scowled and shrugged.

Clovermead counted the men in front of her in her

head. Four living, four dead, but there had been a ninth Yellowjacket who had come with them to the Tansy Steppes. "Where's Sark?" she asked. He was almost as young as Habick, with piercing blue eyes. "Is his arm all right?"

"He died yesterday," said Algere. "We thought he'd be riding with us today, but the slash on his arm swelled up all of a sudden, and a sweating fever burned him up. The doctor couldn't do anything but ease the pain."

"Golion, Dunnock, Lewth, Bergander, and Sark," said Clovermead. *Five dragged along with me to Barleymill and back, and dead now. For a good cause. Oh, Lady, have pity on Mother. There's no way she can remember the names of everyone who died at Yarrow's Bowl.* She shivered. *One day I'll be Lady Cindertallow.*

"His name will be on the monument too," said Algere. "I told it to Milady's clerks." He hesitated a moment. "I'm glad you remember our names," he said at last. He stood to attention and saluted Clovermead, and the other Yellowjackets did too. "It's been an honor serving with you, Demoiselle."

"And for me," said Clovermead, and she returned his salute. She looked at each of their faces, and tried to memorize them. "Good-bye," she said. Algere, Habick, Naquaire, and Quinch murmured their farewells, and then the Yellowjackets were gone.

The next day the remnants of the allied army left for Bryony Hill. There were too few of them left to attempt an assault on Barleymill, but there were enough of them left to tear down the fortress' half-built walls, raze Ursus' temple, and reconsecrate Bryony Hill to Our Lady, and so ensure that Ursus could never again make a silver-bear.

Fetterlock had already sent a screen of horsemen out into the Steppes, to make sure that in the meantime no more quicksilver passed from Barleymill to Bryony Hill.

"How long will you be staying here?" Lady Cindertallow asked Clovermead just before they parted.

"Some weeks more," said Clovermead. "Sorrel will be helping the Cyan Cross Horde set up again. Fetterlock gave the Horde fifty horses, but they want him to do some of the heavy lifting to start out with." Clovermead smiled. "When they saw me carry three folded-up tents on my back in bear-shape, they wanted to make me a member of the Horde too. I said I couldn't do that, but I do want to help them. Some of the freed slaves will be heading off to the Whetstone River, and back to their homes, but we need to take the Tansyard slaves back to their Hordes. And we'll be taking Mullein to the White Star Horde. She's going to stay there for a while. I think she'll take lessons from the White Star Shaman-Mother, to learn more about her profession."

"Your friend Sorrel," Lady Cindertallow began. She stopped and cleared her throat. "I've commuted all charges against him since he saved your life in the battle, but I can't let him back into the Yellowjackets. I know you say you gave him permission to leave you in the Moors, but every soldier in Chandlefort knows the truth: He disobeyed orders and he deserted. No officer would be willing to have him as a trooper."

"I don't suppose that's a problem," said Clovermead. "Sorrel doesn't much want to serve in the Yellowjackets as a trooper anymore."

"I'm glad," said Lady Cindertallow. She sounded relieved. "Of course he is free to return to Chandlefort."

"I'll tell him," said Clovermead. "I don't know if he wants to come back."

"I'm sorry," said Lady Cindertallow. "I know you'll miss him—and with good reason." She smiled. "I gather he has the proper attitude toward mothers—that we are wonderful creatures, beloved by their children, who ought always to be rescued by them from great danger. I'm glad you've chosen a man of such excellent judgment and character to be your friend."

"I'm glad he chose me to be his friend," said Clovermead. She smiled wryly. "Though I'm not sure it shows such good judgment on his part."

"Too much modesty, Clo! I'm sure you deserve each other." Lady Cindertallow gathered Clovermead into a hug, kissed her, then leaped onto her horse. "Come back soon, Daughter. I will miss you."

"I'll be back before you know it—oh, Mother, please say hello to Saraband and Father for me as soon as you get back to Chandlefort! Let them know I'm alive, and that I won't be out here too long, and let them know I've been thinking of them." For a moment Clovermead saw Saraband's head lopped off again, saw Waxmelt weeping for his treachery. *I won't let that happen,* Clovermead swore to herself. *It was a vision of what might have been. Not of what will be.* "Give them my love," she said.

"I will," said Lady Cindertallow. She smiled at her daughter a last time, and then she rode off. Soon the Tansyard warriors and Linstock soldiers rode after her, off to the north.

Late that afternoon Sorrel and Clovermead finally had a chance to walk by themselves, in the clean grass of the hills overlooking Yarrow's Bowl. Sorrel had finally replaced his Yellowjacket uniform. He was dressed in a

russet deerskin shirt and leggings, dark-brown moccasins, and his red fox-fur hat. Around his neck he wore
a necklace of sapphire beads. All in all, he was quite the
handsome Tansyard warrior.

"You always manage to get dolled up," said
Clovermead. "Where did you get those sapphires?"

"They are a gift from Fetterlock," said Sorrel.
"They are the proper regalia of the Horde Chief of the
Cyan Cross Horde." Clovermead's eyes went wide, and
she whistled. Sorrel chuckled. "Oh, yes. I know I am
unsuited for the position, for the Horde Chief is
supposed to be the bravest and the wisest warrior in
the Horde—but after all, I am the *only* warrior the
Horde has yet. I hope we soon may adopt some
warriors from other Hordes, who will be able to take
my place in time, but for the meanwhile I will serve. It
will mean a great deal of hard work and botheration on
my part, though it does have some advantages. I have,
for example, with my unanimous consent, pardoned the
cowardly warrior Sorrel who ran from the bear-priests
at Bryony Hill. He has shown sufficient bravery since
then, and he is an outlaw no longer." His eyes
twinkled. "I believe I outrank you, Clovermead. I am
the leader of my nation, and you are only the heiress-
in-waiting of yours. I want due respect for my exalted
station to be shown in the future. You cannot hit me in
the arm again."

"I've never been good at diplomatic protocol," said
Clovermead. "I might forget." She looked the Horde
Chief up and down. "I don't know how I'll stand being in
Chandlefort without you, Sorrel."

"I will miss you terribly too," said Sorrel. He reached
to his neck, moved aside the sapphire necklace, and

produced a small golden pendant. It was a flaming bee wielding a sword. "A gift from Milady. I will not wear the livery of Chandlefort any longer, but I will gladly wear this token, as a sign of my gratitude and my friendship. It will always be with me, and I will never forget that desert town while I wear it. I will never forget you." He looked Clovermead straight in the eyes, and hesitated for a long moment. Then he smiled. "I recollect that I never told you the end of the story about the red fox. Would you like to hear it?"

"Very much," said Clovermead. "You and your brother were about to slaughter the poor thing, like the blood-thirsty little boys you were, and then your father smacked you on the head and told you to do no such thing. You all sat down and waited, and the fox, conveniently enough, stuck around and didn't run away overnight."

"My father would never have smacked me on the head," said Sorrel. "In other essentials, you are correct." He paused a moment. "We waited all night. Indeed, I thought the fox would run away, but he did not. I fell asleep against my father's side. I woke in the gray light before dawn and I saw two foxes. As soon as I saw them, I knew they were a pair, a husband and a wife. They whined and nuzzled each other like true lovers, like my father and mother did when they thought we children were not looking, and my heart almost broke to think that I had almost killed one of them, from a thoughtless whim. I saw their love for each other and I told myself, 'I want to love like that someday.' I thanked my father, and I thanked Our Lady for letting me know how I wanted to live my life."

"Oh," said Clovermead. Then she said "Oh!" again, and she blushed a very, very deep red.

In the twilight Sorrel held out his hand to her. "Will you take my hand, friend?" he asked.

And it was really remarkably easy. Clovermead held out her hand, and then they were walking side by side. Clovermead's heart had a distressing tendency to skip and lurch, but other than that everything seemed quite normal. *Rather nice,* Clovermead amended to herself. She interlaced her fingers with Sorrel's. *Even nicer.*

"I began to tell you that story without remembering how it ended," said Sorrel. "Then it struck me as I was talking that it was not quite proper for me to tell it to you unless I had made some declaration of sentiment. And to tell the truth, while I wished to say something to you, I was too terrified to speak! I did not know what you would say, and I did not want to ruin our friendship."

"You didn't need to worry. I've been—I thought I was in love with you for an awfully long time. Since we were in the Reliquary Mountains three years ago."

Sorrel's eyes widened. "I had no idea! You gave me no clue." Then he smiled. "I would not have made a declaration to you then anyway, for you were far too young. I have only begun to regard you with, ah, corporeal admiration this last year, when it was decent to think such things of you." He shook his head. "Truly, you are still young."

"I'm glad you didn't say anything until now." Clovermead clutched at Sorrel's hand. "Don't go away! I just mean—for a while I told myself that I was in love with you, and I was just miserable. Then I started wondering whether I really was in love with you, or if it was just a crush, and I was less miserable but a lot more confused. And that's where I was when you started to tell me that story about the red fox. And if you'd kept on speaking that night—I don't know what would have happened. But I'd have, well, I'd have wanted to kiss you." She blushed again. "You're awfully handsome. Did I ever tell you that?"

"I told myself so," said Sorrel. "But I am very glad to hear it from you. And you, Clovermead—you were a pretty girl, but now you are a lovely woman."

"Whoo," said Clovermead. "That made my knees go weak." She squeezed Sorrel's hand even tighter.

"But you are just as glad we did nothing," said Sorrel lightly, a little sadly. "Because it was just a crush."

"Not just a crush. But a good deal of one. And expecting that love and romance was something really different from friendship, better somehow, and I think I was even a little impatient with *just* friendship. But then I hurt you so badly, and you left me, and I didn't think we'd ever even be friends again. That hurt me so much, and I didn't care anymore about anything but our friendship. I'm not exactly glad that happened, but I don't think I valued our friendship properly before. Valued you properly. And you came back to me, and you're still willing to be friends with me after all I did to you, and now I think I really know what to love about you, more than I ever did before."

"Now *I* am weak in the knees," said Sorrel. "I can never say it so well as that, but, yes, I am also glad that I did not make any declarations until now. Until I knew you properly. No, even if I could, I would not change anything. I am much happier to have waited until now to speak to you."

Clovermead turned to face Sorrel head-on. Their fingers were still intertwined, he was only a foot away, and he was even more handsome than usual in the twilight.

Clovermead brought her hand up to brush Sorrel's cheek. Short stubble grew on it, and she luxuriated in its feel. And suddenly, surprisingly, but not too soon at all, he bent down and kissed her. It was a gentle kiss, a hesitant kiss, and, really, a somewhat clumsy kiss. *But I'm sure I'm clumsy too*, thought Clovermead. She kissed Sorrel back, with just as much hesitance and clumsiness. For a second it was really quite wonderful—and then Clovermead drew away.

"I think that's enough for now," she said, a little dizzily. She looked at Sorrel shyly. "If you don't mind? It takes a little getting used to."

"Do not worry, Clovermead. I know you are worth waiting for." Then Sorrel grinned. "Besides, I am sure I will tempt you into another meeting of the lips sooner than you think."

"You are a vain peacock," said Clovermead. "You always have been and you always will be." She hit him on the shoulder.

"Most undiplomatic," said Sorrel. He looked down at Clovermead with affection, with good humor, oh, Lady, with love. It was frightening to see him look at her that way. It scalded her, it was wonderful, it was terribly hard not to look away. Then Sorrel dropped his gaze, and he looked suddenly sad. "There is a third part to that story of the red fox. I should tell that to you as well."

"You killed one of them by accident, and it became your hat after all? I knew it!"

Sorrel chuckled. "No, little tease." He sighed. "When the two foxes had frolicked together for half an hour, they yipped a good-bye to each other, as if to say, 'We will see each other again when we can.' Then one went east and one went west, looking back over their shoulders until they were out of sight. I have never wanted to tell you that part of the story at all, but now I think I must." He gestured with his free hand down at the lights of the Cyan Cross Horde, camped in Yarrow's Bowl. "I told you that I am their Horde Chief now. I cannot abandon them for a good while to come."

"And you should spend some time with your mother and Mullein," said Clovermead. "You should get to know them again." She sighed. "I have to go back to Chandlefort in the fall."

"I know," said Sorrel. "That is why I told you the last part of the story. The two foxes said farewell only for a time. They knew they would see each other again."

"I'll bet one fox wasn't certain. I'll bet she was afraid they would wander the Steppes forever, and never see each other again." Clovermead frowned. "How long?"

"I will be in Chandlefort three springs from now, without fail," said Sorrel.

"Three springs?" Clovermead stared at Sorrel in disbelief. "That's forever!"

"It is a long time," said Sorrel, soberly. "But it is—" He smiled crookedly, bitterly. "It is my duty to stay with Cyan Cross Horde. I think you understand."

"Ha-ha," said Clovermead sourly. "I do. But I don't have to like it." She adjusted her grip and interlaced her fingers even more tightly with Sorrel's. Already his fingers felt comfortable around hers. "Three springs?"

"But no more. And we have a summer together first. Besides, when we are apart, I will send you objects that cunningly tell you whole days of conversation in just a glance. For example, I will send you an egg, and you will know that I spent the day watching birds fly overhead, and that their feathers gleamed beautifully in the sunlight."

"You'd better tell me what the messages mean in advance. I don't think I'd have guessed what an egg meant."

"The first thing I will send you will be a codebook," said Sorrel. He tried to smile at Clovermead. "I do not like the thought of being separated from you any more than you do. But when this time apart is done, we will have all our lives to spend together."

Sorrel turned from her, left her forever, and he walked into darkness.

"I had a nightmare a little while ago," Clovermead began. She looked at Sorrel and opened her mouth. But then she could not bear to tell him her dream. *I healed Snuff and Boulderbash. And maybe thanks to me they still will conquer everything for Ursus. You won't be able to love me then, and you will leave me. I can't tell you. I just can't.*

Don't let it happen, she prayed to Our Lady. *I know I said I'd accept any consequence for what I did, but please keep me from the worst. Let us live. Let us learn to love each other properly. I won't give up. I'll keep my hope. I'll keep my faith in you. But, please, save us from the darkness. I need you now, more than ever.*

The moon was rising over the horizon. It shone its light over the dark world, and Clovermead took some comfort from its light. But the darkness was so large, and the light so very small and far away.

"I'll feel so cold without your hand in mine," said Clovermead. "Oh, Sorrel, never let me go."

"Never, Clovermead," said Sorrel. "I swear it by Our Lady." He put both his hands around Clovermead's one hand. "We shall walk hand in hand forever."

Clovermead let her head rest on Sorrel's shoulder. "Forever," she said dreamily. "I like the sound of that."